RAVE REVIEWS FOR
LIVING LEGEND HUGH B. CAVE!

"Hugh B. Cave is one of the grandest Grandmasters of horror fiction."
—*Rave Reviews*

"Hugh B. Cave is legendary."
—*Hellnotes*

"Cave's influence on horror fiction is important and pervasive."
—*Feo Amante*

"A haunting, suspenseful mini-epic. Cave is a poet of the perverse."
—*Hellnotes* on *The Evil Returns*

"An effective and chilling tale that strikes at the very core of what we think we know about the world around us . . . a hugely satisfying and frightening read."
—*Masters of Terror* on *The Dawning*

STAY OUT OF THAT ROOM

Susan took her time gathering up the cups and saucers and putting them on a tray, Jeff noticed. In fact, she went through a number of unnecessary motions while the others unhurriedly climbed the stairs and disappeared. Then she put the tray on a table and came over to Jeff.

In a voice too low to reach those upstairs, she said while gazing up intently at his face, "After what happened, are you going to sleep in that room again?"

"I was planning to, Miss Susan."

"Shh." She put a finger on her lips. "We don't want them to hear us. I don't think you should, you know. Not after what happened there last night."

"You think it might happen again?"

"Who can say . . . ?"

Other *Leisure* books by Hugh B. Cave:

THE EVIL RETURNS
THE DAWNING

THE
RESTLESS
DEAD

HUGH B. CAVE

LEISURE BOOKS NEW YORK CITY

A LEISURE BOOK®

January 2003

Published by

Dorchester Publishing Co., Inc.
276 Fifth Avenue
New York, NY 10001

ISBN 0-8439-5082-X

The name "Leisure Books" and the stylized "L" with design are
trademarks of Dorchester Publishing Co., Inc.

Printed in the United States of America.

Visit us on the web at www.dorchesterpub.com.

THE
RESTLESS
DEAD

Prologue

Aboard *Barracuda II,* inbound off the east coast of
Florida, a small white man with a pimply face
thrusts his head up from the boat's engine room
and says in a whine, "Joe—jeez—I can't find out
what's wrong with this thing!"

His gaze takes in the seven dark-skinned passengers huddled on deck, then fastens in desper-
ation on the big, bearded white man at the wheel.
"We ain't gonna make it before daylight, Joe!"
The same shrill whine. "We just ain't gonna do
it!"

The craft continues its erratic crawl toward a
string of lights a mile or so distant.

The lights of a coastal highway are giving the

1

man at this old fishing boat's wheel something to aim for. But there is something not so good in this part of Florida these mornings. There is a small army of Immigration watchdogs on the lookout for craft like *Barracuda II*.

The bearded man peers angrily at the luminous hands of his wristwatch—an expensive one with the words LOUVAN, PARIS, on its dial. A Haitian on one of the many trips before this gave it to him, probably after stealing it from some elite home in Port-au-Prince. They are always grateful, some with their emotions pouring out in a flood of tears, when he delivers them safely to the forbidden land of freedom and opportunity.

What the watch tells him now brings a look of panic to his long face. "You sure?" he snarls at Pimples. "You sure you can't fix it?"

"Jeez, Joe, I dunno what's wrong with it!"

Knowing what must be done, Joe really studies the passengers now: an old man, three younger men, a woman of thirty or so, a woman of seventeen with a baby girl hungrily sucking at her breast. All are probably peasants, but they proudly wear their Sunday best in anticipation of meeting old friends or relatives in the "Little Haitis" of Fort Pierce or Miami. How any of them managed to scrape together the five hundred U.S. dollars he charges for this Bahamas to Florida powerboat run is more than he can understand. Even more puzzling is how they ever made it from their homeland to the Bahamas in a rub-a-dub sailing tub that should have tipped over in the first gust of wind.

They have been talking in their native Creole, but the old man speaks English as well. He's a voodoo priest, it seems, and already knows a little about Florida. He was once employed in the Panhandle for a few months, legally, as a farmworker. At all times he carries what they call a *cocoma-caque*—a light, tough stick about the length of a cane that has something to do with his voodoo.

"Hey, you, Lelio," Joe calls to him. "Come here a minute, will you?"

Lelio takes his time about walking over. "Yes, M'sieu Joe?" You never let any of them know your full name, of course. If they get caught after you land them, they might blab it.

"You see those lights over there, Lelio?"

"Yes."

"We should be putting you ashore there right now, but the engine's been giving us some trouble. You understand?"

"Yes."

"So you and your people will have to swim the rest of the way. Otherwise it'll be daylight when we land you, and we'll all be caught and arrested. I guess you know what that would mean. You people would be sent back to Haiti after all it's cost you. My partner and I would end up in jail."

Except for the wheeze of the engine and the slapping of the dark sea against the boat's sides, there is silence for a few seconds. Then the old man says in a loud voice, "No! These others cannot swim! Even Lucille and I swim only a little."

"Hell, you can make it, all of you," Joe says. "It's only half a mile." Times two, he mentally adds.

The old fellow speaks to his companions in Creole, and a babble of that Haitian peasant tongue follows. It stops abruptly when Joe, visible to all of them in the glow of the cabin light, bends down and picks up an M-1 Enforcer he always carries on these trips. That nifty little automatic weapon, made in Florida, is only nineteen inches long but can fire thirty rounds of 30-caliber ammunition before it needs reloading. After all, this is a risky business, and a guy has to protect himself.

"Wait, please," the old man says then. "We beg you, m'sieu—all of us beg you—let me ask the *loa* to help us."

"Ask who?"

"The *loa*. The *mystères*. I am a *houngan,* m'sieu, as I told you. Please!" Though little more than a whisper, his voice quivers with emotion.

Joe is not amused. It was kind of fun talking to the old guy before, about voodoo. Something to pass the time. But this is different. "No way," he snarls. "What we need is a mechanic, not a cackle of crazy chanting that could bring Immigration or the Coast Guard down on us." He levels the Enforcer. "Move, now! Clear out of here and swim for the lights!"

Lelio's bony right hand closes more tightly around the *cocomacaque,* as if he might dare to risk using it as a club. "There are sharks in these waters, m'sieu!"

"Hell, they won't bother you none. Move, now!"

"No!"

"Lelio, I'm telling you for the last time, move or I shoot!"

"No! We paid you to put us ashore. We will not be forced to swim! We—"

With no other boat in sight, Joe can risk a little hard persuasion. Aiming a little to the left of the old man's head, he squeezes the trigger. The blast fills the darkness and races out over the dark sea like a stone skipping from wave crest to wave crest. The old man sucks in a huge breath and stands there like a statue, returning Joe's gaze.

"Go!" Joe yells in a rage, lurching from the wheel and wildly brandishing his weapon. "All of you! Go, goddamn it!"

They know they must obey him or die. The two women go first, sobbing as they stumble to the side and commit themselves to the sea, one with the baby in her arms. The men, with forlorn last looks at their voodoo priest, as if they are disappointed in him, step off the boat in a silence of fatalistic resignation. Only the old man is left. Joe lays the M-1 down and takes him by the shoulders, drags him to the side and, despite the Haitian's attempt to hang on to him, hurls him after the others. As he goes, though, Joe's voice follows him in a yell of angry surprise.

"What'd he do, Joe?" the man with the pimply face asks.

"He tore the watch off my wrist, for Christ's sake! He was clawing me and it went with him!"

"Gee, that's a shame, Joe. That was a real good watch. You suppose he still has it and we could find him?"

They stand side by side, peering into the darkness. The boat's engine still wheezes, and the craft continues to creep erratically through the water. There is no sound from the Haitians in the sea behind them. Presently the engine coughs and gives up the ghost.

"Now what do we do, Joe?" whines Pimples.

"We radio the Coast Guard for help, dummy. But first we make sure those creeps didn't leave any of their junk behind to give us away."

The old man was close to exhaustion when he reached shallow water. He stood up, staggered a few steps toward the beach, and fell to his knees. He finished the last few yards by crawling.

In the water he had long ago discarded his shoes and jacket, so he came ashore barefoot, in an undershirt and black trousers. But while side-stroking his way slowly through the water he had never once relaxed his grip on the *cocomacaque*.

As he trudged along the water's edge, hoping to learn that he was not the only survivor, the early light showed him only a deserted beach littered with seaweed and dead jellyfish. There were no houses here, no people. He had been walking back and forth for more than an hour when a wave deposited a small, black body almost at his feet.

He knew the child was dead even before he knelt and put his ear to her chest. Lifting her from the water, he carried her to a place where the sand was soft and dry and laid her down. Then he covered her with seaweed in case the gulls here, already noisily inquisitive, were carrion eaters like the turkey buzzards of his native Haiti.

Soon afterward he found the baby's mother, also dead, and dragged her to a place beside the child and covered her, too, with seaweed. Then the other woman.

But she was alive. Still clad in the black dress she had worn when she stepped off the boat, she called to him as she rose like a dark shadow from the surf.

After embracing, they stepped back to look at each other. "We seem to be the only ones left, Lucille," Lelio said. "I think we had better call ourselves man and wife."

She gazed at him in bewilderment.

"Because, of course, we must stay together," he went on, speaking in Creole. "First, let's be sure we are the only ones."

No one else from the boat had come ashore, it seemed.

"What probably happened," Lelio guessed aloud, "is that the men fought harder not to drown and made a commotion that attracted sharks. I swam very slowly and drew strength from this." He raised the *cocomacaque*. "You were wise

7

enough to let the sea bring you here. The mother of the child spent her strength trying to save her infant."

Lucille showed her agreement by nodding.

"How old are you, Lucille?"

"Thirty-four."

"I am past seventy. Nevertheless, as I say, we had better be man and wife if anyone questions us." They had stopped walking the beach and were facing each other close to where Lelio had covered the mother and child with seaweed. "Are you prepared to walk a very long way?"

"In Haiti everyone walks, Lelio."

"Yes, of course. Well, I know where we are, but I know too little about this part of Florida for us to remain here. When I was in this country before, I worked on a farm near the town of Clandon, in the Panhandle. There I will know better what to do about us."

"Yes, Lelio."

Turning to the mounds of seaweed, he touched them with his *cocomacaque* while softly breathing words Lucille had heard other *houngans* use at certain voodoo ceremonies. Then, with a strange fierceness in his voice, he said slowly, "Farewell for now, unhappy ones. Lelio will see that you are avenged. Never for a moment doubt it!"

To Lucille, as he turned away, he said more gently, "Come now. We have far to go, and even with the *loa* helping us it will not be easy."

Chapter One

Just before seven P.M. the sweltering June rain
stopped at last, and with a grunt of relief Jeffrey
Gordon shut off the car's windshield wipers.

This was still part of Florida? It certainly was not
the Florida pictured in the travel folders. For
miles now the landscape had been empty except
for scattered clumps of scraggly pines and
gnarled, moss-draped trees whose names he did
not know. All under a smothering blanket of gray
sky.

Were these ominous surroundings trying to tell
him something? That he shouldn't have come all
this way when he was probably not wanted? Everett Everol, after all, had not replied to his letter.
Only after two phone calls had the old fellow reluctantly agreed to an investigation.

Ah, well. College profs who got involved in this kind of research should expect to do stupid things at times. It went with the territory.

Ahead, where the road looped to the right to circle a dark glitter of swamp, a figure stepped from the misty background of trees to flag him down.

He hesitated. A hitchhiker here, with no disabled car in sight? Swinging his foot to the brake pedal, he tensed himself for possible trouble. Then, as the car slowed to a stop, he had another surprise. Though wearing gray slacks, a nondescript shirt, and a floppy hat, the hitchhiker was a young woman. A most attractive one, too.

With a hand on the car door she frowned at him and seemed to hesitate, as he had. Then in a none too steady voice she said, "Hello. Thanks for stopping. Can you give me a lift to Clandon, please?"

Clandon. It was the next town, Jeff Gordon knew, and he was not going that far. The Everol clan lived this side of it. But he leaned over to open the car door. "Trouble?"

Without getting into the car, she said, "My car's in the pond. I nearly went in with it."

"In the pond?"

"Well, half in. What bothers me is that I'm absolutely certain I left it in gear, with the hand brake on. It couldn't have rolled, unless—" She tried to smile but only partly succeeded. "Sorry. I'm not trying to get you involved. If you'll just drop me in Clandon, I'll be grateful."

Jeff peered at her again. In spite of her pallor and the way her mouth trembled, she was indeed a most attractive young woman. About twenty-five, he guessed. He was thirty-one, himself.

"Where is your car?" he asked. "Can we have a look at it?"

Her dark blue eyes appraisingly studied his face, and after another slight hesitation she apparently made up her mind about him. Or about his intentions. "All right. Maybe you'll see something I didn't." Getting into the car at last, she clicked the door shut. "Turn right at the thicket of swamp rose there, this side of the live oak."

When he looked at her with an exaggeratedly blank expression, she laughed. "Oops, I'm sorry. With that New England accent you're probably a stranger here. Turn right at that clump of bushes with the pink blossoms, this side of the big gnarled tree. Okay?"

"Thank you, ma'am." Her delight made him grin.

The side road her directions took him down was no more than a pair of ruts in what seemed to be dark gray sand, and he had to drive at a crawl until they reached a small lake so dark it seemed bottomless. And, yes, her car was in it. Or somebody's car was.

He stopped, and a large, glossy black crow rose flapping and cawing from the solitary red fender protruding from the water.

"I left it over there," his companion said, pointing to the open lower slope of a wooded knoll

11

some forty feet from the pond's edge. "They don't like people prowling around, so I went the rest of the way on foot. Not trespassing, you understand. This is state land and I have permission. Just to make sure they wouldn't think I meant to trespass. Then, when I came back and got into the car, it began rolling backward down the knoll before I even got the door shut."

There was nothing he could do, he decided. Even if he were to wade into the pond for a closer look at the car, he was not likely to learn anything. He certainly couldn't get the machine out of there.

Quizzically, he turned to her. "They don't like prowlers, you say? You mean you think your car was tampered with?"

"Well, I don't know. I mean, yes, of course I do!"

"Who?"

"I don't want to accuse anyone. I can't be that specific. But this is the Everol property—at least, just over there beyond that bayberry thicket is— and the Everols have a thing about strangers. And I left my car in gear; I know I did. I left it in gear, but when I tossed in my knapsack and tools and slid in after them, it started rolling and I almost went into the pond with it."

"Knapsack and tools?"

"I'm from the university. Verna Clark. An assistant professor, sort of. Paleontology."

Jeff gazed at her with even more interest. She certainly didn't look like a collector of old bones and such. "You didn't try to stop the car?"

"Yes, I tried. But the brake pedal didn't seem to work right. It felt mushy. And I panicked, I guess. I did manage to turn the wheel a little before throwing myself out the door. If the car had gone straight, it would have rolled into the pond over there"—she pointed—"where the bottom's supposed to be quicksand."

Turning to gaze at the spot where the car had been meant to go into the water, Jeff wondered how far beneath the dark surface the bottom was. The whole pond was spooky. Along the shore grew a tangle of bushes covered with explosions of white flowers, and beyond that stood a vast jumble of boulders that could have passed for a madman's castle. "So this is the Everol place," he said, rubbing his jaw.

Verna Clark shook her head. "Not quite. As I said, their property begins—" She caught herself and gazed at him wide-eyed. "You mean you know about the Everols?"

"In a way. Like you, I'm a teacher—Jeff Gordon, English Language and Lit—but I moonlight in affairs psychic. Right now I'm here with the Everols' grudgingly given permission to look into what's been happening to them."

"Then you must have made contact with them!" Still gazing at him, she clutched his wrist. "It's incredible that you came along just now! My guardian angel must have sent you!"

"One of us has to be crazy," Jeff countered.

"No, no. Really." Her grip tightened, and sud-

13

denly she was a very mature young woman talking to him calmly in a low, intense voice. "Listen to me, Jeff Gordon. I've been trying might and main to persuade the Everols to let me do some field-work on their property, but they won't talk to me. And I don't dare set foot on their place without permission. You see what happens when I even get close." Turning her head, she scowled at the car fender protruding from the gloomy waters of the pond. "And this isn't the first time."

"You want to search for fossils on the Everol property?"

"Yes! It's a treasure house!"

He shook his head. "Look, Miss Clark, my position here is shaky." Briefly he told her how, after reading about the Everols, he had pressed for permission to come and investigate. "I'm from Connecticut. I've never met these people. I do know Everett was hard to convince and could easily change his mind even now."

"Yet you've come all the way from New England?"

"As I said, I'm probably a little crazy. Have you heard the Everol story? About the unexplained death? The madness?"

"Well, yes." She shrugged. "But in this off-beat part of Florida—"

"Anyway, I know nothing about fossils. So suppose you fill me in on what you're up to while I drive you to town."

She did that. Some time ago, while on a field trip, she had unintentionally trespassed on the Ev-

14

erols' land and made some exciting discoveries, she told him. "I was just scratching around, mind you, and found what could be the start of something big, like those seven-thousand-year-old human skulls, with brains intact, unearthed near Titusville a few years ago. Or the fossil pockets found in that riverbank near Gainesville in 'sixty-one, where almost the first thing discovered was that huge carnivorous bird."

Though not in the habit of taking his gaze off the road while driving, Jeff jerked his head around to scowl at her. "Was what?"

Those remarkable blue eyes were suddenly wider. "A huge carnivorous bird! Yes! And one of the creatures supposed to be preying on the Everols is a huge vulture, isn't it? You don't suppose—no, no, let's not be foolish. Nobody really believes those people. They're weirdos."

"I'll take a rain check until I've met them." Jeff had already returned his gaze to the highway. "Go on with your story."

But she was pointing. "Look. That's where you'll turn in when you come back."

In the dusk he saw two very old stone gateposts rising from a clutter of weeds, with a mailbox on a post beside one of them. The name on the box was EVEROL. "Nothing there to keep out intruders," he observed.

"Oh, the property isn't fenced, if that's what you mean. It's so big, fencing would cost a fortune. What keeps people away is their attitude."

"I see. Well, you were saying?"

"That's it, what I've told you. I found a fossil pocket that could really be important, but the Everols aren't interested. They won't even see me. So I've just been—well, snooping around the edges, you might say, in the hope of finding something not on their property."

A small cemetery beside the road trapped Jeff's attention for a moment. You sometimes learned things from gravestone markings. "How long have you been here?" he asked.

"Since the close of school."

"How long will you be staying?"

She shrugged. "Who knows?"

"And what happened to your car isn't the first trouble you've had? What else have they done to discourage you?"

"Well, I was in a rock pit near another part of their property—not on the property, only near it again—and a boulder came crashing down on me from the pit's edge. It could have killed me if it hadn't hit a ledge and bounced." She moved her shoulders again. "It might have been an accident, of course, but I don't think so."

His frown deepened. "Lady, these are serious charges. Did you see anyone at that rock pit?"

"I thought I saw someone running away."

"Would the Everols really go to such extreme lengths to discourage intruders?"

"Yes," she said, "I think they would. They're not your everyday people, even for this part of the state. They stay by themselves in that huge old

16

house as if they've resigned from the human race."

"Perhaps because they're frightened," Jeff suggested.

"Well—perhaps."

"Sounds as if I'm in for a rough time, anyway."

"I hope not. But do be careful."

The road had become a small town now, and Jeff drove more slowly. Under the gray sky with its scudding lumps of darker cloud, Clandon seemed deserted, even dying, with its broken sidewalks empty of life. "You live here?" Jeff asked with a frown, then answered his own question. "You don't, of course."

"I'm from Fort Lauderdale. I just rent a room here." She smiled at his expression. "It really isn't so depressing when the weather is more cheerful. The countryside roundabout is peaceful and pretty, lots of trees and water." Leaning forward, she pointed. "That's the house I'm staying at, just ahead. That old gray one. And thanks for going out of your way to give me a lift."

"It's been my pleasure." Stopping by a mailbox with the name EARL WATSON crudely painted on it in weathered red letters, Jeff added, "How will you get your car out of that pond?"

"There's a garage in town with a tow truck. Look, will you speak to the Everols for me? Try to make them understand the importance of what I want to do?"

"You haven't told me what you want to do, exactly."

"But I have!"

Jeff smiled. Maybe something good would come of this wild-goose chase to Florida, after all. "Not nearly enough for me to be convincing, if these people are as touchy as you say they are. I need a more thorough briefing, don't you think? Say tomorrow evening, after I've had time to size up the Everols and the situation there?"

After those dark blue eyes had reappraised him for a moment, Verna Clark nodded. "All right. Tomorrow evening."

It was twilight now as Jeff made a U-turn to drive back out of town. With more rain likely to fall, the night promised to be a dark one. He drove slowly, thinking about what Verna Clark had told him.

What would he encounter at the Everol place, anyway? A challenge beyond anything he had tackled before, if the reports were even half true. So far, no one had come up with any plausible answer.

As he passed the cemetery again a light touched his rearview mirror, creating a brief glare inside the car. He looked up. There was a car behind him, coming fast. Coming much too fast.

Careful, his mind warned. Someone tried to drown Verna Clark in that pond. You may have been seen with her.

Chapter Two

The car overtaking Jeff Gordon's was an old, souped-up clunker. With its windows rolled up against the weather, it reeked of marijuana. Seventeen-year-old Dan Crawley had just finished a joint. Sixteen-year-old Nick Indrotti was smoking one as he drove.

The clunker closed in on Jeff's sedan at sixty-odd miles an hour.

In his mirror Jeff watched the weaving gleam of its headlights and was apprehensive. Preparing to take evasive action, he shifted his right foot from gas pedal to brake. His grip on the wheel tightened. His body became a coiled spring. No one but a fool, a drunk, or an enemy, he told himself, would be driving that fast on this road under these conditions.

As the clunker came roaring up beside him, he swung as close to the road's edge as he dared, to avoid being swiped. But the overtaking car swerved and swiped him anyway.

The soft, deep sand of the road shoulder trapped the right front tire of Jeff's car. The steering wheel spun in his hands. His foot was jarred from the brake pedal. Out of control, the car lurched off the blacktop into a shallow, grassy ditch, then climbed the far side of the ditch and lunged into a grove of shadowy trees.

He was a deft enough driver to miss the first two trees the car seemed likely to crash into, but not the third. Striking that one a glancing blow with its right front fender and door, the machine reared over on its side.

After sideswiping Jeff's car, the jalopy had slowed from sixty-plus to barely fifteen miles an hour while the skinny hands of its driver clung to its wheel in panic. The rest of Nick Indrotti's body shook like the wings of a dragonfly clinging to a reed in a stiff breeze.

"Jesus, Nick!" his companion was shouting wildly. "You hit him! You knocked him off the road!"

"I couldn't help it. He swerved into me."

"Like hell he did! You swerved into him! Turn around, for Christ's sake. He may be hurt."

"We can't go back there," Nick wailed. "If he's not hurt, he'll get our license number and report us." But even while protesting, he braked the clunker to a full stop and turned to peer through the rear window.

"Listen, will you?" Dan Crawley was calmer now, more in control of his feelings. "Nobody saw it happen, so nobody can blame us, see? If he says we swerved into him, we just say he's lyin'. And this car stinks. I'm gonna air it out."

They argued a moment more while Dan was opening the windows. Then Nick turned the clunker around and drove back down the road to where they could see the other car's headlights shining through the trees on the far side of the ditch.

"Looks like it tipped over," Dan said. "Halfway over, anyhow."

"I don't see nothin' movin' in there." Nick was shaking again. "Dan—jeez! Come on! Let's clear out of here!"

"Well . . . but hold on a minute. If he's out cold, we could maybe . . . You wait while I go look." Leaping the ditch, which was dry, Dan hurried to Jeff Gordon's car.

To look into it he had to go to the front and peer in through the windshield. The driver was bent grotesquely against the door the car was resting on, with one arm limply draped over the steering wheel. There was no way Dan could open that door.

Climbing onto the car, he worked on the high-side door, badly creased from its impact with the tree. A less husky youth might not have been able to get even that one open, but in the end he succeeded. Leaning in and reaching down for the unconscious man's arm, the one draped over the wheel, he felt for a pulse at the wrist. That was what they did when things like this happened on TV, right?

He felt a pulse, and there was no blood on anything, so the guy was alive and would probably be okay when he came to. Pulling himself farther into the car, Dan took the man's wristwatch and emptied his pockets.

Afraid to take time to look at what he was stealing—he could have done that in the light from the dash, which like the car's headlights was still on—he simply jammed the loot into his own pockets to be appraised later. Then he emptied the glove compartment. Lots of stupid people kept valuable stuff in glove compartments, he knew from the dozens of cars he'd broken into. Finally he snatched the ignition key, which was only one of several on a ring with a plastic tab that glowed in the dashboard light.

Wriggling back out of the sedan like a worm from its hole in the ground, Dan worked with the keys until he found one that opened the car's trunk. There was a suitcase in the trunk—real leather, from the looks of it. He hauled it out and fled with it, leaving the trunk lid open. Stumbling back through the trees and across the ditch to the road, he wrestled the grip onto the seat beside Nick Indrotti and yelled, "Okay, let's go! He's out but alive, and I got us some stuff!" Then, as the old car roared down the road, he pulled the treasures from his pockets and examined them.

"One big, fat billfold, Nicky." Counting the bills in it, he became so excited that his feet performed a kind of dance on the floor mat, even with the suitcase across his knees. "Jeez, Nick! More'n five hundred bucks in cash! And a Visa card, two gas company cards, a driver's license and car registration. That was a Connecticut car, by the way."

"Yeah," Nick said. "I seen the plate before he swerved out and hit me."

"Oh, sure. Before he hit you. Sure. Anyway, the guy's name is Jeffrey Gordon and he's from New Haven, Connecticut." Returning the billfold to a pocket of his black vinyl jacket, Dan eagerly shuffled through the rest of what he had stolen.

That was mostly disappointing. One item was a small notebook containing names and notes. The names were unfamiliar, and some of the notes were just plain weird, such as "Ethel Everol, age 68, was visited by psychiatrist R. J. Walther at the institution where she is a patient. Claimed she actually saw the creature that killed her brother and tried to kill her. Dr. Walther says he is inclined to believe her." A high-school dropout, Dan shook his head and put the book away.

Some coins and a handkerchief made up the rest of the loot from Gordon's pockets, and the glove compartment treasures were even more disappointing. This driver, it seemed, kept only road maps and a car owner's instruction manual there.

Well . . . what about the suitcase?

A key on the ring opened it, and as Nick drove on down the road, Dan flipped up the lid. Nothing. At least, nothing you could hope to sell, and he and Nick sure wouldn't be wearing anything that might tie them in with looting a car. Some clothes, a razor, shaving cream, toothpaste and a toothbrush and even dental floss, for God's sake; a pair of bedroom slippers; none of it worth two cents. Disgusted, he slammed the bag shut.

While putting distance between them and the wrecked car as fast as possible, Nick Indrotti had been watching his pal out of the corner of his eye, knowing he'd be dumb not to. Dan might be a buddy, but this buddy had a fast pair of hands. His tone betraying his disappointment, Nick said now, "That's it? Five hundred bucks?" His earlier panic had vanished.

"More'n five hundred, I told you. And the credit cards; don't forget the credit cards." Dan Crawley shoved the suitcase off his knees onto the floor. "Gimme a joint. What the hell, Nicky, it may not be big, but it's somethin'. When you figure it was just an accident, nothin' we even planned, you got to say we're plain shit lucky."

Chapter Three

Long after the departure of the two teenagers, Jeff Gordon opened his eyes and asked himself what had happened.

He did not remember.

His head throbbed. He put his left hand to his forehead and discovered there a lump the size of a hen's egg. Just touching it caused a stab of pain as bright as a bolt of lightning. He looked at his fingers. There was no blood on them.

Why was he here? What car was this, and why was it resting on its side in the dark with its headlights on and its dashboard glowing? The headlight beams revealed a number of trees, some of them pines, grouped around the machine like giant spiders about to pounce on a crippled insect.

He looked up at the car door above him. Could

he boost himself up to it and crawl out without causing the machine to turn over on its back? He must try. Failing that, he would have to get the window open. Perhaps that would be best: to open the window. A car like this might have automatic window controls, but first you probably had to turn on the ignition. He reached for the ignition key.

There was none.

What now?

He was finding it hard to think straight. When he struggled to concentrate, the throbbing in his forehead became all but unendurable. But the struggle finally paid off. Go back to opening the door, his mind instructed. You can pull yourself up to it.

Squirming out from behind the wheel, he reached up for the door and found he could not work the release. There was a weakness in his fingers. But with beads of moisture forming on his face and salting his lips, he persisted, and the door latch finally yielded.

Now he had to boost or pull himself higher to push the door open, which meant forcing it up. This took time and increased the pounding in his head, but he won the battle, only to find that a tree beside the car, apparently the one the machine had sideswiped, was so close that the door would open only partway. He had to stretch his aching body to the limit and crawl out like a damaged caterpillar.

At last, though, he stood outside the machine

on ground covered with dead leaves and pine needles, and was able to run his hands gingerly over his body in search of injuries.

There seemed to be no major ones except the swelling on his forehead. None that caused any such sharp pain when touched, at any rate. Nor could he discover any rips in his clothing. But again, why was he here? Whose car was this? Most important, who was he?

He was wearing tan slacks and a lightweight brown sport jacket, and had a feeling there should be a billfold in the jacket's inside pocket. But the pocket was empty. All his pockets were empty. Maybe the license plate on the car would tell him something.

He went to look but learned nothing except that the car was from Connecticut. Was he in Connecticut now, close enough to walk home if he could remember where home was? He didn't think so. The trees seemed wrong, what he could see of them. The rest of the vegetation, too. Even the air felt alien.

The trunk lid was open, he saw—perhaps it had sprung open when the car hit the tree—and the trunk was empty except for a spare tire. Well, maybe something in the glove compartment would help him. Climbing back up on the car with the greatest of care, he worked the door partly open again and reached down to the dash.

But the glove compartment, like the trunk, yielded nothing.

Who was he? Where was he? How long would

the pounding in his head, apparently caused by the bruise on his forehead, keep him in the dark about these things?

Anyway, he had to walk out of here and get help somewhere. There was no way he could use the car. Where was the road?

The car ought to tell him that, at least. It must have run off a road into this grove of trees, so the road should be behind the red glow of its tail-lights. Not too far behind, either, or the machine would have hit something else before slamming into the tree here.

Had he simply lost control while driving? A blackout? Or had another driver forced him off the road and then gone on without even stopping to help him? And what time was it, by the way? He had a feeling there ought to be a watch on his left wrist, but there wasn't. Had he been robbed after wrecking the car?

Start walking, he told himself. Just pray there's a house nearby, where you can phone for a doctor and a wrecker.

With both arms outthrust like the antennae of a night-prowling insect, he struggled on through the dark and came to a ditch. On the far side of that was a two-lane blacktop road. A pale moon shone feebly through cloud gaps above it.

Judging by the position of the car, he must have been coming from the left. Had he passed any houses? He didn't remember any. Better go the other way, then.

As he turned to his right and began walking

along the road's edge, the lights of the wrecked car were still visible behind him, among the trees.

For two miles or more there was nothing. No car passed him in either direction. There were no houses. Wherever this road was, it obviously was little used. Then he came to a pair of old stone gateposts that somehow seemed familiar, flanking the start of an unpaved drive or private road that disappeared among tall trees. Beside one post was an old wooden mailbox. In the dark he had to lean close to make out the name on it.

EVEROL.

He stood there frowning at it—gratefully resting, too, because he had not stopped walking since leaving the car. Had he heard the name Everol before? Something far back in his mind, behind the pounding, said he had but supplied no details.

Strange, he thought; I don't know my own name. I don't know where I am or whose car I was driving. But I feel I ought to know who this Everol is.

It was encouraging, at least. Perhaps on coming face to face with the people who lived here, he would remember more. As he straightened from his slouch against the mailbox and went plodding along the drive, he felt his burden of despair lighten a little.

When he saw lights at last, they were the windows of a house far in from the road. A huge house, old and brooding. Two of the windows lit up a long veranda and showed him the steps. Certain he had never seen the house before, he climbed to the door with a strong feeling that he should not be doing so. Then he wondered whether he should be honest about not knowing who he was. What would he do if some hurt stranger appeared out of the dark and said, "Please help me. I've been in an accident; I don't know who I am or where I'm from or where I was going at the time it happened"? Would he let such a person in or quickly lock the door and call the police?

I could give myself a name, he thought. But unable to think of one that sounded right, he put his thumb against the bell button while his mind was still blank.

There was a buzzing sound inside, followed by the sound of slow footsteps on a wooden floor. How should he respond if the person coming to the door asked, "What do you want?"

The door opened. He found himself face-to-face with a small, white-haired woman who simply stood there frowning at him.

Recalling the name on the mailbox, he said, "Mrs. Everol?"

"Yes, I am Blanche Everol. Are you Mr. Gordon? We've been expecting you."

Gordon. That, too, seemed to be a name he ought to know, just as Everol was. Should he claim to be Gordon until he had a chance to tell them the truth? No, no, that could lead to trouble. Better be honest from the start.

"To be truthful, Mrs. Everol, I don't know who

I am at the moment." Feeling weak again, as he had at the mailbox, he put a hand against the door frame to steady himself. "I've had an accident with my car. May I use your telephone to call for help, please?"

She came closer to peer at him. "Accident?"

"About two miles down the road. I don't know what happened. When I came to, the car was on its side in a grove of trees and I had this bump on my head."

She gazed at the bruise he pointed to. "It looks nasty. Yes, you can use our phone, I suppose. Come with me."

Closing the door behind him, he trailed her down a dim hall to a wide archway on the right, and through that into a living room. To his surprise, three of its half-dozen overstuffed chairs were occupied by persons at least as old as his guide. Their attire was old, too, and decidedly old-fashioned.

Mrs. Everol said to the others, "This man says he isn't Mr. Gordon. He's been hurt in a car accident and doesn't know who he is."

The three gazed at him with such intensity that he was tempted to turn and run. Two were women. The third was a tall man with snow-white hair and a wasted face that somehow resembled a skull.

"Don't you have a driver's license, mister?" The man's voice had the gritty timbre of sandpaper sheets being rubbed together.

"No. Or anything else with a name on it. Someone emptied my pockets while I was unconscious."

"Looks like you're in big trouble."

"I want to call a doctor. If I might use your phone—"

"Who you aim to call?"

"If you folks know of a doctor who lives within reach—"

"Won't be none willin' to come out here at this hour, mister." The man jabbed a bony finger at an old brass clock on a marble-topped table. "It's past eleven. We'd be in bed if we weren't expecting Mr. Gordon."

Jeff was startled. Past eleven? How long had he been unconscious there in the woods?

"You better forget about any doctor tonight," the man said. His gaze flicked to the woman who had opened the door, then to the others. "To look at him, I'd say what this man needs most is a good night's rest, wouldn't you? I don't know why we can't let him bed down in Jacob's room. Then if he wants to be looked at in the morning, we can call someone." After a pause, during which the three women exchanged glances in silence, he added in a voice sharp with impatience, "Well, Amanda? Susan?"

"I—suppose it would be all right, Everett," one of the seated women replied with seeming reluctance.

"Jacob's room, Everett?" The other actually whispered the words.

"That what I said. Jacob's room." Everol's raspy tone implied he was the head of the household and would tolerate a discussion, perhaps, but no real argument.

Trying to sort them out, Jeff studied the four in a haze of perplexity. Apparently the man was Everol, first name Everett. The woman who had come to the door was his wife, Blanche. One of the other two—tall, white-haired, with a face full of hollows—looked enough like Everett to be his sister. The other, the one who had whispered, "Jacob's room, Everett?" was tiny, like Blanche, and might be her sister.

Was this the whole household? And was the absent Jacob yet another member of this strange, old-world clan?

Everol, he thought. Everett Everol. Why did the name seem to tug at his memory so? And the other names, too. Where could he have heard them before?

Skull-face turned to him. "Well, mister, what you say? You agree what you most need right now is a good night's sleep?"

"With all due respect, sir, I'd prefer to see a doctor," Jeff protested. "If you don't know one who might make a house call, do you—is there a cab I could call to take me to one?"

"No taxicab in this town, mister."

"What town is this, please?"

"Nearest one is Clandon."

"What state?"

"What state? Florida, o' course. Where you think you are?"

"I didn't know." But the name Clandon had

come close to ringing a bell in Jeff's mind. Clandon, Florida? Yes. If he asked a few more questions . . .

But he was afraid to do that. These people already suspected him of being unstable.

"Well . . . if I can't get to a doctor, perhaps you're right in saying a good night's sleep would be best."

"That's settled, then." Everol pushed himself out of his chair. He was even taller than he had appeared to be when seated. His feet were bare, Jeff noticed for the first time. In long-legged black pants that were held up by gray suspenders, and a long-sleeved white shirt that was patched in places, he could have passed for a scarecrow. "Blanche," he said to his smaller but equally plain wife, "why'n't you fix this feller some hot soup while I show him upstairs? When it's ready, you just bring it on up." He turned to Jeff. "Mister Whoever-you-are, you just follow me, if you will."

Jeff trailed the man up a wide flight of stairs, the carpeting on them almost black with age, and along an upstairs hall to the rear of the house. Halting before the last of several doors, Everol produced a ring of keys and inserted one into an opening under the porcelain knob. Strange, Jeff thought with a touch of apprehension. How many people kept bedroom doors locked, even when their occupants were absent?

The click of a switch under Everol's thumb caused a lamp on a bedside table to glow. The room was larger than Jeff had expected, but this was a big old house, and probably all its rooms were spacious. This one had two windows in the wall facing the door and two more in the wall to his left. The bed was a massive four-poster of dark mahogany. Completing the furnishings were two huge dressers, a bedside table, and two bedroom-type chairs with faded rosebuds on their floor-length skirts of chintz.

"Bed's all made up," the tall man said in his sandpaper voice. "Be a good idea for you to get right into it, I should think. You look mighty peaked."

"Are you sure this won't inconvenience you, Mr. Everol?"

"No trouble at all."

"You said this is Jacob's room. Are you—"

"He don't use it now. Let me get you somethin' to sleep in." Striding to a dresser, Everol dropped to one knee to ease open its bottom drawer. "Reckon these'll fit you good enough. You're about his height and build." He placed a pair of short-sleeved gray pajamas on the bed and turned to peer at Jeff again. "You'll find a razor and shave cream in the top drawer there. While you're makin' ready for bed, I'll just go see what's holdin' up the soup I told my wife to fix you. The bathroom's down the hall to your left."

He went out, leaving the door open. But he was back again by the time Jeff had the pajamas on. On the bedside table he placed an old metal tray advertising Coca-Cola on which were a covered bowl and some sandwiches wrapped in waxed paper.

"Thank you," Jeff said. "I really am hungry."

"But still don't know who you are, eh?"

"No, not yet. But it will come, I'm sure."

"Maybe while you sleep," Everol said on his way to the door. "Things do sometimes. All sorts of things."

This time he shut the door behind him.

Chapter Four

Seated on a chair beside the bed, Jeff gratefully consumed his bedtime snack. Both the soup and the sandwiches were of chicken; the soup was homemade. After a trip along the hall to the bathroom, where the plumbing was as old as he had expected, he turned down the four-poster, got into it, and by switching off the lamp on the bedside table plunged the room into darkness.

Not complete darkness, however. As his eyes adjusted, faint moonlight filtering through the windows brought the furnishings into focus again. The night sky must be clearing.

That was comforting. He had been telling himself he did not trust this room or this house or these people, and was not sure he ought to risk going to sleep here.

Dear God, if only he could remember who he was and what he was supposed to be doing. And why did he feel he had been in this very room before, or at least had had it described to him?

For a time he lay without moving, his eyes wide open, the only sound that of his own breathing. Were the people in the living room downstairs talking about him, discussing his unexpected appearance at their door and his puzzling condition? They must be if they were normally curious folk, but he heard no voices. Perhaps, though, nothing but a very loud noise would pass through the heavy plank floor of this room and the faded, many-colored hooked rug that covered two thirds of it. What kind of planks were they? Not pine. Cypress, maybe? He seemed to have read somewhere that cypress floors were often used in old Florida houses.

Why had he been reading about old Florida houses?

But now he did hear something. He heard a car being started, and the sound seemed to come from below the windows at the side of the room. Sliding out of bed, he hurried barefoot to one of them and peered out through a pane of bubbly glass.

Yes, a car. A car in an old wooden barn that obviously served at least partly as a garage. The doors were open and the car's lights were on. Its taillights seemed to stare out like the red eyes of a crouching animal. Farther inside, its headlights created a mist of yellow.

As he watched, the machine crept out of the barn in reverse and made a turn on a patch of bare earth in front, then growled out toward the road.

To go where at this time of night? *Probably to look for the car I was driving,* Jeff thought. *To see if I told the truth about having an accident. And if he finds the car and isn't stupid, he'll take down the license number and phone the police.*

But all right. If Everol does that, the police will contact their counterparts in Connecticut and learn who owns the car, won't they? And since it probably belongs to me, I'll find out who I am when they come here to talk to me about it.

Good. Except that I should have had sense enough to take down the license number and call the police myself. Or memorize it, rather, since I didn't have anything to write it down with.

Anyway, Everol is not a threat; he's only trying to help. So . . . go back to bed and hope there is still some life in the car's battery and the lights are still on.

In bed he closed his eyes this time and courted sleep by breathing slowly and deeply. When this failed, he forced his mind to repeat over and over, "Who am I? Why am I here?"

It was like counting sheep. After a while he dozed.

And began dreaming.

The dream seemed to be faintly familiar, like the name Everol and the name Gordon—they had asked him if his name was Gordon, hadn't they?—and certain aspects of this house, this room. The room, in fact, was part of it. In the dream he was staring at the very window from which he had seen the car being driven out of the barn.

Something was in motion outside that window now. Something so big it filled the whole aperture. A bird? He had a feeling it ought to be a bird, a huge one, perhaps a huge black vulture.

But no, it was not a bird. It had a mouth, not a beak. A mouth like that of a snake, with a red tongue that kept flicking out to touch the glass. But no snake he had ever seen was that big or that . . . What was the right word? Prehistoric? If real, this thing must be a re-creation of some monstrous creature that had lived on earth thousands of years ago.

Now the jaws were agape and he saw the fangs. God in heaven, they were like stalagmites in a cave! And as the creature's head came closer to the window, swaying from side to side as though preparing to strike at him through the glass, it was so much bigger than the aperture that all he could see was an endless, waxy-white tunnel of throat down which he would be sucked and swallowed after the fangs shot their venom into him.

But wait. Wait. He was not just lying in bed mesmerized, waiting for that to happen. No, by God. In the dream he was out of bed and striding to the window. He was standing before the window on widespread legs, with his right hand outstretched to touch the lower sash. His finger was tracing a design on the glass.

A triangle? Five triangles? No—it was a five-pointed star, a pentagram. And though the glass intervened, his finger seemed to be tracing the design in the very throat of the monstrous snake-thing that was poised there to hurl itself at him.

Now on the upper sash his finger drew a second such star. And with that one finished, he straightened before the window and became a pentagram himself, his feet still wide apart, his arms outstretched, his head the focal point of power. How did he know that a pentagram could be a force for good against evil and might protect him? Where had such knowledge come from?

In the dream he stood there staring down the throat of the snake-thing outside the glass, a sentry on guard at the window, defiant. Then, with a hiss of rage that made the whole window clatter in its frame, the monster drew back.

The red tongue flicked a final time and was withdrawn. The jaws snapped shut. Slowly, very slowly, the hideous head retreated into outer darkness until only the glitter of its eyes remained visible. Then that, too, was gone.

Suddenly weak, Jeff clutched at the windowsill to keep from falling. Had he seen the thing or only dreamed it? Was he standing at the window or still in bed asleep?

A snake. He had seen a huge snake. Not a real one, surely, but a monstrous thing in a nightmare. Like the vulture.

Was he the one who had seen the vulture? No,

no, that had been a woman. A woman named Ethel Everol.

Everol. People in this house were named Everol, too, weren't they? Was Ethel one of the women downstairs?

No. They were Blanche, Amanda, and Susan. But she was related to them somehow. And she had told someone named Dr. Walther, who had talked to her at some institution where she was now confined, that she had seen the vulture twice, first at a window of her brother Jacob's room the night he was so horribly killed, then at a window of her own room before she was put away.

Brother Jacob. This was Jacob's room.

Think, man. Think! You know about this house. It's a house of horror.

Get out of it, for God's sake! Now!

Chapter Five

"Mister, you awake?"

He must have passed out on the floor. The sandpaper voice came to him from the doorway, and the room was gray with daylight. He still wore the borrowed pajamas. The dead man's pajamas. Jacob's.

As the tall stringbean with the gritty voice came into the room, Jeff struggled to his feet without reaching for the hand outstretched to help him. Everol, was it? Yes, Everett Everol. "You all right?" the man said. "You fall or something?"

"I must have."

"Nothing worse than that?" Apparently unconvinced, Everol turned to look around the room. "What's that on the glass there?" Fiercely scowling, he strode to the window from which Jeff had watched the car. "You do this, mister?"

Bewildered, Jeff walked over and stood beside him.

A star? A pentagram? The dream came back to him: the monstrous snake-thing at the window, threatening to smash the glass and do to him what the vulture had done to Jacob. In the dream he had leaped out of bed in a frantic effort to save himself by hurriedly tracing pentagrams on both windowpanes with his finger. Was there something significant about such five-pointed stars? Something that might keep dream monsters at bay?

But had it been a dream? The glass at which he stared now in total confusion was gray with dust and dirt; evidently no one had washed these windows in ages. And something had unquestionably drawn a five-pointed star on each pane.

Well, all right. Even though the threatening serpent had been only a figment of his imagination, he must have stepped here to the window in his sleep and done this. There had been nothing but grime on the windows when he first examined the room, he was certain.

Or . . . had someone come into the room and done this while he slept? Everol, say, or one of the women. Or Jacob, whose room this was.

No, no, not Jacob. Jacob was dead. His twin sister Ethel was in an institution.

Now how did he know that Ethel was Jacob's twin? Had they told him, or were things coming back? They wouldn't have had any reason to tell him such a thing . . . would they?

The tall man at his side was speaking to him. "Mister, let's just forget this for the time being, hey? Why don't you get dressed and come downstairs for some breakfast?" He glanced at his wristwatch. "It's close to nine o'clock."

"I—yes, of course. Thank you."

"How you like your eggs? I have to tell our cook."

"Any way. Any way at all."

"Soft-boiled? We like 'em soft-boiled."

"Fine."

"All right, then. Be ready in just a few minutes, so don't be too long." With a final quizzical look at the marked window, Everol strode from the room, leaving the door open behind him.

Their voices guided Jeff to the dining room when he went downstairs. All four of them were seated at an old, dark mahogany table, apparently waiting for him. Everett stood up and motioned him to an empty chair beside the tiny woman who might be his wife's sister.

" 'Case you don't remember from last night," the man said, "this is my wife, Blanche, this is my sister Amanda, and this is Blanche's sister Susan." He glanced at each as he spoke. So—yes—the two diminutive women were sisters.

"Good morning," Jeff said, including them all in his nod. "I want to thank you again for taking me in last night."

"Did you sleep well?" The question came with an oddly intense look of concern from little Susan, who was seated beside him and spun herself to face him as she spoke.

"About as well as could be expected, I guess, under the circumstances."

"Everett found you on the floor just now, he says."

"Yes. I thought I had only dreamed about getting up in the night, but evidently I actually did it, and fell."

"Getting up to do what?" asked Everett's tall sister, Amanda, leaning across the table as if afraid she might not hear his answer.

"There was something at the window, I seem to remember. I mean, of course, I dreamed there was."

In silence the three Everols and Blanche's sister exchanged glances before the man said with a frown, "What'd you see at the window, mister? A bird, maybe?"

"No, not a bird. A snake. But it was only a dream. Snakes don't climb to second-floor windows, do they? Besides, this one was something huge and—well—I guess the word is prehistoric." With a little laugh, Jeff tried to break what he felt was a growing tension.

They didn't seem amused. Instead, they exchanged glances, as if what he had said disturbed them in some way. Then, "They've found prehistoric things here in this part of Florida," said little Susan. "Scientists have, I mean."

"So I've heard." But where, Jeff asked himself, could he have heard such a thing? Until these people had told him so last night, he hadn't even known he was in Florida.

At that moment two other members of this strange household appeared. A black woman of about thirty-five, followed by a black man much older, came from the kitchen with coffee, toast, and the boiled eggs Everett Everol had promised.

Seeming to feel she had to explain their presence, little Blanche said, "This is Lelio Savain and his wife, Lucille. They're Haitians who live here on the property."

"Bon jou', compère. Bon jou', commère," Jeff heard himself saying. *"Comment ou yé?"*

Freezing in the act of putting the food on the table, the couple turned their heads to look at him. The others stared, too—first at him, then at the Haitians. The black man said, *"Eské ou parlé Creole nou, m'sieu?"*

"Do I speak your Creole?" This time the words Jeff heard himself speaking were English, because he was thinking out loud, not really answering the question. "Well, yes, I do. A little, at least."

In Creole, Lelio said, "You have lived in our country, then?"

"Yes." Was it true? Had he at one time lived in Haiti, or spent enough time there to learn the peasant tongue? He could continue a conversation with this old fellow if he wished to, he realized. But he had better not. The members of the Everol clan were apparently not too pleased. "Perhaps we can talk about this later," he said in Creole, and then became silent.

They were all silent until the two Haitians had gone back to the kitchen. Then Everett Everol said, "Have you lived in Haiti, mister?"

"I don't know. It would seem so, wouldn't it? But I don't remember."

"Can't understand why anyone would want to live in that backward country." Everol shook his head vehemently. "These two people, months ago we found them shacked up in an old caretaker's cottage on the property here and let them stay because they had nowhere to go and offered to help out around the place. He looks after the grounds and she does some of the housework." He shrugged. "Nobody local would have worked for what they were willing to accept, so we let them stay." He shrugged again. "I suspect they're in the country without any proper papers, but that's no business of ours."

Jeff was reluctant to talk about Haiti until he had done more thinking about his unexpected ability to speak Creole. "Tell me," he said, "did you go looking for my car last night, Mr. Everol?"

"Yes, I did."

"And did you find it?"

"Two miles down the road. Banged up, like you said, with the lights still on."

"I hope you took down the license number and called the police. They might be able to tell me who I am."

"There was no license plate, mister."

"What?"

"The car'd been stripped. Keys gone, glove compartment empty. Trunk open and empty, too. And, like I say, the license plate was missing. Somebody must have come along and taken everything after you walked away from there."

Or, Jeff thought, I was run off the road by people who do that sort of thing for plunder on these back-country roads.

"So it looks like you won't find out from the police who you are," Everol said, with another of the shrugs he so liked to use when talking.

"Is there a garage in Clandon that can repair the car?" Jeff asked. For some reason he felt he knew there was.

"Well, yes." The old man really seemed reluctant to admit it. "After we eat, I can call and see if they'll send out a tow truck, I suppose."

"Please."

"Don't want you to think you're not welcome here."

"You've been very kind. But I mustn't impose any longer than I have to."

"Eat your breakfast now," said Blanche's sister, Susan. "You must be hungry after all you've been through."

Silence took over, but when the Haitian woman, Lucille, returned to fill the coffee mugs, Jeff caught himself wondering again where he had learned to speak the peasant tongue of her country. Far back in his mind lay a hazy picture of himself seated on a bench at some kind of ceremony in which women in white robes were doing a slow, rather stately dance around a painted post, and a man in black pants and a red shirt was drawing designs in cornmeal on the dirt floor, and a throbbing of drums accompanied a sound of chanting, and he was taking notes. But it was all too vague. He could not pull the blurred bits of the picture together and make any real sense of it.

Breakfast finished, Everett said, "Well, mister, let me call that garage and see what they can do for you." He rose and went into the adjoining room, the living room in which Jeff had talked to all of them the night before. In a few minutes he was back, nodding.

"Their wrecker's out on a job, so they can't come right off. But they'll be here soon as it's free."

"Would you, then—would you mind very much if I went for a short walk? It might clear my mind."

"Do anything you like."

"But be careful," little Susan warned, leaning toward Jeff and shaking her head at him. "You've been in an accident, remember, and could have things wrong with you that you don't know about. Don't go too far and get lost, now."

"I'll be careful. I promise."

"If the garage man turns up before you get back, I'll tell him where your car is," Everol said.

"I won't be gone that long. But thanks."

Chapter Six

In silence they watched him walk out of the room. When they heard the front door click shut behind him, little Susan frowned across the table at her sister's string-bean husband.

"I just don't understand, Everett. He seems such a nice man, and we know who he is from that picture in the magazine he sent. So why can't we tell him?"

Everett's sister Amanda said, "Susan's right, you know, Everett. You're just not making any sense!"

"And you told him there was no license plate on his car," Everett's wife Blanche said. "You took it off and brought it back here, then told him somebody stole it. I don't understand, either."

Everett prefaced his reply with one of his eloquent shrugs. "Can't you see what will happen if we tell him who he is? He's been hurt and must be scared half out of his mind. He doesn't even know he's at the place he was coming to, for God's sake. If we tell him who he is, he most likely will leave us and go to some hospital to get himself looked at."

"I disagree," said Susan with a toss of her head. "I say he's much more likely to stay here and help us if he knows who he is. Didn't he just about beg us to let him come here in the first place?"

Amanda jabbed a forefinger at her brother. "And if it's beginning again, Everett, we need him! He saw something at his window last night, he said. And I'm telling you I heard something at mine the night before."

"And I say you only dreamed it," Everett shot back.

"Everett, please!" There were tears in Amanda's eyes. "I swear to you I heard—"

"Oh, be quiet!"

"No, you be quiet, Everett Everol." His wife leaned closer to glare at him. "If Amanda says she heard one of them again, I believe her. And you're not making any sense at all about Mr. Gordon. For heaven's sake, just a few minutes ago you phoned Staley Howe to pick up the man's car. If you don't want him leaving here, why'd you do that?"

"You didn't see the car. I did." Everett's hands were clenched on the table now, wrinkling the cloth.

"What's that supposed to mean?"

"It'll be days before Staley and his boy can fix that machine so anyone can drive it. By that time, the way I see this, our man will be over his loss of memory and anxious to get on with his investigation here."

"So why can't we help him get over it?" Susan demanded. "Everett, you're going at this all wrong!"

"Oh, for God's sake, Susan, shut up and put yourself in his place for a minute. Try to see this through his eyes. You've been hurt and don't know who you are or how bad it is. You're scared. Now suppose I was to tell you your name and that you came here from miles away to investigate some hellish things that have been happening here in this house, but you don't even know what I'm talking about. Wouldn't you want to get to a hospital or a doctor and find out what's wrong with you?"

With a petulant toss of her head, little Susan pushed back her chair. "Very well, have it your way. You will anyway."

Blanche and Amanda gazed at Everett in silence, both of them frowning and slowly shaking their heads from side to side.

"What's more," Susan continued, on her feet now, "I think we're not just talking about Jacob being killed and Ethel sent to the asylum and those things coming back to torment us again when we thought we were free of them. There's something going on here in this house that you're

HUGH B. CAVE

hiding from the rest of us, Everett." At the door she turned for one last challenge before marching from the room. "And don't any of you try to tell me different!"

Chapter Seven

Leaving the house, Jeff Gordon started down the driveway with no destination in mind, only the thought that a stroll about the property might help him to remember. In daylight the driveway was most attractive: a curving lane of what looked like gray beach sand, one car wide, through a woodland of tall pines and heavy undergrowth.

He turned to look back at the house and saw that it, too, was attractive in daylight—obviously one of the "old Florida homes" he had read about. Old, yes, and rather badly in need of paint, but impressively big, with a long, wide veranda and many windows.

Windows. Had he, in fact, seen something like a monstrous, prehistoric snake at his window last night? Had he drawn pentagrams on the glass to keep it at bay? Shaking his head, he turned again and went on.

But before he reached the blacktop highway that he remembered walking along the night before, a footpath on his right caught his eye. Curious to know where it went, he turned along it and presently came to what had probably once been a caretaker's cottage. Little more than a shack now, it nevertheless appeared to be occupied. On a line between two pines in its small yard hung some sheets, towels, a white dress, and a man's white long-sleeved shirt.

He stood for a moment, undecided. Then when he saw no sign of movement and heard nothing to indicate that anyone was at home, he crossed the yard to a window and looked in. Yes, despite its condition, the shack was being used. The room he was looking at contained chairs and a table, an old, small TV on a stand. At the far end an open door revealed a chest of drawers and one side of a neatly made double bed.

Was this where the two Haitians lived? "We found them in an old caretaker's cottage on the property and let them stay," Everol had said, hadn't he?

Objects on the table were close enough to the window to catch Jeff's eye and arouse his curiosity. Maracas? Those dried gourds used as rattles in Latin American music? Yes, probably. He had heard such instruments used in Haiti, he remembered. Perhaps the old fellow was a musician.

Curiously, though, the tabletop was strewn with

small colored stones, colored beads, and what appeared to be snake vertebrae.

Take a dried gourd, Jeff thought. Put into it some small stones of different colors and some vertebrae from a snake, because the revered old god Damballah comes in the form of a snake. Then wrap the outside of the gourd with colored beads and you have an *asson*, a sacred rattle used in voodoo by *houngans* and *mambos*. In a way it was even more essential than the drums, flags, ceremonial urns, and other such paraphernalia.

So was Lelio a voodoo priest? Or his wife, Lucille, a priestess? Were they practicing voodoo here?

He shrugged. He evidently knew something about voodoo, just as he had known how to talk to the two Haitians in their own tongue. Ordinary voodoo was no terrible thing, merely a peasant religion dealing with the spirits of gods and the dead. Of course, there were some dangerous deviations on the dark fringe of it, but what the old man and his wife chose to do here on the Everol place was no concern of his, was it?

He continued his walk. After a while he circled a small, dark body of water—a sinkhole, he guessed it would be called here—and climbed a rather steep wooded knoll. Then the sound of voices disturbed the woodland stillness, and he heard the growl of an engine. Turning in that direction to investigate, he found himself gazing down the other side of the knoll at a body of water larger than the one he had just circled.

In it, some fifteen feet out from shore, was a car. At least, he could make out a solitary red fender protruding from the gloomy water. And at the edge of the pond or lake—whatever it should be called—stood a battered old tow truck.

The red fender tugged at something in his memory. Had he seen it before? Almost shoulder deep in the lake beside it, a young fellow appeared to be trying to attach a chain to some submerged part of the car, while an older man, on the bank, called out instructions.

Suddenly a young woman, standing near the truck, saw Jeff on the knoll and waved to him.

With a feeling he had met her somewhere, he walked down to her.

"Well, hi, Jeff!" she said with enthusiasm. "I didn't expect to see you until this evening."

Jeff. Was that his name?

"How are things going at the house?" she asked.

"All right, I think." He knew he was staring in a way that could be frightening to her, but he could not help it. "Look—I've had an accident and don't remember things too well. Do I know you?"

"Do you know me!" She came closer and did some staring of her own. "You don't remember picking me up and giving me a lift last night?"

"Picking you up where?"

"Out there on the highway, the other side of those trees." She turned to point. "Just after my car went into the lake here. You were going to

the Everols' place, you said, but went out of your
way to take me to Clandon."

Clandon. A small town in the rain, and the
name Earl Watson on a mailbox. It was beginning
to come back to him. "Are you—did you ask me
to do something for you at the Everols'?"

She reached for his hand and again looked intently into his face. "You really mean it, don't you?
You have had an accident."

He nodded.

She glanced at the man by the truck, who was
still shouting instructions at the youth in the lake.
"Let's talk," she said, and drew Jeff away from
there, toward a cluster of boulders that, in an old-
world setting, could have been the remnants of
an old castle tumbled by an earthquake. There
she peered at his face yet again and said, "I'm
Verna Clark, Jeff Gordon. Does that mean anything to you?"

He let his mind work on the names awhile. Jeff
Gordon. Yes, he was Jeff Gordon. And she . . .
"You're a professor, sort of? That's what you told
me, isn't it? A professor, sort of. Looking for fossils."

She let out a held breath as an expression of
relief chased the frown of concern from her face.
It was really a beautiful face. "That's right, looking
for fossils. And on the way to town I told you how
the Everols were giving me fits. And you promised
to talk to them about me. Jeff, what happened?
What accident are you talking about?"

He was beginning to remember that, too. A car

behind him in the dark, coming much too fast. Sideswiping his car and sending him off the road, through a ditch, into a grove of trees. He recalled his frantic efforts to avoid hitting the trees as he struggled to bring his car to a stop. Then the crash.

When he was sure he had it right in his mind, he told her about it.

"And you ended up at the Everols' place anyway?" she said. "But that's not surprising. Theirs is the only house along here. So tell me about them, huh? What are they like?"

Delighted that he was able to do so, he told her about Everett, and Everett's tiny wife Blanche, and Blanche's equally tiny sister Susan, and Everett's tall sister Amanda. He mentioned the Haitian couple and the cottage, and his suspicion that they might be into voodoo. And when Verna Clark said, "How would you know that?" he was able to say without hesitation, "Because I spent last summer in Haiti, studying voodoo. Because my hobby—which I hope someday will become more than a hobby—is psychic research. And that's why I'm here in Florida. With the Everols' permission—reluctantly given, but still permission—I'm here to investigate what's been happening in that house of theirs."

"And you have a date with me this evening," Verna Clark said, smiling now. "Do you also remember that?"

"To take you to dinner at the Clandon Inn."

"Right. Phew!" She shook her head in wonder.

"You really had me scared. But will you be able to keep our date? Will your car be okay?"

He didn't think it would be, he admitted. "And I have no money, Verna. While I was out cold after being run off the road, someone took everything I had. So until I can phone a friend to wire me some money, I guess we'd better—"

"No, you don't." Her head shake was emphatic. "We go to dinner as planned. On me this first time. I want to talk to you."

He was delighted. "All right! But now I'd better get back to the house. The garage man is supposed—" He turned to look at the tow truck by the lake. "Oh-oh. This is the garage man, isn't it?"

"I'm sure it is." Verna nodded. "He's the only one around."

The youth in the lake had finished his job while they were talking, and the man on the bank was climbing into the truck now. They were father and son, Jeff guessed. The boy must be about sixteen; the man was big and bearded, with hair down to his shoulders, and wore a gray sweatshirt with HOWE'S AUTO REPAIR on it in red.

The truck's engine growled. The tow chain rose tautly from the dark water, dripping weeds and mud. Verna Clark's little red car crept up onto dry land like an oversized turtle.

All at once Jeff's attention was caught by a movement in a tangle of brush at the top of the knoll. A man stood there, hands on hips, apparently watching what was happening. A man not young, wearing a long-sleeved white shirt and dark trousers. Was it the Haitian? Was it Everett Everol? Before he could see enough to decide, the fellow apparently realized he had been spotted and, with an abrupt about-face, disappeared.

Disappeared so quickly that it seemed a little strange, even unnatural. There one second, gone the next. But before Jeff could think more about it, he saw that Verna Clark's car was rigged for the tow to town and Mr. Howe was beckoning.

"Hey, Miss Clark! Have to talk to you about this, and I got another job to do this mornin'!"

"The other job is my car," Jeff said to Verna.

"Yes. And I have to go." She touched his hand. "Look. I have a borrowed car out on the highway. It's how I got here. Suppose I pick you up this evening, about seven."

"Great."

"I won't come to the house, though. They might try something else on me." Her glance at the car said she still thought the Everols were responsible for its rolling into the lake, with her supposed to be inside it. "I'll wait for you at their gate. Okay?"

"Seven o'clock. I'll be there."

She hurried to the truck, and Jeff climbed the knoll for his return walk to the house. On reaching the top, he wondered again how the man watching them could have disappeared so quickly? By stepping behind a boulder, perhaps? That must be the answer. Many on the knoll were big enough.

He had other things to think about, he realized

as he continued his return journey to the house. Why hadn't the Everols told him who he was? They knew, of course. In urging them to let him come here, he had sent them a copy of a magazine article about him, with a full-page photo. Blanche must have known who he was when she opened the door and said, "Are you Mr. Gordon? We've been expecting you." And the others must have known when she led him into the living room, where they were waiting.

So why had they kept him in the dark about it? And what should he do now? Tell them he knew who he was, and ask for an explanation of their behavior?

No, he decided. Wait. If they were playing some kind of game with him, he would have a better chance of finding out what they were up to if he said nothing.

But he should stay with them if they would let him. Despite their puzzling treatment of him, one Everol was dead and another insane, so they had to be the victims, not the instigators, of what was happening here.

Chapter Eight

According to the weathered sign above its doorway, the Clandon Inn had been erected in 1908. It looked even older.

"And it's not the oldest building in this town, by a long shot," Verna Clark said as she and Jeff walked to it from her car. "I expected to be staying here, actually, but after a fire last month they closed it for repairs. All except the dining room."

"A fire?"

"Some newspaper people were here, investigating the disappearance of a woman. One of them was smoking in bed. Nobody was hurt, thank heaven."

She was happy to have someone to talk to, Jeff guessed. Since picking him up at the Everols' gate she had scarcely stopped for breath. Mostly, so far, she had talked about how uncomfortable she felt at the Watsons', and how she would move in a minute if they weren't the only people in town who took in roomers.

Except for two other couples and a family of two adults and three small children, the Clandon Inn dining room was empty. Jeff indicated a corner table where Verna and he might talk without being overheard, and a waiter in his sixties, wearing black trousers and a white shirt, led them to it. Jeff sent a quizzical look after him as he departed with their order.

"Does every male around here wear black pants and a white shirt?" He, of course, had on the only outfit he possessed at the moment: the tan slacks and lightweight brown jacket he had been wearing when he regained consciousness in his wrecked car. Where, he wondered, were the rest of his clothes now? And his wallet? And the notebook he'd been carrying, with his scribblings about the Everol case and certain voodoo services in Haiti?

"Does every male do what?" Verna said.

"Dress that way, in black pants and a longsleeved white shirt. First Everol. Then the Haitian fellow, and the one I told you about who was watching us from the knoll. Now our waiter."

Realizing he wasn't serious, she let a smile chase the look of concern from her face.

"You were telling me about the sinkhole," Jeff reminded her.

"Yes. Well, as I said, it's on the Everol property,

and the Everols have threatened to fence it off, but people do go there. At least they used to. One Sunday when her husband wanted to watch the Miami Dolphins on TV, a Mrs. Shelby took their two children there. Not to swim, of course. Just for a picnic. And when the little girl's mother and brother were busy laying out the food and not watching her, she disappeared."

"And your Earl Watson found her."

"Scuba diving is his hobby. The police asked him to search the sinkhole and he brought the child up, but of course she was dead. Since then, everyone calls the place the Drowning Pit."

"Even the Everols?"

"Well, I don't know about them. They don't talk to me. But the townspeople do."

"And where is it, exactly?"

"You know where we were standing when you saw the man on the knoll?"

Jeff nodded.

"Well, as I told you when I took you there to look at my car, the knoll isn't on the Everol property and I wasn't trespassing. But the other side of it is theirs, and the Drowning Pit is near the foot of it on that side."

Jeff nodded. "I passed it before I climbed the knoll. A spooky kind of place, like the water-filled quarry pits we have in New England."

"There are three or four others on the Everol property, I've heard. You know what a Florida sinkhole is, don't you?"

"Tell me."

"Well, they're usually vertical shafts created when the roofs of caves give way. If what's underneath is only an isolated pocket in the limestone, the shaft just fills up with rainwater. But if what's down there is a whole network of chambers and tunnels already filled with water, the shaft becomes an entrance to an underwater cave system."

"What kind is the Drowning Pit?"

"Just a deep shaft full of rainwater, Jack Watson says. But we have many underwater caves in this part of Florida, and there have been lots of drownings. I read somewhere that more than eighty divers have drowned here since nineteen-sixty."

Jeff had not tried to change the subject. Verna Clark had a need to talk to someone, he told himself. She was lonely, and as a stranger in Clandon, putting herself at risk in the research she was trying to do, she had every right to be apprehensive as well. Obviously she did not feel she could talk freely to the people at whose home she was staying.

But what a woman she was! The young lady he had picked up on the highway yesterday had been striking enough in pants, shirt, and floppy hat. Now, sitting opposite him in a soft white cotton dress, with her golden hair free to frame her face, she was nothing less than lovely. So let her talk. Let her talk about anything at all. He was content just to sit and look at her while listening.

"Have the Everols mentioned me?" she asked.

"No."

"They haven't warned you to stay away from me? That I'm a terrible creature who keeps threatening their privacy?"

"I haven't talked to them that much."

"Tell me more about them, Jeff. Please."

"First tell me what you already know. About Jacob, for instance. And his twin sister, who's in the asylum."

Before she could answer, the waiter came with their dinners of grouper—fresh caught in the nearby Gulf, if the menu was truthful. He departed, and Verna said, "All I know is what I read in the papers when it happened, plus a few details supplied by the Watsons when I asked them about it." She frowned, as though wondering how much she ought to say, then seemed to relax. "Have you read Daphne Du Maurier's story of the birds that became killers and waged war on people? Hitchcock made a movie of it."

"*The Birds*. Yes."

"Well, last month Jacob Everol is supposed to have been attacked by a huge vulture and just about torn to pieces. That's the story his twin sister Ethel told, anyway. She said she heard a loud noise and glass breaking. Then she heard Jacob screaming and ran to his room, and the bird was on his bed, holding him down with its talons and tearing at him with its beak. It had his whole face torn off, she said. When she screamed, it turned and looked at her, its eyes blazing as if they were on fire, and then it flew out through a big hole in the wall where a window had been. It must have made the hole when it broke in, she said. Is that the story you heard?"

He nodded. "Basically, yes. I only read it, of course. And heard what was reported on TV."

"Well, that's all I did, except for what the Watsons have told me."

"What about the second visit of the vulture?"

"It appeared at a window of Ethel's room the next night, but she was awake and saw it in time to escape downstairs. But it frightened her so much that she went out of her mind. The Everols tried to take care of her at home but ended up having to put her in some asylum."

Again Jeff nodded.

For a moment Verna concentrated on her dinner. Then, looking at him again, she said more quietly, "There's something else I want to talk about, Jeff."

"Yes?"

"About why I'm here. Because I'm frightened and need to confide in someone I can trust."

Pushing his plate aside, Jeff looked at her and waited.

"I'm not a—professor, sort of." Her smile was gone almost before he could be sure he had seen it. "And my name isn't Verna Clark. It's Linda Mason, and I'm only a graduate student of archaeology. My older sister, Kimberly, is the professor."

Jeff only nodded.

"Kim is the one who made the important finds near the Everol property," Linda Mason went on, choosing her words slowly and with care. "We're talking about last month. I was in school, of course. She phoned me and said she had found some fantastic animal remains—fossils—that she thought might be even more important than the seven-thousand-year-old human ones those construction workers discovered at Windover in eighty-two—the ones with complete, well-preserved brains, if you're up on such things. She was wildly excited."

"And?"

"She called me four times in all. Four calls in two weeks, while she was staying right here at the Clandon Inn. Then the calls stopped coming and another week went by, and I had a call from the police up here, asking a whole lot of questions. My sister had disappeared."

"The woman who disappeared," Jeff said. "Newsmen here—the fire at this hotel—"

"Mother, too, had been in touch with Kimberly by phone right along, of course. Our dad is dead. But the people at the inn here, who didn't have any real idea of what she was doing, said she had simply gone out one morning and not come back. Her car was found near the Everol place. Her clothes and things were still in her room."

"This was last month?"

"Early last month. May."

"Before Jacob was killed and his sister went insane?"

She nodded. "I came here with Mother, of course. In Kim's room we found the fossils she had talked about. They've since been identified as parts of a huge carnivorous bird, like the one discovered near Gainsville in sixty-one, and an enormous, equally old wolf. Nothing had been disturbed. But Kim had vanished."

"The police were trying to find your sister, of course?"

"They questioned everyone for days."

"Including the Everols?"

A frown touched her face. "The Everols were first on the list because her car was found near there. And because of their ongoing war against intruders. They said they'd seen her a number of times on or near their property and had warned her not to trespass, but that was all."

"But now you think—"

"Jeff, all I know is, Kim and I were very close. If she were alive, she would never cut me out of her life like this. I want to know what happened to her."

Jeff was silent for a moment. Then he said with a frown, "Did she come here to look for fossils or just happen to find some here?"

"She said in her first letter that she was driving through and stopped because she had to go to the bathroom. She walked in off the road—from her description it might have been near that pond my car rolled into—and found a piece of bone that some dog probably dug up. Easter break was only two days off, so after studying the bone in the college lab she came back here to investigate,

71

intending to make a project of it if it seemed promising."

"And there's never been a clue to what happened to her?"

She shook her head. "I suspect the Everols, of course, because of their attitude toward strangers. Twice before I've been here trying to find out something. Now I intend to spend the summer here if I have to."

He told her about the snake thing at his window. "Probably I only dreamed the snake, but actually, in sleep, got out of bed and drew the pentagram. So far as I know, the Everols haven't had any trouble since the vulture claimed Jacob and Ethel."

"A vulture and a serpent," she said. "Both from a time we know almost nothing about. Jeff, what's going on?"

"Well, if I really did see the snake, someone has opened a door perhaps."

"A door?"

"To the time when these things existed here in Florida." He frowned at her. "What have you found since you came here, Verna? I'd better call you Verna, hadn't I? Otherwise my tongue might slip when it shouldn't."

"I haven't found anything, really."

"But you said when I first met you—"

"Uh-uh." She shook her head. "I didn't know you then. All I've been doing is looking for the answer to Kim's disappearance. The fossils are only an excuse for snooping around. Which re-

minds me, when we leave here I have to go to the
bus station to pick up a package. Come with me?"

"Of course. By the way, where did you get your
car? I may need one."

"From Staley Howe, the garage man."

"He rents them?"

"No, he just lent it to me. There isn't a car
rental place in Clandon."

"Here's hoping he can fix mine, then."

They ate in silence for a few minutes, Jeff pon-
dering the significance of what she had told him
about her sister. Could there be some link between the sister's disappearance and what was going on at the Everols'? It was possible, he decided.
Kim had unearthed remains of prehistoric creatures on the Everol property. Reincarnations of
those creatures were now preying on the Everol
clan. Had she somehow opened a door in time?

"This package you're going to the bus station
for," he said. "Has it some connection with what
you're doing here?"

She nodded. "I asked my prof at the university
to send me some fossils, so I could say I found
them here. If I don't find something, people
might wonder."

"What people?"

"Earl Watson, for one. He keeps asking me if
I've found anything."

"Did he know your sister? He knows about her
disappearance, of course, if the police questioned
the townspeople. I mean did her meet her personally."

"He says no."

"Do you look like her?"

She shook her head. "Not enough for him to have guessed who I really am, if that's what you mean." Her dinner finished, she took a twenty-dollar bill from her handbag and passed it to him. "You pay, will you? In a place like this, it might look funny if I did."

He signaled the waiter, then said as they were leaving the dining room, "Is there a Western Union office in town?"

"Just a couple of doors down from here."

"I have to call a friend back home, ask him to wire me some money."

"There'll be a phone at the bus station," she said.

The bus station was straight out of a Norman Rockwell painting portraying life in backwoods America. Except for an agent almost as old as the building, it was empty. The agent told them the bus was running late.

Using change from the twenty Verna had handed him at the hotel, Jeff made his call. The man he called was a fellow professor who on occasion had accompanied him on investigations. The money he needed would be in Clandon in the morning, his friend promised.

Relieved, he joined Verna on a station bench and they resumed their conversation. And presently he began to realize that Miss Verna Clark, or Miss Linda Mason, was the kind of young woman it was fun to wait with in a bus station.

Her enthusiasms, for instance, were many and contagious. When she explained that Florida during the Ice Age had been a stamping ground for practically every kind of creature then living on the continent, she made it so interesting that he hung on every word. When she told him about her mother in Fort Lauderdale, he would have been happy to board the next bus with her to pay the lady a visit.

He told her about himself—a narrative he had never before inflicted on any woman. About growing up in Massachusetts and going to college in Connecticut, and landing a teaching job there after earning his degree. About some of the investigations he had carried out while pursuing his hobby. "You come up empty more often than not, but it's exciting. I have to admit, though, that I've never tackled anything as scary as this Everol case."

Verna could listen as enthusiastically as she talked, he discovered. That had to mean something. It did to him. It made him take her hand, finally, and look straight into her eyes there on the bus station bench, and say, "Verna Clark, I want to help you. I won't be going back to Connecticut until we've done everything we can to find out about your sister."

She squeezed his hand. He thought he saw a wetness in her eyes, but it was hard to be sure in the bus station gloom. "Thanks," she said softly, as the bus rolled up outside.

They stood up. No one got off the bus, but the

driver handed a package to the station agent and he brought it in. "I guess this is what you're waitin' for, miss," he said. "Miss Verna Clark, care of Jack Watson?"

Miss Verna Clark, Jeff thought as he carried the box to the car. Miss Verna Clark, who is certain her sister Kim did not simply walk out of her life and is determined to find out what really happened to her. And someone who knows or suspects this has already tried to kill her and may try again.

As they were leaving the building, he thought of something. "Hold on a minute, will you? I need a crayon of some sort. Something to mark glass with. Maybe the old fellow here has one he can sell me."

Verna pulled him forward. "I'll bet he doesn't. But I have something at the Watsons', and we have to go by there."

"Good. Maybe I'll get to meet this Earl who keeps asking you if you've found anything."

The Watsons were on their veranda when Verna and he climbed the steps. Verna introduced them as Mr. and Mrs. "Name's Earl," the man corrected with something like a snort. "This here's Marj. Glad to know you, mister." He was a lean, husky man in his fifties, with a face that seemed made of leather and long hair that looked as if it hadn't felt a comb lately. His wife was twice as wide and a foot shorter and obviously didn't care much about her looks either. At their invitation, Jeff sat while Verna went into the house.

"Verna's been telling me how you found that child," Jeff said. "The one who drowned, I mean."

"Yeah?" Earl shrugged.

"We was real proud of him," Marj said. The air on the veranda was warm and sticky; she fanned herself with a folded newspaper.

Jeff fished a little deeper. "I've seen the place you call the Drowning Pit. It's hard to imagine people went there for picnics and such."

"They never swam there, mister." Earl leaned from his chair, scowling. "And let me tell you, that sinkhole ain't no place to mess around with. It's real deep and dangerous."

"Oh, I wasn't planning another visit."

"Better not. You ask me, the Everols ought to fence it in and put signs up to warn folks off." Apparently convinced he had made his point, Earl settled back on his chair again. "You a friend of the Everols?"

Careful, Jeff thought. "Not exactly. I'm—well, I'm a writer, and I thought I might do a book about what happened there." He had almost said, "what's happening" but shifted gears in mid-sentence.

"To Jacob and Ethel, you mean?"

Jeff nodded.

"Got your work cut out for you, I'd say. You ask me, lookin' for the truth of what happened there might be near as risky as swimmin' in that sinkhole. And like I said"—leaning from his chair again, Earl used a knobby forefinger this time to punch home his words—"that Drownin' Pit is a killer, mister. Nobody in their right mind would fool around with it."

"And Earl should know." His wife nodded vigorously. "He come near to drowning there himself, the time he brought up that little girl's body."

"You nearly drowned, Mr. Watson?"

"Well, it was sure deeper'n I'd counted on."

Before Jeff could try for more, Verna reappeared, letting the screened door shut with a slight thud behind her. "Will this do?" she asked, handing him a box of crayons.

He looked at them and thanked her, then turned to the Watsons. "It's been nice talking with you two. We'll meet again, perhaps."

"Yeah," said Earl.

"If you and Verna here are friends, I guess we will," said Marj.

Verna and he went to the car.

"Well, what do you think of them?" she asked while driving.

"What does he do for a living?"

"He's a house painter. Self-employed."

"He seems pretty anxious for me to stay away from that sinkhole. So if I come up empty elsewhere, maybe I'll just have a look at it."

She took her gaze off the road long enough to frown at him. "You're into scuba diving?"

"I've done a little."

"Where would you get the gear?"

"We're not far from the gulf here. There'll be a diving shop somewhere."

"Jeff, if you go there with that in mind, I want

to be with you," she said. "Remember that."

When she stopped to let him off at the Everols' gate, he took her in his arms and kissed her. She returned the kiss, apparently as eager as he was to make it more than a mere good night.

"When do I see you again?" he asked.

"Tomorrow? Here? Same time?"

"Until then, be careful. Please, Verna. Be very careful."

Chapter Nine

Again it was Blanche who opened the Everol door to him. Again the others were seated in the living room. This time they were watching television.

Everett reached for the remote control and shut off the TV, apparently indifferent to whether the others wished to continue or not. He made a face at the watch on his wrist. "It's past our bedtime, mister. If you're going to stay here with us and go out of an evenin', it'd be considerate of you to get back earlier."

"I'm sorry," Jeff said. "I didn't realize."

"No harm done this time. But we're not as young as you."

"There's something else," Jeff said. "I should be paying you for your kindness in putting me up.

Just as soon as I'm able to get some money, I intend to do that."

Everol peered at him under lowered, bushy brows and said, "Where you plan on getting money? From that girl who picked you up at the gate this evening?"

"How do you know someone picked me up?"

"Lelio saw you and told us. It was that Clark girl, wasn't it? The one who's been snooping around here."

Jeff returned their challenging stares in silence while groping for a response they might find acceptable. "I intended to walk to town," he said with care. "Just as I reached the gate, she came along and offered me a lift. To tell the truth, I don't know who she is. I didn't ask her."

"It was the Clark girl," Blanche said, as if the name felt sour in her mouth. "Lelio said so."

"And?"

"Like Everett said, she's not welcome around here. She snoops too much."

"She told me she's—I'm not sure whether she said student or teacher—but connected with some university and looking for fossils."

"Well, she's got no business looking for them on our property," Everett said. "And if you see her again, we'll thank you to tell her that." Rising, he punctuated his remark with a grunted "Good night" and made for the stairs.

Blanche and Amanda followed. Little white-haired Susan, as though performing an assigned nightly chore, began to gather up cups and saucers and put them on a tray.

She took her time doing so, Jeff noticed. In fact, she went through a number of unnecessary motions while the others unhurriedly climbed the stairs and disappeared. Then the tiny, rather pretty sister of Everett's equally doll-like wife put the tray on a table and came over to Jeff.

In a voice too low to reach those upstairs, she said while gazing intently up at his face, "After what happened, are you going to sleep in Jacob's room again?"

"I was planning to, Miss Susan."

"Shh." She put a finger to her lips. "We don't want them to hear us. I don't think you should, you know. Not after what happened there last night."

"You think it might happen again?"

"Who can say?"

"Miss Susan, can we sit down and talk a little? In the kitchen, maybe, with some coffee?"

Her head bobbed up and down. Reaching for the tray, she turned and trotted with it across the living room, through the dining room, into the kitchen. She was like a bird of some kind, Jeff thought as he followed. One of those little ones—sandpipers, were they?—that ran along beaches and always seemed to be in a hurry. But at the kitchen door she stopped to wait for him, then shut the door after him and motioned him to the table.

He sat.

"Sugar and cream?" she asked, trotting past him to the counter.

"No, thanks. Black."

"I like mine that way, too." To the table she came with coffee for both of them. But after seating herself she pushed her cup aside and leaned toward him with a conspiratorial smile. "Tell me something. Does the name Jeffrey Gordon mean anything to you?"

He very nearly dropped the cup he was lifting toward his mouth. "Who?"

"That's your name. Everett said not to tell you but I'm doing it anyway because I think he's wrong." She nodded briskly. "You're Jeffrey Gordon and you're a professor of English in Connecticut. Yes. You're also an investigator of psychic phenomena, which is why you're here in our house. How I know about all this—when you wrote to ask if you could come here, you sent a magazine that had a story about you and a picture of you. Now do you remember?"

Trying to imagine how a character in a play might act in such a situation, Jeff at first forced himself to look puzzled, then slowly replaced that expression with what he hoped was one of understanding. "Jeffrey Gordon . . . Jeff Gordon . . . yes, of course, Miss Susan. That's who I am. Of course!"

"Not Miss Susan, please." She was smiling now, as though delighted to have been able to help him. "This isn't an old Southern plantation, you know, even if it is in Florida and run down. Just plain Susan will do."

"Susan. Yes."

"And you really remember?"

"Yes. Thank you." He reached across the table to touch her hand, remembering how he had felt when Verna Clark did the same to him at dinner. "Now tell me why Everett docsn't want me to know."

"He said if we told you, you'd leave us and go somewhere to find out if your accident caused any serious damage. All of us disagreed with him and insisted you'd leave as soon as your car was fixed if you didn't learn who you are, but Everett is the kind of man who thinks women are stupid."

"Am I to pretend I still don't know who I am, then?"

"Could you say you just remembered?"

"Well, of course, but—"

"That's the way to do it, I think." Susan's white hair and pretty face were bobbing up and down again. "You will stay now that you know, won't you?"

"Yes, I will."

"So tell me . . . what really happened in your room last night, Jeffrey Gordon? You can trust me. I won't tell anyone else."

With care and a frown Jeff said, "I'm afraid it was nothing more than I've already told you. I dreamed I saw a snake at the window and—"

"How could a snake appear at a second-floor window?"

"Yes, how? But anything can happen in a dream, can't it? Anyway, it was a huge snake. Enormous. All I ever saw was its head, and that was so big its body could easily have reached the ground. You know, like that very long African snake—the mamba, is it?—that can make itself so vertical it seems to be walking on its tail?"

Evidently Susan was not interested in snakes that walked on their tails. "Are you certain it wasn't a bird?"

"It wasn't a bird, Susan."

"The thing that killed Jacob was a bird," she said in a low voice, again leaning toward him, though this time with her coffee cup in her hand. "Ethel says it was, and I believe her. A huge, ugly bird with awful claws, she said. And that was what she saw the second time, too. Are you sure you saw a snake, Jeffrey?"

"Well, who can ever be sure about a dream?"

"We have other rooms. You could stay in one of those tonight."

Jeff drank some coffee to give himself time to think. "Are you afraid some harm might come to me, Susan? Because of what happened to Jacob and Ethel?"

"I don't want any more terrible things happening in this house."

"Tell me something: You say Ethel saw what happened to Jacob and then saw the bird again. Ethel is in an institution now, isn't she?"

"Yes."

"Did the bird attack her, too?"

"Yes, it did, but she got away from it somehow before it could kill her. After Jacob was killed she bought some books about such things and was reading them. But the fright did something to her mind and Everett had to put her away."

"Where did this second appearance of the bird happen? In Jacob's room again?"

"No. In her own room, next to his."

"Is that where you want me to sleep tonight?"

"No!" Susan's voice was sharp with indignation. "How could you even think such a thing? I told you I don't want any more to happen in this house!"

"But if the vult—if the bird has already appeared in two different rooms, how can you be sure any room here is safe? What difference does it make where I sleep, Susan?"

Seemingly bewildered, the white-haired little woman gazed at him in silence, then looked into her coffee cup as though expecting to find an answer there. Lifting the cup to her lips, she emptied it, then put it down again. At last she said, "I suppose it doesn't make any difference where anyone sleeps, does it?"

"Besides," Jeff said, "Everett wouldn't like my using a different room without his permission, I'm sure."

She nodded.

"So shall we say good night, Susan?"

"Yes. Good night, Jeffrey."

"Perhaps I won't dream again."

Rising, she reached for the cups and saucers.

But before turning away with them, she looked intently at his face again and said in a voice that was little more than a whisper, "Let me tell you something, Jeffrey. When you saw that thing at your window, it wasn't a dream. If you've really convinced yourself it was a dream, you're a very foolish man. Snake, bird, whatever it was, it was real, and it will be real the next time it comes, too. Believe me."

Before he could answer she had turned her back on him and was a sandpiper again, briskly trotting to the sink.

Chapter Ten

Jacob's room.

The room in which Ethel had seen a monstrous bird, a kind of prehistoric vulture, perched on her brother's chest with its great black wings outspread and its awful claws tearing its victim's face off.

That was Ethel's story, told to him by Verna Clark this evening and repeated just now by Susan. He had seen and heard it first, though, in various media accounts of the "Everol Horrors."

The vulture-thing, when disturbed by Ethel's entrance, had flown out through a great hole where a window had been—a hole it must have made when it crashed into the room from outdoors. Again, that was Ethel's story, reported by the media and repeated this evening.

Should he stay in this room tonight? Yes. He had come here hoping to solve the Everol mystery, and that had begun here in this room. He would learn nothing by running away from it.

Closing the bedroom door behind him, he walked to the window where he had seen the snake. This morning, after returning from his walk with a functioning memory and certain personal questions to be answered, he had carefully examined it. There was no reason now, he decided, for him to change the conclusions arrived at then. This window frame was much newer than the others in the room. The plastered wall surrounding it had recently been patched.

Well . . . if he was going to spend a second night here, he had better get to work. If, as white-haired little Susan insisted, the thing he had seen was real and not a creature he had conjured up in a nightmare, it could come again anytime now.

Of the crayons Verna had given him, he found that a black one made marks most easily seen on the glass. Starting at the lower left corner of the bottom pane, he drew a straight line to the middle of the top, another from there to the lower right corner, a third to a point two-thirds of the way up the left-hand side, a fourth across to a corresponding point on the right-hand side, a fifth back to the starting point. The result was a black five-pointed star with its dominant point at the top.

Stepping back to survey his handiwork, he was satisfied with what he had created. This was a much neater pentagram than the one he had drawn last night with his fingertip in the pane's coating of dust. Stepping to it again, he drew a circle around the star.

When he had done this to every other pane of glass in the room, he removed his shirt and stood before a mirror. With the same black crayon he drew a final star-in-circle on his own bare chest, then put the shirt back on. Tonight he would not be donning the pajamas Everett had lent him. Would not be going to bed. After a final inspection of the room, he sat on a chair to wait.

Would what he had done protect him? Even without the circle it had last night. What else could have deterred that monstrous snake's head from crashing through the window as Ethel's vulture had done? After all, the belief in the power of the blazing star to thwart evil went back at least as far as pre-Christian times. Perhaps it went all the way back past man's beginnings to a time when Florida was inhabited only by the creatures that now seemed bent on destroying the people of this house.

For it to be effective, though, he must make it a thing of the mind as well. Must project it as an astral aura with himself at the center. Seated on his chair, he shut his eyes and concentrated on doing that.

And waited.

Time crawled. There came a sound of wind and rain, the raindrops few but noisy as they drummed the glass of the windows. The intrusion caused his concentration to waver, and from time to time he found himself thinking of Verna Clark, of Verna's missing sister, and, strangely, of Earl Watson and Earl's unattractive wife, Marj. Each time the wavering occurred, he found it harder to reconstruct the aura he knew was so important. Each struggle left him more fearful of falling asleep.

He lifted his left wrist to look at his watch, then remembered it had been stolen from him while he was unconscious in his wrecked car. The time? It was after midnight now, surely, but how long after? You lost track of the hours when you had to concentrate so fiercely on more important things. Except for the sound of the rain, the house was as silent as a tomb.

Then he heard something. From somewhere outside in the rain and dark came a noise that evoked a mental picture of a four-legged animal sitting on its rump with its gaze on the sky and its mouth agape. A wolf. Howling.

A wolf in Florida?

Again the sound, this time closer. And again. And yet again.

Had he in fact ever heard a wolf howl, except perhaps on television or in a movie? He could not remember. But whether from experience or some inherited memory, he knew for certain what he was hearing.

It made his skin crawl. Made the hair rise at the back of his neck. With his gaze glued to the window where he had seen the snake, he sat rigid except for the sudden trembling of his lips and hands.

He saw what was making the sound then. It was not a seated wolf howling at a nonexistent moon, as his mind had suggested, but a shadowy figure loping toward the house through the rain and darkness. A shadowy figure with eerie, glowing eyes.

Around the eyes a head took form as the creature drew closer. The head of a huge gray wolf. Only the head was distinct, though. The darkness and rain still blurred the rest as the animal raced forward.

For a few seconds the whole of the thing's head was visible. But those oncoming eyes were like the headlights of a speeding car. Almost at once the window became too small a frame for the picture, and he knew that had he not been awake and watching from the beginning—had he been awakened from sleep only when it was there at the window—he could not have been sure what he was looking at when the glass, or what he had drawn on the glass, caused it to stop. How could he possibly have known that what looked like stalactites and stalagmites in a cave were actually the gleaming white fangs of a monstrous wolf?

Behind those fangs, what looked like a subway tunnel was in fact the creature's throat, scarlet near the glass and darkening to black in its depths.

If that huge head came at him the way the vulture must have hurled itself at Jacob, it would smash through the wall as easily as an army tank. Fighting back his fear, Jeff forced his mind to concentrate on the aura he hoped was still around him.

The thing grew larger. Now the window revealed not a whole head but only a solitary eye that blazed like a sun as it peered in at him.

Was the pentagram holding it at bay, or had it only paused like any confident predator to enjoy its victim's helplessness?

In his mind, while waiting, he had rehearsed certain other measures he might take if attacked. There were incantations and prayers that were said to have worked sometimes against assorted evils. He dredged them up now and tried to use them while struggling to maintain the star-shaped aura around him. At the same time he knew, or thought he knew, that his life depended on what he had already done. No man facing a horror such as this could be expected to think straight.

The eye moved sideways.

He had been like an actor on a stage with a spotlight on him. Now the spot was gone. His sensation of relief was a sudden warmth flowing like hot new blood through his body. Still staring at the now empty window, he went limp on his chair.

This time it had not been a dream. It had been real. He had seen a wolf. A gigantic, probably prehistoric wolf, seeking prey.

Not a vulture. Not a serpent. A wolf.

God in heaven, what was going on here at the

Everols'? What kind of door in time had been opened? How? And by whom?

Suddenly he snapped out of his slump and sat bolt upright, every nerve tingling again. Someone in the house was screaming. A continuing shriek of sheer, soul-wrenching terror was ripping the stillness to shreds. Like a sound produced by some fiendish machine, it shrilled through the hall outside his door. Somewhere close by, a woman was either frightened out of her mind or suffering some awful physical agony.

He stumbled to the door and got it open. Lurched into the dark hall. The sound came along the hall from his right. Turning in that direction, he ran in search of its source.

Whose door it was that he assaulted, he had no way of knowing. All the bedrooms in the house were on this floor, off the one long corridor. The door shuddered open and let him go lurching into a room that should have been dark but was not. At one of its windows blazed the solitary eye he had seen through the glass in his own room. The eye filled the room with an unnatural scarlet light. Then, as he stumbled toward it, tearing his shirt off, the eye suddenly grew larger.

The window and the wall around the window exploded into the room, spraying him and the floor and the bed—and the screaming woman on the bed—with shattered wood, plaster, and glass.

The woman still screamed as he dropped his shirt on the floor. Her voice of terror still rocked the room as he thrust his marked bare chest at the intruder. Had it been leaping, it could never have stopped. It would have destroyed him in mid-leap on the way to its screaming victim. But that final assault had not begun. Only its head was inside the room. The rest of that huge gray body was still straining to enter through the shattered wall.

With its gaping jaws only a foot from the star on his chest, the head stopped its forward motion. Both blazing eyes focused on the pentagram. Or were they seeing that other pentagram, the astral aura he was again creating with a mind that seemed likely to snap from the demands he was placing on it?

A sound like the rumble of an earthquake welled up in the thing's throat. As though fueled by fury, the eyes blazed more brightly as the creature backed away. Into the room stumbled Everett Everol, barefoot, in pajamas, reaching out for a light switch as he crossed the threshold.

The old man skidded to a halt. "Great God!" His outcry at that moment was the only sound in the room. The wolf was retreating through the shattered wall. The woman on the bed had at last stopped screaming.

Rain and darkness reclaimed the wolf. Everett stumbled to Jeff's side. "God almighty, what was that thing?" This time his voice was only a hoarse whisper.

Jeff picked up his shirt and turned to the bed. Everett's sister Amanda was the one who lay there. On her back as though she had fallen in a faint, silent now except for a sucking rattle in her throat as she struggled to breathe, she gazed with wide, unblinking eyes at the ceiling.

"I think you'd better call a doctor, Mr. Everol."

"That thing I saw . . . was it a wolf?"

"I don't know what it was. Something very big, very old. Your sister needs a doctor. Can you phone for one?"

Everett went to the bed and sat on it, leaning forward to peer at Amanda's face. "Yes, yes, a doctor. We can't get one at this hour."

"Take her to a hospital, then. She's in shock."

"A hospital. Yes, of course. Let me get Blanche to help me."

"I can help, Mr. Everol."

Everett jerked himself around, violently shaking his head. "No, no, not you. You don't even know who you are. Go back to bed. I can handle this." He stood up, his face a tangle of mixed emotions, his long-fingered hands pawing at his pajama jacket. "Just stay with her while I get my wife, will you? She's awake. The screaming woke her. I'll only be a minute." He hurried from the room.

Jeff stood there for a moment, gazing down at the woman. She did not move. Her eyes stayed wide open. Turning away, he walked to the gaping hole in the wall where the window had been. That was no flimsy wall. Of seasoned cypress with a thick layer of old plaster on sturdy laths, it would have given a wrecker problems. The wolf-thing had crashed through it as though it were made of paper.

Hearing voices in the hall, he turned back to the door. Everett came into the room again, followed this time by his wife and her sister Susan. "All right, mister," the old man said. "We can take care of this now."

"I'd like to help."

"No, no, we can handle it." He looked at the watch on his wrist. "It's after two o'clock and you have problems of your own, in case you've forgotten. You go on back to your bed."

"Very well," Jeff said. As a guest here, what else could he say? But as he passed them on his way to the hall, he caught the eye of Everett's sister-in-law, Susan.

Was it a warning look she was sending him? Or was it a silent plea for help?

Chapter Eleven

Physically and emotionally drained, his head pounding in a way that alarmed him, Jeff returned to Jacob's room and stretched out on the bed. Not to sleep. Afraid to sleep.

You were in a car accident, buster. You still have a bump on your head to prove it. If Amanda needs a doctor—and God knows they'd better get her one—then for a different reason so do you.

In college he hadn't been a football jock; he'd only helped edit the college magazine.

Tomorrow, as Susan had suggested, he had better pretend to remember who he was and try to protect this whole house. But what was to prevent those prehistoric predators from seeking prey elsewhere?

In spite of his determination not to, he fell

asleep. When he awoke, the sun was shining through the grime of his marked windows. On his way to the bathroom at the end of the hall, with the razor Everett had told him he could use, he paused by the door he had all but broken down the night before.

There was no sound from within. After glancing along the hall in both directions, he put a hand on the knob and turned it. He would not go into the room, of course. No way. But if they had taken Amanda to a doctor, her bed would be empty. It had to be empty. After her behavior last night, any doctor worth the cost of a stethoscope would want her in a hospital, under observation.

The knob would not turn. He tried again with the same result, then stooped to peer at it. In this house the bedroom doors had locks. At least, this one did. And this door was locked.

Well . . . that didn't have to mean anything, did it? There was a hole in the wall in there that you could drive a truck through. Maybe they had taken Amanda to a doctor or hospital but wanted the door locked in case the wolf-thing returned. A locked door wouldn't help much if it did, but it might give them some peace of mind, no?

He shaved. Would have showered but felt he shouldn't take the time. Besides, he would have no clean clothes to put on until he could pick up his money at the Western Union office and buy some somewhere. When he went downstairs, wearing the same tan slacks and lightweight brown jacket he had been wearing when run off the road half a lifetime ago, he found Everett and Blanche and Susan seated in the living room, sharing what must be the morning newspaper. Was it delivered daily to the door, he wondered, or was it left in some box he hadn't noticed out near the gate?

With a "Good morning" that included them all he, too, sat down. Their only response was a nod as they stared at him. Then the two women looked at Everett, and Everett said, "The doctor came last night when we called him. He gave Amanda some stuff to quiet her nerves and she's to rest until he comes again tomorrow. She's in one of the spare rooms, of course. Her own has to be fixed." He paused. "I knocked on your door to see if you wanted him to look at you, too, but you must've been asleep."

Quietly Jeff said, "I've remembered who I am."

Everett and Blanche gazed at him in silence. Little white-haired Susan said brightly, "Oh, that's wonderful! Tell us!"

"My name is Jeffrey Gordon, and this house was my destination when I had my accident. Call me Jeff, please; everyone does. I'd written to you, Mr. Everol, and talked to you on the phone. You had agreed to let me try to help you. I teach at a college in Connecticut, and for some years I've been doing psychic research."

The expression of astonishment Everett tried for did not quite come off, Jeff thought. Nor did the false gasp that preceded his, "So you're the one! We thought you'd given up on us!"

"But how can you help us?" Blanche challenged. "You saw what happened here last night. If you remember who you are, you know what happened to Jacob and Ethel. How can anyone help us?"

"There are things I can try, Mrs. Everol."

"What things, for heaven's sake?"

Taking his time about it, Jeff carefully explained what he had done to protect himself in Jacob's room, and how he could try to apply that protection to the whole house. "One thing that puzzles me, though, is that these creatures have attacked only this house. Can any of you think of an explanation for that?"

"There aren't any others nearby," Everett said.

"Which is the same as saying the door that's been opened must be somewhere on this property. Perhaps even in the house. The door in time, I mean, because these creatures are certainly from the distant past."

"I wouldn't know about any door." Everett turned to scowl at his wife's sister. "Susan, why don't you take Mr. Gordon to the kitchen and fix him some breakfast." The scowl shifted to Jeff. "We've had ours, Mr. Gordon, and it's after nine. You must be hungry."

Susan said brightly, "Of course! Come along, Jeffrey!" Again reminding Jeff of a sandpiper, she trotted ahead of him from the room.

The kitchen was to be their place for conspiratorial get-togethers, Jeff decided a moment later. With the door shut and two eggs boiling and bread in the toaster, she sat with him at the table. "It came again last night, didn't it?" she said in a low voice. "The vulture. They said no, but I think they're lying. It was the vulture, wasn't it?"

"No, Susan. It was a wolf."

"I'd ask Amanda to her face, but Everett won't let me in to see her. She's in the room next to the bathroom. The one Blanche calls her guest room, except we never have any guests."

Something in the intensity of her stare made Jeff wonder how much he should trust her. Why, really, had she chosen to disobey Everett last evening, right here in this kitchen, and tell him who he was?

"They didn't call any doctor, you know," Susan said accusingly. "That was a lie Everett told you just now. They didn't call anyone—just moved her out of her room into that other one. They say she'll be all right, but I wonder. Ethel didn't get over it when she saw the vulture." The toast popped up in the toaster and she glanced at it but remained seated, in fact leaned even more strenuously across the table. "Everett isn't going to put away another sister of his, I can tell you. He's been living in shame since he put Ethel away, and he'd rather die than have two of them in a crazy house. What he's going to do is keep her here and hope she gets over it. But I don't think she will."

"Are you suggesting I talk to him?" Jeff asked.

"Not that. I just want you to know. Don't let on you do know, though."

"But—"

"Uh-uh. If Amanda isn't crazy, she'll get over it, won't she? If she is, what difference will it make whether she's here or where Ethel is? But we should keep an eye on Everett. He needs to be watched."

Leaving him with that to think about, she jumped up and fluttered about like a bird again, getting his breakfast to the table. Then, after pouring coffee for both of them, she again sat down and leaned toward him. "Everett did call a carpenter this morning to come and fix up Amanda's room. He'll be around today sometime. And Staley Howe called to say he'd be bringing your car around this morning. You'll be glad of that, I know. What will you do about a license plate for it?"

"I don't know."

"Well, let me tell you something: The plate is right here in this house. Everett took it off the car, not whoever robbed you. Like I said last evening, he thought the longer you didn't find out who you were, the longer you'd stay here and help us. I mean that's what he said he thought. What I can do now is try to persuade him to give you the plate and say he found it along the roadside where your car was."

"It would save me a lot of trouble."

"I'll do it, then." She finished her coffee and stood up. "You eat your breakfast while I go talk to him."

* * *

Staley Howe was a man of his word, or nearly so. Though he missed a morning delivery of the car by twenty minutes, he did bring it.

Susan, too, had been true to her word. Half an hour before the car came, Everett returned from what he called "a trip to the village" and handed Jeff the missing license plate.

"Seen something shiny in the grass while I was drivin' by where you went off the road," he said with a straight face. "Stopped to see what it was. You bein' from Connectucut, no doubt it's yours."

With the plate on the car, Jeff headed for town, again passing Clandon's little cemetery and promising himself this time to stop there on his way back. You sometimes learned things in cemeteries. At the Western Union office he picked up the money he expected. Then he drove about town looking for somewhere to buy an extra pair of slacks, a shirt, underwear, and some drugstore items, including a razor to take the place of the one he had used that morning.

A diving shop now, he thought. He needed a phone book.

There was a phone booth outside the drugstore, and he found some diving shops listed in the book's yellow pages. The nearest was in a town half an hour or so distant.

He called it.

Could he rent the gear he needed?

He could, a cheerful male voice informed him, but "not today, buddy. I run a school here and I got a class goin' out for a dive in five minutes. Be gone the rest of the day. Why'n't you come 'round tomorrow, hey?"

"I'll do that. Thanks." And he would probably have to put down a sizable deposit, Jeff told himself. What he needed was the checkbook that had disappeared with his suitcase, or the bank credit card stolen with his billfold. Come to think of it, he had better report the card stolen right now, before the thief or thieves used it for more of the drugs or booze that were probably responsible for their running him off the road in the first place.

He did that. At the same time he arranged for the bank to wire him more funds and mail him some emergency checks. Thank God for telephones, and for bank managers who recognized your voice over them. It was getting to be quite a day.

On the way back to the Everols' he stopped at the cemetery.

Judging by its stones, it was a very old one. Woods still hemmed it in on three sides. As he walked among the graves, he read some of the inscriptions on the stones.

Close to the trees in the far right corner he found a cluster with the name Everol on them. In front of the newest one, Jacob's, he stood for several minutes.

It was important, Jeff felt, to get the timing of various events fixed in his mind, and with Jacob's death date as a starting point, now would be a good time to do it. All right. Verna Clark's sister,

Kim, had discovered fossils in Clandon in April and with Easter break coming up had stayed to look for more. She had disappeared soon afterward, just before Jacob was killed. Ethel Everol had encountered the vulture the night after its attack on her brother.

When, exactly, had Earl Watson dived for the child's body in the Drowning Pit? In February? Someone, either Verna or Watson, must have told him. Anyway, it was before the Haitians had come on the scene and before the disappearance of Verna's sister. What he remembered most was not a date but the determined way Watson had warned him to stay away from the sinkhole.

Thinking about these things, frowning over them, he finished his return trip to the house and found that Everett and Blanche had gone out. Susan was alone and eager to talk.

They sat in the old-fashioned living room, Susan perched on the edge of her chair, one hand uplifted and a forefinger seeming to fire the words at him like a toy gun as she unburdened herself.

"Soon as my sister and that man were out of here, I looked in on Amanda," she said. "She was awake, just lying there looking at the ceiling, and she didn't know me. I've seen that look in a woman's eyes before, Jeffrey. In Ethel's eyes. I know what it means."

"Did you try to talk to her?"

"Yes, I did, but she couldn't or wouldn't answer

me. All she did was lie there." Susan nearly fell from the chair as she leaned farther forward to bring the toy gun forefinger closer to his face. "Now before I say what I'm going to say next, Jeffrey Gordon, just remember that I'm not an Everol. I'm only Blanche's sister and my name is Susan Casserly. So! What I'm going to tell you is that I think Everett is somehow mixed up in all these terrible things that are happening here. And I want you to think about it."

"What proof have you?"

"Well, I don't have any real proof, of course, or I'd be talking to the police. But I'm afraid of that man. Yes, I am; I'm frightened half to death of him. Let me tell you something. There was a girl disappeared from around here last month. Her name was Kimberly Mason and she was a professor or something from some college. She was here to—well, the way I heard it, she was looking for old bones and such things. Lots of prehistoric remains have been found in this part of Florida, I guess you know. Even people. Anyway, she disappeared and hasn't ever been found, and I think Everett knows more about it than he's ever admitted."

"What makes you think that?"

"The way he's been acting. Like the way he changed about wanting you to come here, for instance."

Frowning, Jeff waited for more.

"Oh, I know, I know. He wasn't ever too keen

about letting you come here. That's because none of us have ever been too comfortable with strangers. But he did let you come in the end. And then before you even got here he began acting as if he wished he hadn't." She paused for breath because she had to, but at once went into high gear again. "And after your accident he hid the license plate off your car and told us not to tell you your name, so's you'd want to leave and go away to find out what was wrong with you—all the time telling Blanche and Amanda and me he thought it would make you stay, mind you, as if we'd be stupid enough to believe black was white." The toy gun finger was still wagging furiously. "If you ask me, Jeffrey Gordon, my brother-in-law is up to something."

"Are you saying he might have had something to do with the Mason woman's disappearance?" Jeff said carefully.

"Well, I don't know, but I wouldn't be at all surprised, I can tell you." Susan's pretty face was suddenly pale and there was a tremor in her voice. "I just don't trust him anymore."

"Did you before?"

"Well, I suppose so, though I never liked him much. Since that woman vanished, though, he's changed. I mean he acts like a man who's hiding something. I'm telling you this so you'll be on your guard." The finger at last stopped shooting holes in the air between them and went limp, as if it had suddenly become tired. "You will be careful, Jeffrey? Won't you?" Susan whispered.

"I will, I promise." Jeff stood up.

A look of alarm touched her face. "Are you going out again? Leaving me?"

"Just to visit your Haitians for a few minutes." He glanced at the inexpensive watch he had bought in the Clandon drugstore. "This should be a good time for it, don't you think? But I'll be back soon."

Chapter Twelve

"There, Lucille. It is finished."

In the shack he occupied with his woman, Lelio
Savain took up the object he had been working
on for the past two hours and gave it a shake. "At
last!" he said.

The object in his long-fingered hand resembled
a maraca, one of those percussion instruments
used by musicians in his native Haiti to add
rhythm to some of their dance tunes. Of course,
it was nothing of the sort. Inside its gourd shell
now were snake vertebrae and small stones of
many colors to provide a chattering sound when
it was shaken. Fastened to its outside, like the lace-
work of mace around a nutmeg, were strings of
colored beads.

Lelio looked at his watch. "Are you ready to go

110

to the *hounfor?*" He spoke in Creole. Always when alone with Lucille he used the peasant tongue of Haiti.

She turned from the sink to see what he had done, then walked to the table to peer at the *asson* more closely. "This is nicer than the one you made before, Lelio."

He grunted. "*Nice* means nothing, woman. What matters is how correctly it is made." There was, of course, no point in trying to explain to her what an *asson* really was: how its very shape called into being the two major symbols of magic in all the universe, the gourd being a near-perfect circle and the handle a smaller version of that vertical rod, the *poteau-mitan,* that linked the world of people with that of the spirits. Or how, when the *asson* was ritually shaken, the snake vertebrae inside it had the power to summon the *loa.* "What we cannot know yet," he said with a scowl, "is whether the person who stole the first one also defiled the *pé.* That remains to be seen."

"Yes," she said.

"The wrong word or behavior in that sacred place could mean hours more work for me." He let out his breath noisily. "Which of them did it, I wonder."

"Who knows? And you can only hope for the best," Lucille said. "In any case, there is not time enough to go there now. We are expected at the house."

"What for?"

"Lelio, I've told you! Amanda is in a different

111

bedroom now. One that has not been used for a long time and needs cleaning."

The old man's broad nose expelled a snort. "Cleaning! A respected *houngan* is to wash windows and scrub floors?"

"We agreed to do what they asked, Lelio. We can go to the *hounfor* later. Even tonight, if you wish. Night and day are all the same in that place."

Like a small boy sulking, he made a face at her, then slumped in his chair and gazed at the *asson* again. "It is wrong for us to wait a moment longer than we—"

A sound of footsteps outside the shack caused him to turn his head. Someone knocked.

Lucille went to the door and opened it. The person standing there was the white man who had talked to them in Creole at breakfast the day before.

"May I come in?" He spoke in the peasant tongue again.

She hesitated only briefly, then stepped aside and motioned him to a chair at the table. "Of course, m'sieu. Please sit down."

As he did so, she saw him look at the *asson* Lelio had made. Then he smiled and said, "I suppose you know about my accident, and how for a while I did not know who I was."

They nodded.

"Well, I know now. And another thing I've remembered is that I spent all of last summer in Haiti, studying your voodoo." Again he glanced at the *asson*. "You made this, Lelio? You must be a *houngan*."

"One of no importance, m'sieu."

"From what part of Haiti, may I ask?"

"A small village on the southern peninsula, called Les Irois."

The white man nodded. "I've heard of it but have never been there. I have, however, been an invited guest at a number of voodoo services. To learn something about voodoo is why I went to Haiti."

"Services in Port-au-Prince, you mean?" Lelio tried to keep the sneer out of his smile but knew he had failed.

The white man laughed. "No, not those affairs for the tourists. And not, I'm afraid, anything as difficult to get to as La Souvenance or Nan Campeche. I did attend a *kanzo* service, though, and one for 'Zaca, and several at which family *loa* were summoned and honored."

Lucille said with a frown, "Why were you interested in our gods, m'sieu?"

"I'm interested in everything of that nature. Have been for years. It's why I'm here at the Everols' now."

Lelio said carefully, "Because of what has happened here, do you mean?"

"It is still happening. You know, I'm sure, that another something came last night."

They nodded. Lucille said, "M'selle Susan told me this morning."

"What are these creatures? Where are they coming from?"

They shook their heads.

"You are a *houngan,* Lelio. You must have thought about it."

"Voodoo, m'sieu, has nothing to do with the kind of horrors that have been happening here. We in voodoo simply call upon the *loa* to help us with our problems."

"Your gods, yes. But you also call upon the spirits of the dead."

"Sometimes."

"The things attacking the Everols are very old, Lelio. Like your oldest voodoo *loa.* Could they be the spirits of dead things?"

"In voodoo we call up the spirits of people, m'sieu, not monsters."

"Isn't there a *loa* who is known to assume the shape of a vulture, Lelio?"

"I have not heard of any such."

Aware from his many hesitations that her man was anxious to end the conversation, Lucille came to his rescue. "M'sieu, we are expected at the house," she interrupted. "If you would be so kind as to excuse us now . . ." She smiled to show him that she was truly regretful. "You will come again, perhaps?"

Their caller stood up. "I'm sorry. Thank you for talking to me."

After shaking hands with them, he departed.

With fear on her face, Lucille turned to the old man. "What do you think, Lelio?"

"He believed me. That I am unimportant, I mean."

"I hope so. Can we go to the house now, so there will be time later to do what we must in the cave?"

He nodded.

"Let me put away the *asson*." She reached for it. "Someone might look in through a window and see it here."

At the house Jeff found Susan seated in the living room, looking as though she were still annoyed with him for having left her. Taking from his pocket one of the crayons Verna Clark had given him, he handed it to her. "Would you like to help me?"

After he had explained what he proposed to do, they began marking the downstairs windows as he had marked his own the night before. Before they had even finished the living room, Lelio Savain and his wife arrived. Susan instructed the Haitians to go upstairs and clean the room Amanda was in.

"She'll be asleep. At least she was when I looked in on her a little while ago. But don't let that stop you. The room's a disgrace."

Lelio frowned at her. "Disgrace, m'selle? I do not know—"

"She means it's very dirty," Jeff supplied.

"Oh."

The Haitians went to the kitchen for what they needed, then climbed the stairs. When Jeff and

Susan had finished all the downstairs windows, they, too, went upstairs.

In Amanda's room the Haitians watched them as they drew the five-pointed stars on the windows. On the bed, Amanda appeared to be in a sound sleep with her eyes shut. After awhile Lelio said, "The stars are to keep those things out, m'sieu?"

"We hope so."

"I do not understand."

"It's a belief that goes back to the days of your oldest voodoo gods, the ones even your most learned *houngans* admit they know little about," Jeff said. With a feeling that Susan, too, would want an explanation, he stopped work for a moment. Of course for Lelio, with his limited grasp of English, the explanation must be kept simple. "Inverted pentagrams are a symbol of evil used in almost every Satanic cult the world over. But when drawn right side up, with the single point at the top—blazing stars, they are sometimes called then—they are thought by many people to be a powerful force *against* evil."

Lelio frowned. "*Against* evil, m'sieu? How, please?"

"When you draw a *vèvè* on the peristyle floor at a voodoo service, you believe there is power in it, don't you?"

"Certainly. Without question."

"The five-pointed star has a similar power. There are many ways of using it, just as there are many ways you use the *vèvè*. Its five points, with one at the top and two at the bottom, have been thought to represent many different things down through the ages. One belief, for instance, is that they are the five wounds of Jesus when he was crucified."

Gazing at a pentagram already drawn on one of the room's windows, Lelio only nodded. Then with a quiet "*Merci*, m'sieu," he motioned to his wife and both went to work at cleaning the room again.

Jeff and Susan finished the upper rooms and went back downstairs. "Is that all we can do?" Susan demanded.

"I'll do the rest myself." Tempted to add, "The mind probably has more to do with this than any symbols on windows," Jeff decided that such a remark would require more explaining and let it go. "When will Everett and Blanche be back?"

"They didn't say. Once a week they go shopping together. With Amanda in bed, Everett gave me strict orders not to leave the house while they were away." She frowned. "Why? Does it matter?"

"Not now. But I have to go out later." Jeff tried to keep it casual. "By the way, do you suppose you could lend me a key, in case I'm a bit late again? Everett wasn't too happy last night."

Seemingly displeased herself, she rose without answering him and went into another room. Returning, she handed him a key in silence, then sat down, frowned at him, and said, "Just when will you be going out?

"Before seven." She would, of course, ask him

where he was going. Should he confess he was
seeing the *prowler* they so disliked?

She did not ask it. "Well, seven's a long way off
yet," she said. "So why don't I make us some tea?"

"We are finished upstairs," Lelio said. Lucille and
he had come down together, and Lucille had
gone into the kitchen to put away the cleaning
things they had used. "Unless there is something
else, we will be going now, Miss Susan."

Alone in the living room, Susan looked up from
a magazine. "Mr. Gordon is in his room. Did you
ask him if he wanted you for anything?"

"He said no."

"Is Amanda still asleep?"

"Yes, m'selle."

"I suppose it's all right, then. Everett didn't tell
me anything different. Lucille needn't come at
suppertime, remember."

Returning from the kitchen, Lucille heard that
and said, "Yes, m'selle. I know." On their weekly
shopping day, Everett and his wife always brought
back a ready-cooked supper from a fried chicken
place. With a quiet *"Bon soir,* m'selle" she nodded
to Lelio and headed for the front door.

Outside the house Lelio said to her, "The cave
now."

"Yes, Lelio. Don't forget the *asson.*"

They stopped at their shack only long enough
for her to go in and get the sacred rattle for him.
Five minutes later they had circled the sinkhole
called the Drowning Pit and were climbing the

knoll from which Lelio had watched the wrecker pull Verna Clark's car from the pond.

The pond, Lelio reminded himself, from which their employer, M'sieu Everol, had warned them to keep away because there were places where the ground at its edge was a kind of quicksand.

Atop the knoll, Lelio went straight to one of several large boulders that seemed to grow like huge gray toadstools among the clumps of high grass and brush. When he put his shoulder against it and pushed with his legs, the boulder rocked.

It rocked sideways, then ponderously rolled just far enough to reveal a vertical slit in a wall of rock behind it. With a nod to Lucille, Lelio stepped aside.

Wriggling into the opening, Lucille disappeared in darkness. But in a moment a light from inside played over the entrance to guide the old man as he followed her.

A little way in he found her waiting for him, holding a flashlight, and she reached into a niche for a second one that she handed to him. Then, with Lucille in the lead, they continued.

The niche had become a passage, gently sloping downward. For a hundred yards or so it was no more than that: a tunnel about a yard wide, leading into a world of stone beneath the knoll. They went along it with care, the old man acknowledging his age by reaching out with his free hand at times to steady himself. They passed dark holes in the walls that could have been side passages.

Ten minutes later, one of these side tunnels led them into a more or less circular chamber about twenty feet across. Here their flashlights revealed the voodoo *pé* or altar that Lelio had built months earlier, though not in this chamber, after stumbling on the entrance to the cave one day when the boulder had been rolled away from it. Only since the theft of his first *asson*, the day before the coming of the man called Jeffrey Gordon to the Everols', had Lucille and he moved the altar to this room.

Its legs were tree limbs that Lelio had obtained on the property. The boards that made up its top, covered now with a white sheet, had been salvaged from the remains of a chicken coop behind the caretaker's cottage. On the cloth now were earthenware jars—*govis*—made and painted with ritual designs by Lelio as he had patiently labored to create something like the altar over which he had presided in Les Irois.

A small village, Les Irois. He had not lied to their caller about that. No four-wheeled vehicle could reach it, and the journey on foot or by mule from the nearest real road was long indeed. Yet people had come there from all over Haiti to attend the services of Lelio Savain, or to seek his counsel.

Why, oh why, had he let himself believe the United States would have more to offer him?

Lucille had finished lighting candles on the altar and in niches about the room. Now Lelio stepped to the altar and took up two of the objects lying there. One was a *govi* adorned with the cross of Legba and filled with small stones. When summoned, the spirit of Legba could be expected to enter it. The second object was the *cocomacaque* he had brought from his homeland—the stick whose power had helped him to survive when he and the others were put off the boat to drown.

Carrying these objects to the center of the chamber, he placed the jar on the floor and carefully thrust the stick into it. The stones held the stick upright. In that position it became, like the handle of the *asson,* a symbol of the *poteau mitan* or central post by which the gods would come from their home in Ifé when he called them.

Now, returning to the altar, he took up a white soup plate full of yellow cornmeal and carried it to the *poteau-mitan.*

Bending from the waist with his knees stiff and his legs wide, he held the plate with his left hand, took some of the meal in his right, and proceeded to draw designs on the floor around Legba's *govi* by letting the yellow powder dribble between his thumb and forefinger. Slowly, with infinite care, he drew the *vèvé* of Legba with its elaborate cross—the same symbol that was done in paint on the jar—and the *vèvé* of Erzulie with its dominant heart. Legba and Erzulie, the sun and the moon, were the ones most likely to help him in this hour of need. But the *vèvés* must be correct, the *cocom-*

acaque must do its job again, and the new *asson* must meet with the *loas'* approval.

The drawings finished, he straightened and returned the plate of cornmeal to the altar. Then he took up the *asson*. Again bending from the waist, and chanting in a barely audible monotone as he did so, he lightly struck each of the *vèvés* several times with the gourd rattle.

"Papa Legba," he sang in a moaning monotone, "I beg you to close the gate. Beloved Erzulie, help us, help us, I implore you." Still chanting, he fell to his knees and bent forward to touch his lips to the *vèvés* while Lucille watched him in silence.

On her face was a look of profound melancholy.

Chapter Thirteen

What, Jeff Gordon asked himself, should he do about his date with Verna Clark? Now that he had a car again, should he ask Everett's permission to use the phone and call her to say she would not have to pick him up as planned? Everett and Blanche had returned from their weekly shopping trip an hour earlier.

No, he decided. With more than one phone in the house, someone might eavesdrop, and for now at least he did not want the Everols to know that he and Verna were seeing each other.

At five minutes to seven, saying he was going to town on an errand and would have dinner at the inn before returning—and that Susan had lent him a key in case he got back late—he drove out to the gate and found Verna waiting there in her borrowed car.

"Are you in a hurry for dinner?" he asked her.

"Uh-uh." She shook her head and smiled at him. For that kind of smile from this kind of woman he would have risked far more than the Everols' disapproval, he knew.

"I want a look at that sinkhole before it's too dark for us to see anything," he explained. "Why don't you drive back to the Watsons' alone and let me follow you? We can leave your car there and use mine. I don't want you having to drive me back here again when the evening's over."

She nodded. "Shall we take both cars to the Drowning Pit or leave one here?"

"Both, I think. The Everols might come snooping."

"You don't want them to know we're friends?"

"Not just yet. They've a thing about you."

She made a face. "And I was hoping you'd be able to convince them I'm harmless. Well . . . do you remember how to get to the sinkhole from here? The ruts that lead in to the pond, I mean?"

"I'll follow you."

She turned her car and drove up the highway in the direction he had been coming from when he first picked her up. When she swung in along the road to the pond, he was close behind her. This time she stopped well short of the water.

Getting out, she walked back to him and opened his door. "Let's go it on foot from here, shall we?" she said. "I don't want another car tampered with."

"Check. Is the garage fellow going to be able to put yours right, by the way?"

"He said yes, but it will take a few days. He's had to send for some parts."

Jeff looked back along the ruts. His car could be seen from the highway, he realized, and he had encountered trouble along that route before. "We'd better play safe and lock these."

"Jeff"—her voice revealed anxiety—"just why are you doing this? You're not thinking of diving, are you?"

"No, no. I don't have any diving gear yet. Just want a good look at the place so I can be thinking about how to tackle it."

"Oh." She let out her breath. "Well, all right, then. You had me scared for a minute." Reaching for his hand, she voiced a nervous little laugh.

Hand in hand, they walked to the pond and climbed the knoll.

The top of the knoll was an eerie sort of place in the evening light. With so many huge boulders, it reminded Jeff a little of England's Stonehenge, which he had visited in pursuing his interest in the occult. Not that the stones here were laid out in a Stonehenge circle. But they did seem to speak to some part of his mind or consciousness, the way that ancient, mysterious ring of rocks had.

There was no time now to explore the knoll, though. With Verna following, he made his way down the slope on the far side and advanced to the rim of the sinkhole.

The Drowning Pit. It was like an almost circular swimming pool some thirty feet in diameter, carved out of limestone and so full of water that it seemed about to overflow. At this hour the water was almost as black as tar. Standing there at the edge, he looked down and wondered how deep it was.

"Hey, Danny! That was a car in there!"

The speaker was Nick Indrotti, the younger of the two youths who had run Jeff Gordon off the road. Dan Crawley was driving this time. Nick sat beside him with a joint between his lips.

The souped-up clunker had just passed the rutted side road where Jeff and Verna had left their cars.

"Pull up, I tell you, Danny! Maybe we found us an easy one!"

The clunker coughed to a stop. "You didn't see no one around?"

"No!"

"Okay." Dan shoved the shiftstick into reverse and sent the machine weaving backward. At the entrance to the pond road he braked it again. Both youths peered up the road in silence, straining to see what was in there where tall trees cut down the light.

"I think there's two cars," Nick said.

"Yeah. Me too."

"Let's go."

Shoving the doors open, the pair leaped to the blacktop and went racing down the ruts into the woodland gloom. With live oaks and other big old trees all but crowding the road out of existence, there was little daylight left here. Probably only eyes that knew what they were looking for would have spotted Jeff's car in the first place.

On reaching the car, seventeen-year-old Dan Crawley said with a frown, "Hey, didn't we hit this one before? Take a look at it. The one you ran off the road."

Nick looked and said, "Yeah. Whaddaya know?"

"There wasn't nothin' in it. We got some cash off of him, but nothin' in the car except a suitcase, and only crap in that. Let's try the other one, huh?"

"The other one. Yeah."

They went to the car in front, and Nick tried the driver's door. "Locked," he said. "Shit."

"So we bust it. Nobody's around to hear nothin'."

"Gotta find a rock." Letting go of the door handle, Nick looked up and down the almost dark road but saw nothing big enough. Try a dumb thing like busting a car window with a rock too small, you could ruin your hand. He turned and peered into the roadside trees, then took the joint that was still dangling from his lips and let it fall to the ground. "Wait up," he said, and walked into the off-road gloom with his gaze on the ground.

Slouched against the car, Dan Crawley sent uneasy glances up and down the road while waiting.

After a few minutes he called out in a hoarse whisper, "C'mon, c'mon, will you? We don't need a rock as big as a fuckin' gravestone, for Chrissakes!"

"Keep your shirt on," Nick called back. "I got one."

He was some thirty feet from the car, in a little clearing surrounded by trees tall enough to turn dusk into dark. At the edge of a hogplum thicket in front of him lay a whitish stone the size of his fist. He bent down and reached for it.

But before his grimy fingers with their black-tipped nails could make contact, a loud hissing sound beyond the hogplum caused him to suck in a breath and jerk up his head.

He found himself gazing into an open mouth.

A wide-open mouth. Huge. With a multitude of cone-shaped teeth that resembled pickets in an eight-foot-high, once-white fence that had turned dirty yellow with age.

For perhaps ten seconds the mouth yawned there without coming any closer, like a cave entrance waiting to be explored. Nick leaned forward with his head upthrust, staring at it in abject terror while his breathing became an irregular flutter and his eyes swelled to the size of table-tennis balls.

The monstrous throat he stared into, between two huge, gaping jaws, had to be ten feet deep. The gray, black-spotted horror that loomed behind it was a jumbo-jet body with scales, on short legs as big around as old oak trees.

Nick Indrotti finally got his lungs full of air and let out a scream that all but tore his head off.

He screamed again.

He screamed a third time.

That was all.

The awesome jaws had opened wider. The monstrous, scaly body behind them rose on its tree-stump legs and began to sway from side to side. Some part of Nick's half-paralyzed brain told him it was a 'gator. A 'gator too big to be real. Get out of here! his mind shrieked. Run!

He somehow succeeded in making his feet obey the command and, stumbling around, began to run.

But he was too late. And, despite his terror, much too slow.

With incredible swiftness the huge creature hurled itself after him. The wide-open jaws shot forward and snapped shut with a cannon clap that shook trees and made the earth tremble. Half of Nick's body was inside them when the conical teeth began grinding.

The teeth of a 'gator, any 'gator, are designed not so much to chew the creature's food as to tear it into big, bloody chunks for swallowing.

Leaning against the car, waiting for Nick to come with the rock to smash a window, Dan Crawley heard the screaming and snapped out of his slouch.

"Hey, what the hell—"

As the screaming ceased, he stepped away from the car and saw something dark moving like a big black stain among the trees. Something much too big to be his buddy. Puzzled, scared enough to be shaking, he went toward it slowly, ready to turn and race out of there if he had to. To hell with being a hero.

When he saw what it was, he stopped as though he had walked face first into a wall.

Born in a part of Florida where 'gators were common, he had seen his share of them. Never one as big as this, though. Jesus, it must be fifty feet long! But was it a 'gator? Alligators had broad snouts, and this one's was long and tapered. A croc, maybe. He'd read about those. Were there crocodiles in Florida? Christ, who cared? Who could care about anything except what was hanging from this thing's jaws!

His buddy's legs. The rest of Nick was inside, out of sight. And even as Dan began to choke on his own vomit, the huge head swung almost vertical, the jaws opened, and the rest of Nick Indrotti disappeared into the monster's maw.

The jaws snapped shut again.

Dan spun himself around on one foot and raced back to the road. Without even a glance at the two cars parked there, he sped past them and down the road to the clunker on the blacktop. Sobbing out his terror, he threw himself into it and fumbled frantically with the ignition key until he got it started. Then he sent the car weaving down the highway toward Clandon in such a way that anyone seeing it would have thought its driver was on the point of passing out drunk.

*   *   *

Jeff Gordon turned from the dark, still waters of the Drowning Pit to frown at his companion. "Did you hear something, Verna? Someone yelling?"

Verna nodded. "Yes, I think I did."

"It seemed to come from where we left the cars. Let's go. We're through here anyway."

They climbed the knoll and made their way through the fantasy world of boulders on its crest. They hurried down the other side and along the pond road to the cars.

"Over there." Jeff pointed into the woods. "What could—" Puzzled, he ventured in a few yards, then stopped. "Good God, it looks as though a tank went through here!"

Something at least as big as a tank must have made that track through the trees and under-growth. From the way the brush was packed down and small trees bent over or broken near the base, something low to the ground and huge must have passed through here while Verna and he were at the sinkhole.

With a glance back at Verna, he went forward a few feet more, alert and ready to run at the slightest sound. This time when he stopped it was to stare down at a footprint. Not a very distinct one, but still a print.

The foot of a huge bird, perhaps? A giant liz-ard? An equally oversized alligator? He thought of the wolf he had seen at his window. Of the vulture that was supposed to have killed Jacob Ev-erol and driven Jacob's twin sister mad.

There were other prints. The enormous weight of the creature had compacted brush, stones, and leaves in impressions more than a foot deep. Judging by their direction, the creature had come from the pond and gone back there.

Shaking his head, Jeff returned to the cars.

"What did you find?" Verna Clark asked.

"The tracks of a big 'gator, I think. But 'gators don't yell."

"No." Her hand was out, holding something for him to look at. "People who smoke these things might, though."

He took it from her and lifted it to his nose. "Marijuana?"

"I found it here on the ground." She frowned at him. "Come to think of it, wasn't there another noise after we heard the yell? Didn't I hear a car—?"

"Start up and take off at high speed? I think so. Yes. But out on the highway, not in here."

"Well, someone's been here. I'm sure this joint wasn't here before." Unlocking her car, she leaned in. "Nothing of mine's been touched, though. What about your car?"

He went to his and found it still locked. But suddenly he wanted out of there in a hurry, and the feeling was so strong, it almost made him shout a warning.

"You ready?" he called to Verna.

"Yes, Jeff."

"Then I'll see you at the Watsons'. Let's go."

Backing his car out to the highway, he waited

for her. Then, to be close if anything unexpected happened, he let her drive ahead of him toward town.

They dined at the inn again, this time on what the menu called "our famous Southern Fried Chicken." They asked each other what could have made the tracks back there near the pond. Failing to come up with any likely answer, they turned to the subject of the Everols.

Jeff told Verna what he had done to protect the Everol house. "If, of course, *protect* is the right word. If something comes tonight in spite of the pentagrams, there are some other things I can try."

"But you believe the pentagrams may work?"

"When you're fooling around with psychic phenomena, love, you never know what will happen. I went to Haiti, for instance, convinced that the powers of voodoo existed mostly in the imaginations of certain writers. Then in two months I saw enough—not just heard about it, mind you, but saw it—to make a believer of me."

"Such as?"

He told her about some of the voodoo services he had attended.

"How were you able to get into such affairs?"

"I was staying with the family of a wealthy young Haitian I had in class—a fellow you'll be hearing a lot about someday because he wants to be a writer and is going to be a good one. He took me around, taught me some Creole, translated for me when I needed help." Jeff flapped a hand in the air between them. "Whoa, fair lady. Let's talk about us."

"Well, we are, aren't we?" She smiled the smile he would have driven from Connecticut for. "At least, we're talking about you."

Through the rest of dinner, though, he made sure the conversation centered on her. Not on her missing sister or the Watsons, as it had the evening before, but on Verna Clark, whose real name was Linda Mason, and the things she thought about and believed in and liked to do when she could do what she liked. It was an interesting evening. At the end of it, their goodnight embrace in front of the Watsons' house took even longer than the one at the Everols' gate.

So long, in fact, that he saw a movement at an upstairs window before it ended. A hand inched a curtain aside; a face peered down at them for a few seconds. Then, when he drew Verna's attention to it and she turned to look, the face abruptly vanished and the curtain flapped back into place.

"They probably heard the car pull up and are wondering why I'm taking such a long time to come in," Verna said. "It's natural, I suppose."

He wondered.

At the Everols' house, letting himself in with the key Susan had lent him, he found the downstairs dark and silent. Evidently the family had retired. Climbing the stairs to the room he was using—Jacob's room, he reminded himself again—

he inspected the markings on the windows. Satisfied that they were untouched, he undressed and went to bed—not in Jacob's pajamas this time but in new ones he had bought in Clandon.

And he dreamed.

In the dream he saw dark shapes outside his windows. They were not distinct enough for him to make out what kind they were; they could have been blobs of darkness visible only because they were blacker than the night itself. Except for the eyes. At every window were eyes, some red, some yellow, some an eerie green.

In the dream the pentagrams on the panes of glass began to glow yellow, then deepened through orange to scarlet. When the scarlet was intense enough they caught fire, and each of them became a blazing, five-pointed star.

The shadow shapes disappeared.

In the morning, while breakfasting with the Everols, he mentioned the dream and saw a meaningful glance pass between Everett and Blanche. With a scowl that warped his long face and half shut his eyes, Everett said in his sandpaper voice, "There was something at a window in our room, too, mister, and it wasn't a dream. Blanche and me were both awake. We saw it."

"And?"

"The thing you drew on that window caught fire, same as you say yours did. Drove the thing away, seems like."

"What kind of thing was it?"

"Hard to say. Looked to me like a bat, sort of,

135

if there ever was a bat that big. We used to have bats here, too. Lots of 'em. Had to pay an exterminator to get rid of 'em."

Jeff turned to Susan. "You, Susan? Did you see or hear anything?"

She shook her head. "I was tired. I slept right through."

"I wonder if Amanda . . ."

"She didn't say anything when I took up her breakfast," Blanche said.

"How is she, by the way?"

"Well . . . some better, maybe, but there's a lot she doesn't recall. She hasn't any idea what happened to her. What you aim to do today, by the way?"

"For starters I'll just walk around a bit more, I think."

"Thought you already done that."

"Well, yes," Jeff said, "but you have a big place here. There's a lot of it I haven't seen yet, and that's what I'm here for, isn't it? To look things over and decide what we can do."

But he would not be just "walking around," he knew. Next on his list of things to "look over" was that sinister sinkhole called the Drowning Pit. Nor would he wait to rent scuba gear before going there.

Chapter Fourteen

The air was like milk, Jeff discovered on leaving the house. A cool, damp mist lay along the paths and blocked out all but the nearest trees. At the sinkhole he nearly walked off the edge into the water before realizing he had reached his destination.

The Drowning Pit. Even at this hour it was a sinister-seeming place, the water barely visible as a sheet of dark glass under the drifting layers of mist, the silence so complete he could hear his heart thudding.

With a glance up at the knoll to be sure no one was watching, he quickly shed his clothes and shoes and stood naked at the pit's edge.

Now with the stone cool and smooth under his curled toes, he took in a slow, deep breath, held it, let it out, and took in another. He was a better-than-average swimmer, but how deep was this sinkhole? And how dark? At least he had bought a flashlight at the drugstore and taken the time to waterproof it with a wrapping of plastic. With adhesive tape he had bought at the same time, he fastened it now to his left wrist and hoped the waterproofing would work. Then he filled his lungs with air and dived.

Almost at once he knew the water of the Drowning Pit was clean and clear, with only the mist reducing its brightness at the moment. Good! His light worked better than he could have hoped for, too, revealing a faint blueness in the rocky walls, as though they were of pale blue bottle glass through which light could pass. Surprised and pleased by the strange, unreal beauty of his surroundings, he swam on down.

But it was deep. He had still not caught a glimpse of the bottom when his chest began to ache and he had to return to the surface.

After clinging to the edge for a while, he swung himself up and sat motionless, resting, with his feet in the water. But suddenly a bird cry shattered the silence—a screech so unexpected and shrill that he was almost startled into falling from his perch.

He recovered and looked around. The mist was thinning here. He saw a ghostly dark-gray bird, as large as a gull, planing down from the knoll—that knoll with the Stonehenge boulders, down the other side of which Verna Clark's little red car had rolled into the pond.

The bird vanished into the mist and the stillness returned. Jeff began breathing deeply again in preparation for a second plunge.

This time he knew at once he would go much deeper. He hadn't properly prepared himself the first time. He was bolder, too, now that he knew what to expect. The circle of milky whiteness contracted above him. Below, the walls of the pit acquired more character, developing patches of shadow where they became irregular with knobs and niches.

But again he had to go back up.

He was diving for the third time when it happened. Deeper than he had gone on the first two tries, he was exploring the irregularities of the wall and saw just below him what appeared to be an opening, a tunnel, the entrance to some sort of grotto, perhaps, that wholly intrigued him. It was beyond his reach, he realized, and would remain so until he came here with equipment.

With a longing look at the cave mouth, if that was what it was, he turned back. His chest ached again. The circle of milky daylight above seemed small and remote. Then, in the glow of his light, just above his upthrust hands, a ghostly pattern of crisscrossed lines took form, sinking slowly toward him, and he sensed danger.

With a powerful backward push of his arms, he sought to propel himself clear of the thing, not knowing what it was but vividly remembering that someone had tried to turn Verna's car into a death trap. The pattern of lines seemed not quite to reach the wall. There was a gap between web and stone. He tried desperately to reach it, and almost succeeded.

Almost. Not quite. The sinking net fell across his furiously churning legs. His head and arms were in the gap and he tried to make himself vertical to glide through it to the light above. But one foot, moving too slowly, became entangled in the sinking strands.

When he thrust himself up toward the surface, the foot pulled the net after him. The weblike thing rose in a swirling cloud above his knees. For a few yards only he carried it up with him. Then its weight overcame his momentum and it began to sink, inexorably pulling him down with it.

He had to breathe!

Afterward, he wondered where he had found the strength or determination, whatever it was, that enabled him to live without air for the next twenty seconds or so when he knew it was impossible. For hours he relived that moment when he doubled himself over, got his hands on the net where it was wrapped about his foot, and worried the strands apart with his fingers until he was able to pull the foot free.

You were supposed to recall the highlights of your life when facing death, weren't you? He hadn't. It was all a little vague, but he was certain of one thing: Part of his mind, at least, had been fixed on Verna Clark. All the time he was battling the string trap that held him, he saw himself sitting with her at the Clandon Inn and the bus station. Not talking to her, exactly. Not really doing anything. Just sitting there, being with her.

He also remembered a crazy urge to yell in triumph, even underwater, when the foot came free. Then at last he was clinging to the edge of the pit, gasping for air, turning his head in search of some clue to what had happened.

There! On the knoll from which the bird had taken wing after startling him with its eerie cry . . . wasn't that a human figure standing by one of the boulders, looking down at him? He struggled to his feet and took an unsteady step toward it but was weaker than he thought. His knees buckled. He went sprawling.

Before he could rise again, the figure dissolved.

One moment it was there and he was gazing straight at it as he struggled to get his knees under him. The next moment it had vanished. The effect was uncanny. Or had it only stepped behind the boulder?

Still weak, he slowly toiled up the slope to investigate. Why had his assailant come up here, anyway—if, indeed, that figure in the mist had been the person who dropped the net on him? And what kind of net had it been?

He thought he could answer the second question. In Haiti he had seen fishermen walking the beaches with nets they threw out into the surf to catch small fish. Driving down to Florida he had seen the same kind of nets used by men on bridges that spanned ocean inlets. Here, so close to the gulf, many men might own such nets.

At the top of the knoll, confronted by the boulders, he thought he knew the answer to his assailant's disappearance, too. After dropping the net on him, the fellow must have come up here to watch the pool. Then, on seeing that his murderous scheme had failed, he must have performed his vanishing act by running down the offside slope to the road that led from the pond out to the highway.

Unless, of course, it had been one of the Everols, wanting to put an end to his investigation. Verna Clark's sister had disappeared while looking for fossils near here, hadn't she? And Verna herself had very nearly gone into the pond with her car. If his assailant had come from the Everol house, he or she probably would have run down the other side of the knoll and hurried back there.

Chapter Fifteen

The friendly voice at the diving shop turned out to be that of an ex-navy frogman from, of all places, New London, Connecticut. "Hell," he said with a grin, "no one in Florida was born here. If it wasn't for outsiders coming in, this state would belong to the 'gators and water moccasins. Where you planning to use this gear?"

"In a sinkhole."

"You mean an underwater cave? Better be extra careful if you're new at it. We lose half a dozen people a year in those things. Here, take this." He produced a ball of white string. "Tie the end to something at the cave mouth and play it out as you go in, so you can find your way back out. I'm not kidding. There'd be guys alive today if they'd done that. You get down inside one of those caves,

HUGH B. CAVE

everything looks the same and you're out of air before you can find your way back out."

Jeff had stopped at the Western Union office in Clandon to pick up money the bank had wired him. He paid the deposit on the diving gear and after a few minutes more of friendly counseling let the shop owner help him carry it to his car. "I'll try to return this tomorrow," he said.

"Check, Professor."

Driving back to Clandon, he reviewed what had happened at the house after his close call at the Drowning Pit. He had not mentioned his attempt to explore the sinkhole itself, of course; only that he had seen someone, perhaps a trespasser, on the knoll near it. But Everett and the two women had not risen to the bait.

After the three had exchanged glances, the white-haired little bird woman said in her bouncy voice, "It was probably only some trick of the mist, you know, Jeffrey. Strange things seem to happen here sometimes when the mist is heavy."

"More likely it was our lady scientist looking for dinosaur bones, or whatever it is she's really looking for," Blanche said with a sarcastic snort.

Everett, seated at a table with some bills and a checkbook in front of him, stopped work to listen but made no comment.

Who else might have dropped the net on him? The Haitian, Lelio Savain, perhaps? But why would Lelio want to?

Nearing Clandon, Jeff glanced at the car clock, reset since his accident, and saw that the morning was about over. Should he stop at the Watsons' and brief Verna on what had happened? Ask her to accompany him to the sinkhole in the morning and stand guard while he dived again? He should, he decided.

Earl Watson's fat wife opened the door to him while he was still climbing the steps.

"Oh, it's you, Mr. Gordon," she said. "I thought it was Earl comin' home." She stepped back and motioned him to enter. "You come to see Miss Clark, I guess, huh?"

"Yes."

"She ain't here. Staley Howe brought her car back a short time ago and she went to the store. Said she'd be right back, though. So sit down, why don't you? I was just makin' some coffee. Can I get you some?"

Sinking into one of the shabby overstuffed chairs, Jeff shook his head. "Thanks, no. But I'll wait."

"Well, I'll just get a cup for myself if you'll excuse me a sec. I guess I'm hooked on coffee the way some folks are on booze 'n' cigarettes." Waddling from the room, she left him alone.

Close to Jeff's chair stood a table littered with things of the Watsons' world: a folded newspaper that Marj apparently used for a fan; the remains of a greasy cheese sandwich on a plate; an ashtray full of butts; a catalog from the university where Verna was a student. (That belonged to Verna, of course.) Returning, Marj cleared a spot for a mug

145

of coffee and said to him, "I brought you some anyhow, just in case."

"All right. Thanks." But he heard a car outside at that moment and, rising, hurried out to the veranda.

It was not a car but a pickup truck, old and battered, and the person who got out of it was the man with the leathery face and shoulder-length hair, Marj's husband. Over one shoulder he carried a roll of old, stained canvas that, before climbing the veranda steps, he let fall by lowering the shoulder and stepping aside. " 'Lo there," he said with apparent indifference. "You here to see Verna?"

"Yes."

"She was right behind me. Should be here any second now." He went into the house and, yes, Verna's little red car came into sight at that moment. Jeff met her at the top of the steps with his hands outthrust, but, after touching her hands, stepped back instead of embracing her. The Watsons were watching, without a doubt.

When Verna and he went inside, Earl had disappeared into some other part of the house, but Marj was standing by the table on which Jeff had left his coffee mug. The mug had been moved, he saw, as Marj picked it up and handed it to him. No. Something else on the table had been moved.

With the table so cluttered, he had put the coffee mug down on top of the college catalog. But what was under it when Marj picked it up was a

146

copy of the *National Enquirer* that had been under the catalog.

The catalog had disappeared.

"Can we?" Verna was saying. "I think I need a second opinion."

He had missed what preceded the question but knew he had to answer. "Of course," he said quickly, without any idea of what he was agreeing to.

"Come on, then." She took his hand and drew him toward the door.

"And how about lunch, too?"

"All right. I'm hungry."

"Mrs. Watson, thank you for the coffee," Jeff said as they went out.

In her car Verna said, "I just want to talk to you, I guess you know. There's nothing wrong with the garage bill."

"And I want to talk to you. Where are we going? The inn again?"

"Well, there are a couple of fast-food places in town."

"We need to talk."

"The inn, then."

As usual, the old-fashioned dining room was all but empty. They sat at a corner table, and over lunch Jeff told her about the attempt on his life at the Drowning Pit and his seeing someone watching from the knoll when he surfaced.

"But who would want to kill you?" Verna said. "You came here to help those people!"

"Evidently someone doesn't want them helped

or is afraid I'll find out something. Anyway, I've rented scuba gear and want to try again tomorrow morning at daybreak, before anyone is likely to catch me at it. Can you be there?"

She reached across the table to touch his hand. "I'll be there. Count on it."

"Now tell me what you've been up to."

She said quietly, "I wanted to make a phone call without running the risk that Marj might hear me, so I went out to a booth. You remember the box of fossils we picked up at the bus station?"

He nodded.

"I called the prof who sent it to me. What I want him to do now—and he's agreed to do it—is tell the *Miami Herald* that I've made a significant discovery here. I need an excuse to stay here and keep on looking, and that will give me one. And Jeff"—she was frowning now—"he said something strange. He asked if I'd gotten the college catalog I'd written to him for. I never wrote to him for a catalog. When I told him so, he said he'd received a letter, typed, signed Verna Clark. Even the signature was typed. It was in quotes, too, as if to say 'I know I'm not really Verna Clark, but don't forget you mustn't use my real name.' "

"I saw a catalog from your college on a table in the Watsons' living room just now," Jeff said.

"What?"

"Do the Watsons have a typewriter?"

"Yes, they do."

"Is there a list of the faculty in your college catalog?"

As she nodded, her expression changed from bewilderment to alarm. "They must have guessed that with a catalog they could find out—"

"If there really is a Verna Clark on the faculty. Yes. And now they know there isn't. What's more, they must have suspected even before they wrote for it. Where did they get your prof's name and address?"

"Off the package we picked up at the bus station. It's in my room."

Again Jeff nodded, this time frowning deeply. "Probably they got the idea when they saw the package. If they'd thought of it before, they'd have written to the college, not to your prof personally. Then, when they did get the idea, they wrote to him thinking he'd respond faster. But why should they care whether you're looking for fossils or not? Tell me—you said Earl is a house painter. Is he also a fisherman?"

"If you mean does he go fishing, yes."

"Then the net that was dropped on me . . . Verna, you've got to get out of that house."

"There's nowhere else in town."

"Outside Clandon, then. A motel somewhere."

She shook her head. "It would be too inconvenient. Besides, is it really that important? Couldn't we be making a mountain—"

"Verna, they've gone to a lot of trouble. And even if they don't yet know who you are, they know you're not who you say you are. There's got to be a reason for what they're doing. How well do the Watsons know the Everols?"

"There's no social contact, I'm sure."

"But the Everols might be behind this?"

"Well, I suppose if they suspect I'm looking for something other than fossils, they might have talked to the Watsons about me. I mean, I . . ." Verna let it go and shook her head in frustration. "Oh, Lord, Jeff, I don't know. Maybe we'll learn something when you explore the sinkhole tomorrow."

"Yes," Jeff said. "Maybe we will."

Chapter Sixteen

"Are you going to eat your supper tonight, Miss Ethel?"

"Yes, of course."

"You said that last night, you know. Then you never even touched it."

"I'll eat tonight. I'm hungry."

With a shrug, the young woman with the tray of food walked past the foot of the bed to a small table by the room's only window. She put the tray on the table. "It's a real good supper tonight, Miss Ethel. Cream of broccoli soup and chicken and a nice tapioca pudding. And your tea, of course. You be sure and eat every bit of it, now." Turning, she wagged a finger at the older woman on the bed. "When I come back, I'll be expecting to find every dish clean as a whistle. You hear?"

"I hear you. Get out."

Marching to the door, the other woman shook her head in reproach but said no more.

Ethel Everol waited for the door to close, then stuck out her tongue at it. Taller than average, like the rest of the Everols, she was already several pounds lighter than she had been when she had come here last month to what those in charge smugly called "the home." In fact, she had now lost enough weight to be ready tonight if everything else came together, she told herself. She'd been thinking about it all day. But in case she couldn't do it tonight, she must be more careful about disposing of the food they brought her. Last night, for the second time in a week, she had stupidly neglected to put her supper down the toilet.

Anyway, tonight she ought to eat something, just in case. Not the whole supper, of course—not enough to put back any of the weight she had so carefully shed—but enough to keep up her strength. Getting out of bed, she lay face down on the floor in her nightgown and began to do push-ups.

"Twenty-eight, twenty-nine, thirty . . . There, that's enough." She could do more if she had to, now that her arms were stronger, but it would be a mistake right now to use up too much of her strength. In the beginning she had been able to do only four, she recalled with a twisted smile. How little they knew about her in this miserable place! Rising, she went to the table by the window and sat down to eat.

Of course, she did not leave every dish clean, as the woman had demanded. After just enough to keep her from being hungry, she carried the tray into the bathroom. Thank God she had her own bathroom in this ghastly place and didn't have to go out into the hall like some of the other patients. After four flushings, there was nothing left to arouse the suspicions of those who kept tabs on her behavior.

Now to wait for them to come for the tray, by which time it would be dark outside.

She sat in the only comfortable chair the room contained, a rocker done in black enamel with pink roses airbrushed on the top of its back. They had placed it facing the window so that she would expand her horizons while sitting in it. Yes, that was what they'd said: expand her horizons. Dear God—in a room only fifteen feet square that was no better than a prison cell!

Closing her eyes, she tried to concentrate on what she must do next.

But, as so often happened, her mind went back, instead, to the night of horror when her twin brother Jacob had been taken from her.

They had been so close, she and Jacob. From the very beginning they had been able to communicate in ways even the family had not understood. That evening he had complained of a headache and gone to bed early, and she had stayed up late with a book. But, of course, she had gone to his room before retiring, to see if there was anything he needed.

It came back now in every grisly detail, like a dream, but much more vivid than a dream, as she sat in the rocker with her eyes shut. How she had opened the door quietly, so as not to disturb him if he were asleep. How she had glided in and stopped short, confronted first by the shattered wall where the window had been, then by the bird. The bird was a monstrous vulture, night black, perched on Jacob's chest. It held his body helpless in terrible talons while its beak tore away his face . . . just like the turkey buzzards tore at run-over dead raccoons or snakes or armadillos on Florida highways.

She could still see the chunk of meat lying on Jacob's bloody pillow, with one of his brown eyes in it. And the hole in his head from which the other eye had been gouged out by the thing's pounding beak. She could still hear her own screams as she slammed the door shut behind her and ran.

And then the next night. Terrified that the thing might return, she had made a trip to the attic. Up there in an old trunk were some books she had collected years before when she enjoyed reading about vampires and werewolves and other such things. Books she had had to put up there, out of sight, because brother Everett and sister Amanda just wouldn't leave her alone about them. Even Jacob had frowned on them.

From one of them she had gotten the idea of

the crucifix. In olden days a crucifix was thought to keep one safe from vampires, the book said. She knew that Blanche, Everett's wife, was or had been a Roman Catholic and had a handsome one made of silver in the top drawer of her dresser. She had sneaked in and borrowed it. And hung it around her neck when she went to bed.

And, yes, in the middle of the night the vulture had come again. It appeared like a great black cloud outside a window of her room. In her fear she had been unable to sleep. At the sight of it she sat bolt upright in bed, screaming, with the crucifix dangling from its silver chain about her neck.

The crucifix had saved her. Or something had. The vulture went away.

Of course, they said that she was crazy now. That her being a witness to the death of her beloved Jacob and then seeing at her own window the hideous creature that had killed him had driven her out of her mind. But they were wrong about that. She might have been mentally ill for a while, but she was over it now. Maybe tonight she would show them.

Now think, she told herself angrily. Put away the remembering and concentrate on what's happening here and now. She was doing that when the woman who had brought her supper came back for the tray.

"Well! You did eat it. Good for you, Miss Ethel."

"I told you I was hungry."

"I'm glad. You've lost weight since you came

here, you know. Now, is there anything else I can get you?"

"No."

"I'm off tonight, I guess I told you. So if there's anything you want, I'll have to get it now. Do you have something to read?"

"Yes."

"Well . . . I'll say good night, then."

"Good night."

The door clicked shut. Alone again, Ethel looked at the watch on her wrist. She would wait half an hour. Exactly thirty minutes, no more, no less. They came back sometimes after saying good night—no doubt deliberately, to see if you were doing something you weren't supposed to do. Meanwhile, what should she wear?

Rising from her chair, she went to the room's only closet and opened its sliding door. Everything she owned in this place was here: a blue and white indoor dress for when she went down to the lounge to watch television, a brown outdoor dress and gray sweater for when she was permitted to walk in the yard, a pair of sensible black shoes to replace the bedroom slippers she always wore here in her room. Her underthings were in the dresser.

The outdoor dress was the thing to put on, of course. And the sweater and shoes. God help her if it rained hard, as it so often did this time of year. She would just have to find shelter somewhere.

Looking at her watch again, she closed the

closet door and returned to her chair.

Where had the vulture come from?

They said she was crazy. Even Everett said she was crazy. But if that were so, why was she the only one asking that question? Everything had been fine up to a certain point, hadn't it? Papa had died and left the house to Mama. Mama had died and left it to her children: Everett, Jacob, Amanda, and herself, Ethel. Then that Blanche Casserly had wormed her way into the family by persuading Everett to marry her, and had brought her sister Susan to live there, too. And the Haitians had come to work on the place, and that woman from the college had disappeared and the police had asked a million questions, and then the vulture . . .

The Haitians, the woman from the college, the vulture. That had to mean something, didn't it? So why couldn't they see it, instead of calling her crazy and locking her up here?

I'll show you. Just wait.

Her watch said she had waited the half hour. Now, then. Rising from the rocker, she went to the door and opened it. Looked along the hall. They didn't lock you in here, but of course you couldn't get out without going downstairs where there was always someone on duty who would see you. The hall was empty now. Good. She closed the door and hurried to the closet.

Be careful now. Remember, you've thought this all out and know exactly what you have to do. Take off the nightgown. Roll it up and stuff it in the bed with the pillow so it will look like somebody's asleep there. Not really, of course, but the most they'll do is open the door and peek in; they won't come all the way in to check. All right. That's done. You've really lost some weight, you know that? Wonderful. Now some underthings from the dresser . . . okay . . . and the outdoor dress and sweater from the closet. And the shoes. And the extra sheets they always keep on the top shelf in the closet, for when those on the bed have to be sent to the laundry.

Four sheets. How many times had she counted them? And measured them? And leaned out the window to see how far down the ground was? Four sheets would reach, if you tied them together properly and you didn't weigh too much. If you weighed too much, the knots might slip or the cloth might tear, and that would be the end of it.

Lifting them off the shelf, she dropped the sheets on the floor and knelt there, rolling them, twisting them for added strength, then tying them together.

So I'm crazy, am I, Everett? When I'm the only one of you who could see a connection between the Haitians and the missing college woman and the vulture? I'm the crazy one?

The window gave her no trouble. She had opened and closed it so many times, practicing, that doing so now was as mechanical as brushing her teeth or washing her face. Or flushing her food down the toilet, for God's sake. But dragging the rocker to the window and upending it and tying one end of the four-sheet rope to it was a little more complicated than she had counted on.

By the time she was finished she was out of breath and needed to urinate so badly she didn't make it to the bathroom in time.

Damn. Goddamn. Now you've wet yourself, Ethel. What's the matter with you, anyway? But get on with it. You'll be a lot wetter if it rains tonight, as the TV weatherman promised!

Everything was ready at last: the sheets knotted, one end fastened to the rocker, the rocker wedged against the wall. She put her head out the open window and looked up, then down.

Nothing. If there was a moon tonight, it was hidden by clouds. Below, in the dark, the lawn was invisible, but of course it was there.

Not a sound anywhere. Nothing.

Dear God, help me! All I want is to go home!

The one thing she hadn't practiced, of course, was climbing out the window and inching her way down the knotted sheets. Would she be able to do it? Would the sheets come apart?

Dear God, I've almost starved myself so I wouldn't weigh too much! I've done push-ups every day to make my arms and hands strong. You have to help me now! Don't I deserve it?

She was through the window now and going down. Down, down, down. The knots were holding, and so was the rocker. Her feet touched the ground. She let go of the rope of sheets and threw up her arms in a silent yell of triumph.

Free! She was free!

Hallelujah!

But suddenly a heavy drop of rain splashed on

her upturned face, and another, and a third. And then—oh, dear God!—lightning flashed and thunder boomed through the blackness above her, and the drops became a savage, blinding downpour.

All at once the whole world was water.

Chapter Seventeen

Jeff arrived at the pond road first, hoping none of the Everols had heard his car start at such an early hour. He had purposely left it some distance from the house last evening so they wouldn't. Daylight was still twenty minutes away.

In the quiet darkness he carried his scuba gear over the knoll to the sinkhole. Then as he worked on it with a flashlight, the beam of a second flashlight moving down the side of the knoll caught his attention. He rose and went toward it.

In a moment Verna Clark was in his arms.

"Did the Watsons hear you leave?" he asked.

"I hope not. I parked away from the house, as you suggested. What about you?"

"My people seemed to be sleeping. Let's hope."

Returning to the sinkhole with her, he finished

readying the diving gear while she watched. He would be carrying a proper diving light this time, plus a second one at his belt in case the one in his hand became temperamental. To his belt he also fixed the reel of line the dive shop man had urged on him.

"It feels like rain," Verna said. She had dressed for rain, he saw. Her dark slacks were tucked into boots, and she wore a waterproof gray jacket. "Do you think it might?"

"The paper said there's a storm moving in. Let's hope we're out of here before it hits."

"Jeff, be careful down there!" There was a tautness of concern in her voice, perhaps of apprehension. "Remember what Earl said."

"About its being deep and dangerous?"

"Yes."

"I wonder."

"Wonder what?"

"If maybe he was just trying to discourage me from doing this." With her help, Jeff had donned a wet suit he had rented with the diving gear. "And you be careful up here," he warned. "If you hear anyone coming, get out of here fast." He was thinking of how her car had gone into the pond and how, before that, someone had tried to drop a boulder on her. Before putting on his mask and snorkel he took her in his arms again. "Be very careful, love. We don't have a clue as to what any of this is all about, remember."

She reached out to touch him. "Good luck, Jeff."

With tanks and mask in place, Jeff let himself fall backward into the water. Then, turning, he swam slowly down into a murky silence broken only by the burbling of air from his regulator. The water was cool. About 70 degrees, he guessed.

His rented light was much more efficient than the jerry-rigged thing he had carried before. By its glow he was able to see much more. The rock wall gliding upward beside him was not all pale blue bottle glass this time but speckled with greens, browns, even reds.

There was comfort in knowing that Verna Clark—not just anyone, but Verna—was waiting there at the sinkhole's edge for his return. How quickly he had become fond of her, he thought. If you believed that certain events in your life took place because they were foreordained, then her presence in Clandon might have been the real reason for his coming here, no?

Now, as he swam on down, the sinkhole wall began to take on character. There were deep cracks in it. There were points of rock jutting out, some so long that his tanks scraped alarmingly against them. His ears began to ache but, pressing the mask in against his nose, he blew against the pressure and the pain left him.

He swam on down.

Below him, at last, he saw the opening he had tried without success to reach before: the cave mouth or whatever it was. Reaching it, he clung to an overhang of rock to steady himself while aiming his light into it.

A cave, yes. Or at least a tunnel. And it was nearly at the bottom of the sinkhole, for when he aimed the light downward, he could see the floor below him.

He swam down to investigate.

It was a Salvador Dali world, the floor of the Drowning Pit. Boulders. A huge octopuslike creature that turned into a tree stump lying on its side with gnarled roots upthrust. A dozen or so beer cans and a dark wine bottle grouped together in an out-of-place still life. And finally, in folds and drapes, the net that had almost trapped him.

It was, indeed, the kind of fish net he had thought it might be.

He swam slowly back up to the tunnel mouth and shone his light into it. The beam revealed nothing that resembled a back wall. Now was the time to use the line the dive shop man had pressed on him. Testing a jagged outcrop of limestone to be sure it would not break off, he made one end of the line fast to it before pushing on in.

As he swam on now, the line unwound from the reel at his belt, a guarantee that he would be able to find his way back out. But still he must be careful. Those seemingly solid walls just might hold booby traps in the form of unstable rocks that could break loose and damage his gear if he brushed too hard against them.

About twenty feet in from the sinkhole the tunnel expanded and became an underwater chamber. In it he swam slowly upward until, had he

been back in the sinkhole itself, he must have
been fairly close to the surface.

Suddenly he was at the surface of this shaft, too,
treading water and looking about himself in
amazement, with his mask pushed up.

The cavern was the inside of the knoll, obviously—that same knoll where so much had happened. Where the figure in the mist had so
mysteriously vanished after the attempt on his life
with the fish net. The walls continued on up for
another fifteen feet or so and formed a dome.
Was he feeling currents of air from the cracks he
could see in it? One such current definitely came
from an opening just above the water—a tunnel
similar to the one that had led him here, but dry.

Swimming to the tunnel, he clung to its lower
edge and aimed his light beam into its depths. It
was another passage, yes. Could it be part of something bigger?—an unknown but extensive underwater cave, say, like the known ones for which this
part of Florida was famous? Pulling himself out of
the water, he removed his flippers. With the mask
still up and the flippers in one hand, he pushed
on. The only sound was the whirring of the reel
at his waist as the line unwound from it.

The tunnel became a snake, twisting its way
deep into a world of limestone. Then it became
two snakes, and he stopped. Which one should
he follow?

The one that slanted upward toward the top of
the knoll, he decided. But soon he had to make
a second such choice, and a third, and found him-

self aiming his light into a small chamber on his left. Though it was otherwise empty, its floor bore some strange markings.

He went in to look at them and thought he knew what they were. They were the remnants of what had been voodoo *vèvès,* done with cornmeal and obviously drawn with care but partially rubbed out since, as if by someone who had wanted to defile them. Of course, at a voodoo service, once the *vèvès* had been used in the rituals, they were no longer sacrosanct. The *houngan, hounsis,* and other servitors walked and danced on them. But these appeared to have been deliberately smeared.

Still, there was nothing else here to indicate that this room had been used for a voodoo service. Without an altar and a *poteau-mitan* it was simply a small, bare room with the remains of a *vèvé* on its stone floor.

Was it, perhaps, a *hounfor* that had been abandoned? It certainly seemed so when he discovered, against the far wall, the remains of four crudely made black candles.

He went on for another few minutes and stopped again. From the right-hand wall of the passage a face peered out at him. A face? Well, part of one. There was something frighteningly familiar about it.

He took a step toward it and saw that it was not something separate from the wall. Imbedded in the stone, seemingly a part of the stone, it resembled a wolf's head. Or, rather, the skeleton of one. After another forward step, with the hair tingling at the nape of his neck, he realized he was looking at a fossil.

A fossilized wolf's head? Yes. The same kind of head, though not so large, as the one that had appeared fully fleshed and very much alive at his window.

What Verna wouldn't give to be here with him! Because even if she were not actually looking for fossils, she was a student of paleontology and the sister of a professor of that exciting science. And this, the almost perfectly preserved head of a prehistoric wolf, had to be a find as great as those unearthed at the Windover dig she talked about.

Should he go back and tell her? No, it was better to keep going, he decided. The wolf would still be here. His job was to solve the mystery of what was happening at the Everols'. And to learn why Earl Watson wanted people to believe the Drowning Pit was only a sinkhole when, obviously, he knew it was part of a complex cave system.

Suddenly Jeff came upon other fossilized remains, some imbedded in the wall as the wolf's head had been, others strewn about the tunnel floor. From the looks of them, these, too, were parts of animals. One group had surely been a huge bird, another a snake.

The vulture . . . the snake he had seen . . . But he did not know enough about such things. Picking up a piece of bone small enough to carry, he tucked it into his belt and went on.

The tunnel branched. Feeling he must be

somewhere near the top of the knoll by now, he again chose the passage that slanted upward. Perhaps on the knoll there was an entrance to this eerie underworld. There had to be a second entrance somewhere if the Haitians were using the cave for their voodoo. And if so, the person who had dropped the net on him and then abruptly disappeared from sight might simply have stepped into it. But first, he had another chamber to investigate.

It was a second voodoo room, this one complete with a cloth-covered altar on which were more candles—white ones this time. On the floor were two *vèvès,* one to Erzulie, one to Legba, both newly drawn by someone who knew his business. He went forward to look at them more closely and found himself staring instead at a *cocomacaque* stick standing upright in an earthenware *govi* just in front of him.

A *cocomacaque.* One of the lesser known tools of a *houngan,* but a thing he had seen used in Haiti in the performance of some remarkable magic, if magic was the correct word. Here it was the source of silent but undeniable vibrations that made his whole body tingle as he gazed at it. As if—yes—it were warning him!

Sensing a threatening presence behind him, he swiftly turned his head.

It could not be real, the thing his light revealed. Yet after the vulture and the other horrors, how could he question it? According to Verna, Florida in those bygone days had been home to almost everything that walked, crawled, or flew. And from visits to museums of natural history he knew what the thing blocking the chamber's entrance must be. Not exactly, of course, because the family must have been large, but it was a saber-toothed cat of some kind.

His light showed it in a crouch, about to spring, with its awesome jaws agape and upper canines gleaming. Upper canines that looked like curved swords and were certainly capable of tearing him into bloody bits.

So why was he not paralyzed with terror? Why was he lurching around again and reaching for the *cocomacaque?*

He had seized the sacred voodoo stick without even thinking. When he turned with it to face the thing about to spring at him, he, too, was in a crouch, legs wide, the stick horizontal in both hands and thrust out in front of him.

The snarl that issued then from those gaping jaws seemed capable of bringing the ceiling down and shattering the cavern's walls.

Jeff took a step forward. Until now the scuba gear had been only an awkward burden limiting his freedom of movement; now it was a hazard that caused him to stagger. Still, like a house cat confronted by something it feared, the saber-tooth lowered its crouch and wriggled backward. Its haunches quivered. Its claws scraped the stone. Its jaws dripped froth.

Aware that the *cocomacaque* was making his hands tingle, Jeff dared to take another step forward. Then, straightening, he swung the stick like a cutlass as he stumbled forward.

The huge cat whipped itself about and was gone. Gone with such swiftness that he wondered if it had actually been there at all.

Had it been there? It had, of course. Why else would he have snatched the *cocomacaque* out of the *govi* and now be clutching it in both hands again while poised like a batter awaiting a pitch?

Motionless except for his trembling, he continued to wait. Then, when the silence seemed to indicate that the beast would not be coming back, he walked slowly forward to the tunnel and continued his journey through the cavern. After awhile, finding himself at a junction of passages again, he chose the one on his left because there seemed to be a draft of air flowing from it.

Again he found himself trudging up a slight incline, slowly now because his encounter with the thing in the chamber had left him drained of energy. With every step he took, the current of air became stronger. Then the passage ended at a wall in which his light revealed a vertical, man-high slit not wide enough for him to squeeze through.

It was through here, though, that the air was entering—along with, now, the sound of rain. A very loud, ominous sound of rain.

Was the wall movable? If this was the answer to the disappearance of the person who had dropped the net on him, it had to be. He worked his way up to it and found he was right: It was a boulder that yielded when he put his strength to it. It rocked sideways, then ponderously rolled far enough to create an opening through which he might be able to squirm. Removing the tanks from his back would make the squeeze-through easier.

He took them off and laid them down. If he got out, he could reach in for them. The sound of rain was as deafening, now, as if he were standing behind a waterfall. Never mind. At least he would not have to retrace his route through the cave and the sinkhole.

Taking in a big breath, he stepped out into the downpour.

There was a new sound then, a more ominous one, as something whistled at his head. At the same instant he saw lurching toward him a blurred human shape whose upraised arms terminated in some sort of club. Instinctively he counter attacked with the only weapon he had: the *cocomacaque.*

The two sticks came together with a noise like a crack of thunder. His assailant's, apparently a dead tree limb, broke into fragments that flew in all directions, some into Jeff's face. The slashing stroke of his own weapon continued until the side of the man's rain-blurred head stopped it.

With a howl of pain, the fellow stumbled back off balance. But before the *cocomacaque* could finish the job, he had regained his footing, lurched about, and fled.

Recovering, Jeff wiped bits of pine bark from

his eyes and looked around. Obviously the man had been waiting here for him to emerge from the cave, so he must have witnessed the dive. Who had it been? Everett? The Haitian, Lelio? But surely neither of those aging men could have swung that tree-limb club with such force. Earl Watson, then. Yes.

He looked at the *cocomacaque*. There was blood on it.

After retrieving the tank and rolling back the boulder. he stepped away for a better look at the cave mouth. Had he not known it was there, he never would have suspected its existence. But of course Watson, using scuba gear, had brought the child's body up from the Drowning Pit and would have seen the underwater entrance at that time. No doubt he had explored the cave either then or later and found this outlet on the knoll.

And the Haitians, too, knew about the cave. Unless someone else had turned those two chambers into *hounfors*.

Who else might know?

He was standing there in the downpour like an idiot while trying to think, he suddenly realized. The rain that had hidden the identity of his assailant was pounding down now as though determined to drown him. With a shake of his head he turned and trudged down the side of the knoll to the sinkhole, where he found Verna pacing back and forth at the water's edge with her jacket held over her head. She had not seen him coming and was startled when he called her name. Then, obviously bewildered, she turned to peer at the water.

"Talk to you at the cars," he shouted. "Come on!"

It was a relief to reach his car and an even greater one to shed his scuba gear and wet suit and get them safely stowed in the trunk. Out of the rain at last, he sat with Verna on the front seat and told her what had happened to him. To be heard above the hammering of rain on the car's roof, he had to shout.

After telling her about the voodoo chambers, the saber-tooth, and the man who had tried to ambush him on the knoll, Jeff showed her the bone he had brought back. "And there are others in there. Lots of others. Is this something big, do you suppose?"

She studied the fossil in silence, then said excitedly, "This has to be from some bird or animal, but I can't even guess what kind. Can we go look at the others?"

"Later."

"But—"

"Love, we've got to get you out of that house first. Right now, this morning!"

"But where can I go?"

"There's a motel in the town where I rented the diving gear. I saw it. It's old, but it will do. You can't stay at the Watsons'."

"Jeff I—"

"Verna, he went to all that trouble to find out if you're really what you say you are. It's almost a sure thing that he's the one who tried to kill me just now." Jeff suddenly realized he was shouting even more than he had to, and lowered his voice a little. "I know you want to find out what happened to your sister, but can't you see your safety is important, too?"

She looked at him in an agony of indecision.

"We won't stop working on your sister," he promised. "All it will mean is that you'll have to drive a few miles more each day. But you'll be safe."

"Well—" She reached out to touch his hand. "If you're sure I ought to . . ."

"You ought to, love. You have to." Turning, Jeff put an arm around her and held her close. Her safety, he realized, was now number one on his list of priorities, topping even his determination to solve the Everol mystery.

"Come on," he said then. "Get in your car and head for the Watsons'. I'll be right behind you."

Chapter Eighteen

When she had finished applying a bandage to her husband's left ear, Marj Watson stepped back and scowled at him. He sat grimly silent on a straight-backed chair in their kitchen, fiercely glaring into space.

"There," Marj said with an explosion of pent-up breath. "That's the best I can do, and I still say you oughta see a doctor."

"To hell with a doctor," Earl growled. "It'll heal."

"I doubt it, without some stitches. A little more and you'd be minus an ear, if you ask me, not to mention you could have a broken bone or somethin' under that swellin'. Now are you gonna tell me what happened?"

Earl pushed himself to his feet and almost lost

his balance, but caught himself by grabbing the stove. Dropping back onto his chair, he turned his glare on her. "I told you, didn't I, for Christ's sake?"

"You told me and I don't believe you. Not a word. You never got that bruise and that mashed-up ear by fallin' over a bait bucket on any pier. I don't believe you went near any pier. I don't believe you went fishin'."

"Go to hell, then," Earl growled.

With her arms folded, Marj leaned against the kitchen counter and studied him appraisingly. "You want me to tell you what really happened?" she challenged. "Okay, I will. When you heard that girl's car start up—same as I did—you jumped out of bed so quick you just about fell on your face, and you pulled your clothes on even quicker, and you ran downstairs. The next thing I knew, I heard you start up the pickup and go tearin' down the road after her. Now are you gonna tell me where you went?"

"I told you. Fishin'."

"Earl, that ain't the way a man goes fishin'. You think I'm stupid?"

He did, she knew. He thought she was stupid and always had. All he'd married her for was her cooking; she was a damned sight better cook than a lazy bastard like him deserved. And for sex, of course. For something handy to put it in that wouldn't give him an argument. Yes, he thought she was stupid.

But he was wrong. She was smart enough to

know he was up to something. Smart enough to know he didn't have any real interest in getting work at painting anymore, yet still had money in his pocket. Where was the money coming from? Not from any fish he caught and sold, like he said. She knew better than that.

Oh, sure, he was out of the house a lot. Almost every day he climbed into the pickup and went somewhere without telling her where he was going or when he'd be back. But she'd been watching pretty close. He never took any paint or tools, and there was never a fish smell in the truck when he got back, either.

Now this.

He'd been real shook up when he got back an hour or so ago. He'd had one hand pressed to the side of his head and there'd been blood oozing out through his fingers and a real wild look in his eyes. A bait bucket on the pier, he'd said. He'd tripped over a bait bucket on the pier and hit his head on a piling. Ha. Oh, sure.

He'd been in a fight, more likely. Some kind of fight or brawl brought on by whatever he was up to with all the running around lately. Someone must have grabbed a piece of pipe or a bottle or something and caught him on the side of the head with it. He was lucky to—

The front door had just opened. With an angry glance at Earl, Marj went to see who had come in. It was the Clark girl and her boyfriend, Jeff Gordon, and they stopped on their way to the stairs when they saw her coming from the kitchen.

"Mrs. Watson, may I talk to you for a minute?" the girl said.

"Sure." Marj stopped a yard away and scowled at them. "What's goin' on?"

"I have to tell you I'm leaving."

"Leavin'? What for?" Both of them were soaked, as if they'd been out in the rain a long time. For the past hour or so it'd been raining so hard the house windows were all steamed up.

"I have to go home," the girl said. "Someone's ill and I'm needed."

"That's too bad." It was a lie, of course. There hadn't been any phone call, and she hadn't had any mail yesterday, and today's mail hadn't come yet, so how would she know if someone at home was sick? An outright lie. Had Earl been trying to make time with her? It would be just like him. "I can't give you no refund, if that's what you're lookin' for. Know you're paid up till the end of the week, but I don't have it."

"Miss Clark doesn't want a refund," Jeff Gordon said. "We just want to get her things."

"Oh. Well, all right. Go ahead."

"I'm sorry," the girl said.

"Yeah. It's okay."

"Can I say good-bye to Mr. Watson, do you suppose?"

"He's in the kitchen."

They both went down the hall to the kitchen, and Marj heard them talking there for a minute; then they returned and went on upstairs. She stood by the foot of the stairs, waiting, and when they came back down with the girl's two suitcases, she stuck out her hand to the girl and said, "Well, it's been nice havin' you, Miss Clark. Maybe we'll see you again sometime."

The girl said, "Yes," and "Thank you," and the two of them went out into the rain again.

It was called Four Pines Motel, no doubt because of the four tall slash pines that grew in a clump in front of the office. There were six bungalows, all the same size, all painted white with a dark green trim. The lady proprietor, tall and bony in her fifties, watched Verna sign her name and handed her the key to number four.

"Just one of you?" She tipped her head and squinted at Jeff. "You sure?"

"Just me," Verna said. "He's only a friend." Smiling, she put her credit card back into her handbag. "As you see, he has his own car."

The rain had stopped. The office door was open. The woman glanced out at the two cars and nodded. "Right. Well, my name's Gwen—Gwen Towson—if you need anything. Hope you enjoy your stay, Miss Clark."

They walked down to bungalow number four and unlocked the door. It was a good-sized room, old but adequate, with a TV set, a double bed, a dresser, and two overstuffed chairs. Jeff sat while Verna opened her luggage on the bed and began to put things away.

"We agree that Earl is the one who tried to ambush me?" he said.

179

"Yes, Jeff."

"The question, then, is why does he want me dead? And if he's the one who dropped the boulder on you and tried to drown you at the pond, again why? What are we doing that's bugging him?"

"Snooping?" she suggested.

"All right, snooping. But what is it that he doesn't want us to find?"

She turned at the dresser to frown at him. "Could it be something in the cave, Jeff?"

"Mmm. If it were only a cave, he wouldn't be keeping it a secret, would he?" Jeff got up and began pacing. "That should be our next project, don't you think? To find out what's in there."

"I don't know much about cave-crawling," Verna said with a frown. "Do you?"

"It can't be that big."

"And what about the creature? The cat you met in there."

"Of course." He sat on the bed. "But that's what we're trying to find out, isn't it? The connection between the creatures and the fossils, if there is one. We'll have the *cocomacaque*. There are other things we can do for protection, if we're dealing with something unnatural."

Gazing at him, she said very quietly, "When should we go there, Jeff?"

"Well, we seem to be starting our days early. How about meeting me there tomorrow morning, same time? Or maybe an hour later, since you'll have farther to drive than I will."

"Why do I feel we should go back there right now? That if we don't, Earl Watson may get there before we do and take what we're looking for?" With her things put away in dresser and closet, she came to the bed where he sat and closed the two suitcases, then stood there looking at him, waiting for his answer.

He shook his head. "With the head he must have, Earl won't go back there today, Verna." She, too, must be badly needing a rest, he thought. He knew he was. The bed here was mighty tempting.

"Well, yes," she agreed. "I suppose."

Jeff took the suitcases to the closet. When he turned, she was lying on the bed with her shoes off and her arms outstretched to him.

"Let's lie here and talk a little about this, huh?" she said. "And if we decide to wait, let's at least go somewhere for lunch before you leave me?"

With his own shoes off, Jeff lay beside her and took her in his arms. Holding this woman close was getting to be a habit, he thought. A good one, that he had no desire to break. Yes, he would take her to lunch. And after lunch he would return the scuba gear he had rented, because from now on they would be using the cave entrance on the knoll, not the one in the Drowning Pit.

Then tomorrow, early, they could try to find out what was in that cave in addition to voodoo and fossils.

Chapter Nineteen

It was her birthday.

They said she was mentally incompetent, which was just another way of calling her crazy, but if she were all that crazy, how would she know it was her birthday?

"You sure?" she asked the man.

He was leaning over his cash register, staring at her. Pointing over his shoulder with his thumb at a calendar on the wall behind him, he said without turning his head, "Look for yourself, lady. Today's June the twenty-ninth."

"And that's my birthday." she said. "Yes. And my name is Ethel Everol and I live in Clandon. I mean Clandon is the nearest town to where I live. What's your name?"

"Gus Atkinson. And like I told you, it's that

way." This time he pointed out the window, at the highway. "About fifty miles."

"I'd better be going, then."

"I guess so, if you plan on walkin' it. Why'n't you take a bus? There's a Greyhound station down the road a ways. Be better'n walkin', lady. You're soaked a'ready and it's gettin' ready to come down hard again, looks of it."

"I don't like buses." Meaning she hadn't enough money for one. Looking down at her dress and shoes, she shook her head in annoyance.

He was right, of course: She looked like a cat that had been fished out of a pond. She put a hand up to her hair and that was soaked, too. When had it finally stopped raining, anyhow? About an hour ago? The clock on the wall, next to the calendar, said it was seven-ten now.

She had walked all night in the rain.

How many miles had she come in that time? It seemed like a thousand, but how many, really? She couldn't ask Gus—what was the name? Atkinson?—how far away the home was or he might guess she had escaped from there and call the police. He might even try to hold her here until they came. Anyway, what difference did it make? She'd at least walked in the right direction, because he wasn't telling her to go back the way she'd come.

"Well, thank you," she said, and picked up the pita bread and cheese she had bought.

"It's on your right, about half a mile," Gus Atkinson said.

"What is?"

"The bus station. You may have to wait awhile for the next one goin' that way, but it'll sure beat walkin' fifty miles."

"Yes," she said, with no intention of stopping there. "Well, good-bye."

Through the window, Gus Atkinson watched her walk toward the road "Nutty as a fruitcake," he said aloud. "Jesus."

Her birthday. She was sixty-nine.

And not crazy, no matter what they said.

He'd been a nice man, though, hadn't he? Not everyone would have been so kind.

Halfway to the road she turned and saw him watching through the 7-Eleven store window and smiled and waved to him. He waved back. Fifty more miles to Clandon, though? That was a long way. An awful long way.

As she walked along the edge of the highway she tore open the package of pita bread and unwrapped the cheese. The cheese was already sliced. If she were crazy, she wouldn't have thought to buy it already sliced, now would she? So there. Putting a slice into a piece of the pocket bread, she nibbled as she walked.

About now, back at the home, they were probably just finding out she wasn't there. And they would know what happened, of course, because the sheets would still be hanging from the rocker at the window. What did they do when someone got away? Call the police? Probably, yes. And a man at the station would notify all the police cars to be on the lookout for her, the way they did on television. She must be careful.

She finished the sandwich, made another and ate all of that, too, and began to feel better. The ache in her stomach went away. Reaching into a pocket of her dress—and if she were crazy, why had she asked Everett's wife, Blanche, to send her a dress with pockets?—she took out what remained of her money and counted it.

She'd had seven dollars and twenty cents when she escaped. That was all there'd been in Miss DaCosta's office desk when she sneaked in and opened it. What she had now, after stopping at the 7-Eleven, was four dollars and sixty-four cents. So no, she couldn't take a bus. And it wouldn't be safe to ask anyone for a ride, either. Even if someone would stop to pick up a woman her age who looked half drowned, most cars had radios and it might have been on the news that she had escaped.

A car was coming up behind her now. She turned her head. If it were a police car . . .

How would she know if it was a police car? In Florida did they have lights on the roof, like the ones in the TV movies? She couldn't remember. That didn't mean she was crazy, though. If you were to ask a hundred people in the state of Florida that question, probably not even half of them would know, now would they?

The car was an old gray sedan driven by a man

about her age with a mop of gray hair, and he was alone in it. It stopped beside her and he leaned across the seat to open the door on her side.

"Where you goin', lady?"

There wouldn't be a radio in a car that old. If there was, he didn't have it on now and probably wouldn't turn it on if she kept him talking. You could always keep a man talking if you wanted to. Just ask him about himself and what he did.

"I'm going to Clandon," she said.

"Clandon, hey? Well, I ain't goin' but a few miles, but it'll save you some. Get in."

She got in and shut the door but it didn't shut right and he told her to open it and slam it. The car smelled of tobacco and beer. "How come you're afoot?" the man said as he drove on again.

"I was robbed."

"What?"

"I gave a man a lift, just as you're doing, and he took a gun out of his pocket and ordered me to stop. Then he made me get out of the car and drove off in it."

Turning his head to stare at her with his mouth open, the man almost let the car go off the road. The right front tire actually did go off the black-top into soft sand, but he was able to jerk the steering wheel in time to bring it back. When he had it under control again, he said, "Lady, what you want is the nearest police station!"

"No, I don't. I just want to get back to Clandon," she said. "My brother is chief of police there." With Clandon a whole fifty miles from here, there wasn't much chance he would know she was lying. "I don't want to deal with any strange policemen," she said. "My brother will take care of everything."

"Then why don't you phone him instead of waitin' till you get there?" the driver argued. "By the time you get to Clandon hitchhikin', the guy that made off with your car could be long gone from these parts."

"I can't phone. The man with the gun took my purse."

"Well, I can lend you money for a phone call."

"Would you? Really?"

"Sure." He reached into his hip pocket for a billfold and, opening it with one hand, glanced into it. "Well, the smallest I got is a five, but what the hell. A hard-luck lady like you . . ." He thumbed a five-dollar bill partway out so she could take it.

She took it and thanked him.

"There's a phone in front of the Winn Dixie in the next town," he said. "The folks in the store'll change it for you."

"You're very kind."

"That's all right, lady." He stopped glancing at her and concentrated on his driving.

So her brother was a chief of police, huh, he thought. Jesus. And he'd been thinking she was about his own age and not bad-looking, and being down and out and wet and probably hungry, she'd most likely jump at the chance to go home with him. Not that he'd forgotten Alice, but it was more than three years now.

But the sister of a police chief? Good grief, no.

He stopped in front of the Winn Dixie and watched her walk to the door. The moment she was inside, he stepped on the gas hard and sent his old car growling away from the curb.

He never looked back.

Inside the store, Ethel took a shopper's cart and began walking up and down the aisles. With no intention of using the telephone outside, she took her time for fifteen minutes or so without putting anything at all in the cart. Then she returned to the front of the store and saw through the window that the car was gone. Maybe he'd only parked it, but she didn't think so. If he'd done that, he would be waiting out front.

She took the five-dollar bill from her pocket and smiled at it. So she was crazy, was she?

It was a shame, though, that she'd got a lift of only two or three miles. Why couldn't the nearest telephone have been ten miles closer to Clandon?

Out on the road she began walking again.

She walked all morning.

She bought lunch at the drive-in window of a Kentucky Fried Chicken place with some of the five dollars he had given her and remembered, while walking along eating it, how Everett and Blanche went shopping once a week in Clandon and almost always brought home something for supper from a fried chicken place there. Then she remembered the vulture.

Off and on, all through the rest of that day, she thought about the vulture, how it had torn off Jacob's face and appeared at her own window. Then, when she realized the day was about over, she made herself stop thinking about the vulture and began to look for a place to spend the night. It wouldn't be safe to keep on walking in the dark. She could be hit by a car, or some policeman could come along in a car and ask who she was.

She was on a wooded stretch and hadn't seen a house in half a mile or more when she spied a place that seemed suitable. In a clearing well back from the road, with the woods on both sides and behind it, stood a house under construction. The yard was only a patch of churned up black mud—churned up by trucks delivering materials, no doubt—but the walls were up and the roof was on. The windows were in place, too, but there was no front door yet. She trudged through the mud of the yard and went inside.

There, seated on the floor of what would be a rear bedroom, with windows looking out on nothing but woods, she sat on a sheet of plywood to keep out the cold of the conrete floor and ate the last of her fried chicken and then lay down with her head on one arm and remembered it was her birthday.

My birthday, she thought. I'm sixty-nine and look at me. All alone, wet, hungry—well, no, not hungry anymore—and they think I'm crazy. Oh, God. Oh, dear God, look at me. Help me, please.

Would the vulture come for her here? Every

night at the home for the longest time, she'd been afraid to go to sleep, but now the terrible fear was gone.

Just as she had called on her wits today to get money for food, there was now some secret strength or courage inside her that she could call upon if the vulture or anything like it came again. She couldn't explain it, but she knew it was there.

She wasn't crazy. Not now. But she had been for a time, and this was something her mind had brought back from wherever it had been then. God had special ways of talking to His failures.

Don't you, God? Yes. Thank you.

Holding on to that thought, she closed her eyes and slept.

Chapter Twenty

On his way back to Clandon, Jeff asked himself if he should tell the Everols about the cave on their property. No, he decided. First, they probably already knew about it—the Haitians certainly did— and if they had wanted him to explore it they would have told him about it. Second, if he mentioned it at all there would be a whole barrage of other questions for him to answer.

At the house he opened the car trunk and reached in for the *cocomacaque* he had put there along with the diving gear. The gear was no longer there. He had returned it. But on second thought he had better not take the stick into the house. It undoubtedly belonged to Lelio Savain, and though it was now after nine o'clock and the

Haitians were probably not still at the house, he could not afford to take the chance.

Nine o'clock. The end of an exciting and memorable day. After the adventures of the morning he had taken Verna to lunch at a little roadside café near her motel. Then, after spending the afternoon on her bed talking—and not too much of that—they had returned to the café for dinner. She was a very special woman. The longer he knew her, the more special she became.

Closing the car's trunk, he walked empty-handed into the house and found the Everols waiting for him.

All of them, even Amanda, were seated in the living room, looking like some kind of court waiting for a condemned man to appear for sentencing. The faces of Everett and his wife were especially fierce. Amanda looked like a painting of her own ghost done in grays and whites. Only little Susan, the bird woman, seemed human.

Knowing he had to sit and be questioned, Jeff tried to hide his apprehension behind a smile. "Well, good evening. Amanda, it's good to see you up and around again." Did they know he had found the cave?

"Mister," Everett said, "do you mind telling us what you've been doing since you left here this morning? And why you left before daybreak?"

"You heard me go out, did you?"

"We did."

It was like being nailed to the back of his chair by their relentless stares. The only one of the four who seemed not to be a declared enemy was Susan, and she seemed unduly nervous, even frightened. "I wanted to be outside, watching the house, when daylight came," Jeff said carefully. "I had done everything I knew how to do inside. It seemed important to be out there where I would see anything new that might threaten us."

"If you just wanted to watch the house," Blanche said, "why did you drive off in your car?"

He had to dig deep. And fast. "So that anyone out there would think I'd left. I drove up to the road that runs in by the pond, left the car there, and walked back over the knoll." As he spoke the word *knoll* he made a point of watching their faces. If they knew about the cave at all, they had to know about the entrance there. None of them would ever have gone in by way of the sinkhole.

Everett was the only one who seemed to react. His bony, long-fingered hands definitely gripped his knees a little harder, and he leaned farther forward in his chair. "And did you see anything?" he demanded.

"On the knoll, do you mean? No."

"Here at the house! Did you see anything like the God-awful things that have been driving us out of our minds here?"

"No. Nothing."

"Then where'd you go? You didn't come back in the house."

"I went to town and had breakfast, then took care of some needs of my own. Remember, I was robbed. Lost my luggage, my money, everything."

"You took care of all that before," Everett said darkly. "You offered me money for staying here. Which, if you remember, I refused."

A mistake, Jeff realized, and tried to repair the damage. "Yes, of course. But there were other things I needed—"

"Mr. Gordon—" It was Blanche taking over now, with her head atilt and her arms folded. "Just why did you come here, anyway? The truth, I mean. To write about us and our problem?"

"No, Mrs. Everol. Not at all."

"That magazine you sent us said you'd written about other people with such problems and would put it all into a book someday."

"That isn't why I came. As I told you when asking your permission, I hoped to be able to help you."

"Well, you've helped," Everett said. More than ever his wasted face resembled a skull. "At any rate, you put those things on the windows here. But that's about all you can think of to do, it seems, so we think you'd better leave now."

Jeff looked at the others. The silence lasted long enough to become embarrassing before he stood up and said quietly, "Of course, if that's what you want. I'll just go upstairs for my things." He would stay at the motel, of course. If by chance there was no unit available, he would have a bed there anyhow.

"He doesn't mean now!" Little Susan's voice was shrill with protest. "Do you, Everett?"

"Yes, he does," Blanche snapped.

"No!" Jumping to her feet, the bird woman angrily faced her brother-in-law. "You can't expect him to start driving back to Connecticut this late in the day, Everett! That would be cruel!"

The silence took over again while Everett looked at the others. He finally lifted his bony shoulders in an exaggerated shrug. "All right, all right. You can stay the night, mister. But I'd be obliged if you cleared out first thing in the morning."

"I can leave right now, Mr. Everol."

"No, no!" Susan cried. "You mustn't, Jeffrey."

Jeff glanced at her. She was violently shaking her head at him while her eyes and the forward thrust of her tiny body tried to tell him something. Remembering his earlier talks with her—her confession that she was afraid of her sister's husband—Jeff nodded.

"All right. I'll say good night and go upstairs now, though, if you folks don't mind."

Susan's "Good night" was more like a sob. No one else spoke as he turned and walked out of the room.

In his room he shut the door and threw himself on the bed, lying on his side with his gaze on the marked window where the wolf had appeared. So they had heard his car this morning, in spite of the precautions he had taken, and now they wanted him out of here. Why? Had they somehow found out that he had become friendly with Verna, whom they regarded as a most unwelcome intruder?

Well, so much for his efforts to help them. And they were right, of course, in saying he hadn't done much. At least Amanda was up and around again, even if she only sat there like a ghost and stared at him, saying nothing. He had saved her, hadn't he, by bursting into her room in time?

Why had little Susan been so determined that he should stay the night? What did she want of him?

He had the answer to that question a little more than an hour later. Sitting there in his room, still dressed after gathering his few possessions together to be carried down to his car in the morning, he heard footsteps as first several persons together, then one alone, climbed the stairs and walked past his door on the way to their rooms. Those together, he guessed, were Everett, his wife, and his sister Amanda; the one by herself was Susan.

Silence took over. But before half an hour had passed, someone tapped softly at his door and a whispery voice said, "Jeffrey?"

Rising, he went to the door and opened it, instinctively making no more noise himself than he had to. And Susan slipped in under his arm, rather like a kitten darting into a room after scratching to be admitted.

He shut the door and turned to find her standing by the bed, facing him. Downstairs she had worn a frilly blouse and a long, dark skirt. Now she had on a nightgown trimmed with lace.

"Jeffrey, we have to talk," she whispered. "Right

now, because we won't have a chance to in the morning, before you leave here."

With a movement of his hand he indicated she should sit on the bed. She obeyed, staring at him.

He sat beside her. "Talk about what, Susan?"

"About you, and why they want you out of here. Do you know what I think?"

"No, Susan," he said gently. "What do you think?"

"You remember me telling you about that woman who disappeared last month? Early last month? I did tell you, didn't I? The woman who was looking for fossils on this property? How she vanished, and the police came and talked to us every day for days?"

"The college woman. Yes, I remember."

She leaned toward him and poked his arm with her forefinger. "Jeffrey, I think one of them is responsible for doing away with her."

"Why? I mean, why would they want to?"

"Because she was nosing around the property here and they don't like people doing that. They never have."

"And what do you think they did to her?"

"Well, of course I don't know. I mean, how could I know, for heaven's sake? But it wouldn't be hard to make someone disappear around here. There's the pond, with its quicksand. And the sinkhole, where that little girl drowned. And other such nasty places."

"And?"

"What do you mean, *and?*"

He had expected her to say, "And the cave." But perhaps she didn't know about the cave. "Tell me something, Susan," he said. "How long have you been living here with your sister and the Everols?"

With her head atilt and her eyes half shut, she did some mental arithmetic. "Four and a half years."

So, yes, perhaps they hadn't told her about the cave.

"And I'm still an outsider, as you can see," she said. "I mean, I'm only Everett's wife's sister, not a real Everol."

"Which one of them do you think is responsible for Ki—for the woman's disappearance?"

With an accusing frown she leaned away from him. "You were going to say *Kimberly,* weren't you? I never told you the woman's name was Kimberly Mason. I'm sure I didn't. Jeffrey Gordon, have you known about this all along?"

"After you talked to me the last time, I asked a few questions in town," Jeff lied. "Thinking, of course, that there might be some connection between her disappearance and the happenings I'm here to investigate."

"Oh." She let out her breath. "Well, all right. But as for which one of them might be responsible, I don't pretend to know. What I do think is that the others know and are protecting the guilty one. And they want you to leave before you stumble on the truth."

"If you're right," Jeff said, "I'm surprised they let me come here at all."

"Well, I am, too. I mean, why did they? But they don't want you here now, and I just felt I ought to tell you why, so you'll be on your guard."

"On my guard." Jeff reached out to touch her hand. "I will be, Susan. Thanks for the warning. And listen: If you need to get in touch with me about anything, I'll be at the Four Pines Motel. Do you know where that is?"

She nodded. "Yes, I know. And now you listen: I've told you all this, Jeffrey Gordon, because I like you. No matter what the others say, I like you." Suddenly she leaned forward and touched her pale, thin lips to his cheek. Then, just as suddenly, she slid off the bed and ran to the door.

Inching it partway open, she first put her head out to be sure the hall was clear, then stepped out and silently shut the door behind her, thrusting a tiny hand back in to wave good-bye as she did so.

Chapter Twenty-one

Earl Watson had set his alarm for three A.M. before turning in for the night. When it went off, he reached out and shut it off before it could wake his wife. From the early days of their marriage, anyone reckless enough to ask him about his wife's sleeping habits had been informed with a sneer that the best thing Marj did was sleep.

She slept now while Earl got up, put on clothes and boots, and went downstairs, where from a cupboard under the kitchen sink he snatched an almost full bottle of bourbon and tipped it to his mouth.

His need for what he would have called a good stiff drink satisfied, he hurried out to the yard. Moments later his aged pickup growled down the road with Earl hunched over its wheel and the bottle beside him on the seat.

Carrying only the bourbon and a battery lantern, he left his truck on the pond road at the edge of the Everol property and climbed the knoll. There he rolled aside the boulder at the cave entrance, tipped the bottle to his mouth yet again, and went groping into the cave.

The bourbon was already more than half gone.

On his way to where he was going, Earl passed the second of the two voodoo rooms Jeff Gordon had discovered—the one Lelio Savain and Lucille had set up when their first was defiled—but in his haste he passed it without even a glance. On he went for another half mile or more, past the mouths of smaller side tunnels, until he reached a place where the ceiling dipped so low that he would have to get down on his hands and knees if he hoped to continue. On his right now was a man-high niche, a yard or so deep, on the floor of which lay what appeared to be a roll of canvas tied at both ends with rope.

Here Earl drank again from the bottle and tossed it away, thinking he had finished the bourbon but actually leaving an eighth of an inch. On his hands and knees, with no small output of effort, he dragged the roll of canvas toward him and checked the ropes wrapped around it. Then, grumbling, he entered the low-roofed stretch of tunnel backward, still on his hands and knees, dragging the roll after him.

The crawl-stretch was a long one, a hundred yards at least, and by the time he reached the end of it he was cursing the canvas with what little breath he had left. He was also all but drowning in his own sweat, though the cave was cool. For a while he simply sat there with his back against a wall and his head on his chest. Then he went on again, still on his hands and knees because he was too drunk and too tired now to lift the roll of canvas to his shoulder and walk with it.

Some ten yards in from where the ceiling had risen he came to a niche that at first glance appeared to be similar to the one from which he had taken the roll. The tunnel continued on into the darkness, but this was his destination. With no little difficulty he removed rocks and rubble from the opening, then stepped inside. But this was not a simple crack in the wall like the other. A part of it that could not be seen from the main tunnel angled to the left for another three yards. It, too, was strewn with rocks, some of them good-sized boulders.

He moved enough of these to clear a passage, and then with much muttering dragged the roll of canvas into this hidden part of the niche. Having pushed it against the back wall, he used the rubble and rocks to create a barrier that would hide it from anyone who might decide to look in. At the main entrance to the niche he created a second such wall to further discourage any intrusion. He knew this cave well, and the wall, when finished, looked as though it had always been there. But by then he had labored for more than an hour and had to rest again before returning the way he had come, through the crawl-stretch to where he had tossed away the bottle.

When drunk, Earl Watson was not a man of good humor. As his wife often pointed out, alcohol inevitably made him first moody, then sullen, then angry, and finally violent. He was in the next-to-last stage when he again reached the Haitians' second voodoo room and stopped to rest.

This time, catching a glimpse of what was in the room when he slouched against the wall at the entrance, he straightened again and played his light around inside. What he saw caused his red-flecked eyes to become slits and turned his heavy breathing into a snarl.

He lurched into the chamber and went storming around it, to rub out the cornmeal *vèvés* so meticulously drawn by Lelio Savain as part of the latter's invocation to the *loa*. He snatched up the earthenware urn in which Lelio had placed the *cocomacaque* stick taken by Jeff Gordon. He hurled the urn against a wall, where it exploded into fragments. Then he staggered drunkenly to the altar, swept it clean of other urns and the *asson* on which Lelio had labored with such patience and devotion, and threw the white cloth halfway across the room before reducing the altar to chunks of splintered wood by slamming it again and again against the floor.

Only when his rage began to subside did the animal sounds Earl had been making break down into words and become comprehensible. "Keep the Goddamn hell out of my cave!" he was shouting in his fury. "I found it and it's mine! You hear, Goddamn it? It's mine!" A number of variations on this theme followed, some much more colorful and violent, before he finally lurched about and left the wrecked *hounfor*.

His cave? Yes, by God, it was! A few others might know about the entrance on the knoll now, but he was damned sure that he alone had explored this whole underworld, challenging every possible crawl, sump, sink, and boulder choke to reach the actual ends of tunnels that less experienced cavers would have thought ended sooner. He alone knew how many old bones it contained—fossils that had to be worth a pile of money or there wouldn't be so much about them on TV and in the papers. He had explored other Florida caves in his day and knew what he was doing here. Using compass and measurements, for instance, he had decided that one passageway ran somewhere near the Clandon cemetery. Another went close to the Everols' house, maybe even under the house.

Someday, by God, he would figure out how to make real money out of all this knowledge. Not just the miserable few bucks he was making now. Damned right he would. To hell with painting houses for a living.

He was still spewing out his anger, though only in mutterings, when he made his exit from the cave and rolled the boulder back into place. Was still muttering as he went reeling down the side of the knoll to his pickup. On the way back to town he barely had control of the truck, letting it swerve all over the road, but luckily he met only one car, and it gave him a wide berth.

At home he found his wife, Marj, still asleep.

As he carefully eased himself back into bed beside her, the alarm clock that had woken him at 3:00 A.M. now said 4:20.

Just east of the Clandon cemetery the car Earl Watson had passed suddenly lost its purr and began to cough. With a muttered, "Oh God, not again!" Fiona Deering pulled it to the side of the road and shut off the ignition. Her eight-year-old daughter, Corinne, turned to her with a frown and said, "What's wrong this time, Mommy?"

Mother and daughter had left their motel early because the car had twice before given them trouble on their journey from Mobile, Alabama, and Fiona was determined to reach Walt Disney World before dark. The trip was a birthday present for her daughter, and today was Corinne's birthday, and, by God, she intended to be there even if the damned car did keep misbehaving.

"We'll just let it cool down awhile and see what happens, honey," she said. If Schuyler were here, he would have done something under the hood by now and everything would be okay again. But she and Corinne's father had been divorced for more than a year—he was already married to the other woman—and what lay under the hood of a car was pretty much a mystery to her. She worked in a bank, not a garage.

Taking a map from the glove compartment, she peered at it in the light from the dash. "That town we passed through a little while back, honey—it's called Clandon. Do you suppose they'd have an all-night service station there?"

"It looked awful small, Mommy."

"Well, you never know. And if the car won't start, we'll have to do something. We can't just sit here."

"We could wait for daylight," the child said.

"That's a long way off. Maybe they'll have an all-night fast-food place, at least. We'll feel better if we have a bite to eat, don't you think?"

"Well—all right."

"I'll just try the car, and if it doesn't start . . ."

She turned the key. The starter made an unnatural humming sound and nothing else happened. She tried again and then stopped, afraid that if she continued she would only add to the problem by running down the battery. With a shake of her head she took the key from the ignition and dropped it into her handbag. "Well, honey?"

"All right," her daughter said without enthusiasm.

"Let's go, then." Getting out, Fiona waited for her daughter to follow suit, then locked the car and took the child's hand. "Watch out for cars, now." There hadn't been one in the past hour, but you never knew.

There was a moon, or part of one, in the night sky, but clouds kept sliding under it and allowing the warm, sticky darkness to take over. Next time she would remember to put a flashlight in the car, she promised herself. And from now on, before undertaking any trip as long as this one, she would have the car checked, too. She'd been unforgivably careless this time. But as they walked along the road's edge Corinne began to sing, and she had to laugh as she joined in. The song was "Hi Ho, Hi Ho," from Walt Disney's *Snow White*, which they had on a video tape at home.

A swift-moving cloud let the moonlight through again, and she saw they were approaching a roadside cemetery. They had passed it in the car, she remembered; probably it belonged to the town of Clandon.

Back where it ended in a wall of woods, something was in motion. A long black shadow of some kind.

She stopped in her tracks, jerking Corinne to a halt with her.

"What's the matter?" the child asked.

Fiona lifted her free hand to point. "Look." Then, in a shrill wail, "Oh, my God! What is that thing?"

Never before had she seen anything like the creature that was rushing toward them. It looked like a lizard, but the moonlight must be playing tricks on her because there were no lizards that big. Its enormous feet either smashed the gravestones in its path or, like pile drivers, pounded them deep into the earth.

"Run!" Fiona screamed. "Run!"

She looked back as they did so. Common sense told her to save every ounce of energy for running, but terror made her turn her head. And, yes, the creature was a lizard. Born in the south and having majored in biology, she knew all about that suborder of reptiles, even the names of the various kinds.

But this one was far more hideous and much, much bigger than any she was familiar with. Bigger than the largest alligator, it had a horny head and great, gaping jaws, and a monstrous, flicking tongue. Old; that was the word. Ancient. Like something you saw in one of those museum displays of giant birds and saber-toothed cats and Tyrannosaurus Rex, the carnivorous dinosaur whose head was four feet long.

But this monster was alive! Horribly alive! It was overtaking them with the speed of an express train. In only another few seconds it would reach the road.

She stumbled, dragging her more nimble daughter down with her because she would not let go of the child's hand. Scrambling up again, she felt the road shudder under her feet as the creature thundered from the cemetery grass onto the blacktop. The night was full of her screams.

Suddenly a cloud slid under the moon again and total darkness returned, as though a giant hand above had poured black ink on the earth.

And the ink filled with sounds—grinding, crunching, crackling sounds—before silence returned.

When the moon reappeared moments later, the road was empty.

Chapter Twenty-two

No alarm clock waked Ethel Everol that morning. What did was the clatter of a truck dumping sand at the unfinished house in which she had sought shelter for the night. Rubbing her eyes, she sat up and looked around in bewilderment, then remembered where she was and struggled stiffly to her feet. Dust motes danced in a shaft of sunlight from a window.

When she appeared in the doorway a few seconds later, the man at the truck's wheel was lighting a cigarette and a second, younger man in the yard was zipping up his fly as he turned to climb back into the cab. Both men looked at Ethel in astonishment.

They saw a thin, sharp-eyed woman who looked at least eighty years old, wearing black shoes, a wrinkled brown dress, and a dark gray sweater. As she returned their stares, she mechanically brushed cement dust and wood shavings from her clothes, then lifted her hands and ran her fingers through her hair in a hopeless attempt to make that more tidy, too.

The man on the ground finished zipping his fly and took a step toward her. "Lady, is there somethin' you want here?"

"No, thank you." Ethel shook her head.

"Then what are you doin' here?"

"I needed a place to sleep. Really, I haven't touched anything, and I'm going now." She stepped from the doorway and began the long, muddy walk out to the road, smiling as she passed them.

Neither man spoke until she reached the highway. Then the one on the ground looked up at the one in the cab and said while scratching his reddish hair, "Holy cow, Wayne, what you think of that, huh? A broad that old on the road. And sleepin' here without no bed or nothin'."

"You got to give her credit, Lennie. I hope I'm as tough when I'm that old."

"Yeah. Me, too."

"We got no time to worry about old ladies, though. Come on, we're runnin' late."

The truck growled out of the yard. When it passed Ethel a moment later as she strode determinedly along the road's edge, both men waved. She waved back without breaking her stride.

An hour later, at a small gas station restaurant,

she again bought bread and cheese for her breakfast. Soon after she had finished eating it—while
continuing her pilgrimage, of course—a young
man in a pickup offered her a lift. He worked on
a dairy farm twelve miles ahead, he told her, and
let her off when he turned in there. By that time
the sun was bright and hot. Her clothes no longer
felt clammy, and she had stopped shivering.

As she trudged along a deserted stretch of highway a little later, a small black kitten came trotting
out of some woods just ahead and paused to eye
her. Welcoming the excuse to rest for a moment,
Ethel broke her stride.

The kitten came to her feet and looked up at
her with yellow eyes.

"Hello, little one," she said, extending a hand
to it. "I don't see any house around here. Where
are you from?"

The kitten rubbed itself against her ankle.

"You're pretty," Ethel said with a smile. "About
six months old, aren't you? What's your name?"

The kitten looked up at her again and meowed.

"Blackie?" Ethel said. "I bet some little girl or
boy named you that. Well, come on, Blackie. I
haven't passed a house in quite a while, so you
must live somewhere ahead and we can walk there
together."

They had gone about a quarter mile, the kitten
trotting along beside her and looking up every
few seconds, when the pine woods ended in a
field fenced with wire. The fence posts leaned

every which way and looked rotten. The wire was rusty.

An old white house at the end of the field seemed sadly neglected, too—in fact, about ready to fall down. In the tall grass between it and the road were an abandoned car many years old, a discarded bathtub, an old wood-burning stove, and other rusting junk.

As they approached the house Ethel looked down at her companion and said, "Oh, dear, I hope you don't live here, Blackie, a nice, clean little kitty like you. You don't, do you?"

Apparently sensing some danger that Ethel did not, the kitten all but glued itself to her leg and voiced a series of faint cries. Suddenly Ethel saw why.

There were three of them—three large, tawny dogs as muscular and mean-looking as any she had ever seen. From somewhere behind the old house they came at a full run, their jaws already dripping saliva in anticipation of the kill.

She knew what pit bulls were. In country parts of Florida they were common. She knew, too, that many were bred solely for illegal dog-fighting. The more vicious they were, the more their owners prized them.

Pit bulls bred to fight would attack anything that moved. Once their powerful jaws clamped shut on a victim, nothing short of death could make them let go. Children had been victims more than once. Even grown-ups. Small animals were easy prey.

These three had obviously seen the kitten.

Suddenly Ethel felt something like hot needles piercing her leg and looked down to see what was happening. It was the kitten, whining in terror as it clawed its way up under her dress.

"Well, you poor little thing," Ethel said calmly.

Reaching down, she held the tiny creature with one hand while easing its claws out of her leg with the other, then lifted it in front of her face and smiled at it before pressing it to her breast. Her gaze fastened on the onrushing dogs again.

"Don't be afraid, baby," she said. "I won't let them hurt you."

She wouldn't, either. Something she had learned when she was in that other world would protect both of them. She knew it as surely as she knew her name was Ethel Everol. All she had to do was keep the kitten from squirming—so it would not hurt itself, poor thing—and aim an unblinking stare at the oncoming brutes while silently commanding them to halt.

Without even a thought of running away, she spread her feet and put her mind to work.

Not ten feet from their target, the three pit bulls braced their legs and skidded to a stop as if suddenly aware that they were in danger. One of them tumbled rump over head before finding its feet again. Then all three crouched there in the road, looking at Ethel as though she were the killer and they the ones threatened.

"Go away," Ethel said without raising her voice.

They continued to stare. All three had stopped

slavering and were trembling now. Their eyes were cloudy, like marbles made of milk glass. Cringing, whining, they retreated with their bellies rubbing the road, then turned and raced back the way they had come.

"There," said Ethel, holding the kitten in front of her face again. "We've nothing to be afraid of, have we? In fact, I believe we make a good team, you and I. If we don't find out where you live, you can stay with me."

As she trudged along the highway, Blackie once more trotted beside her, looking up every little while.

A boy on a bicycle overtook them. Ethel asked him if he knew the kitten and where it lived. He didn't.

She stopped at a house and rang the bell, asking the same question of the woman who came to the door. The woman did not know, either.

After that there was no point in even thinking about it, she decided, because they were too far from where she and Blackie had first become friends. So from now on it would be the two of them.

Ethel and Blackie. Blackie and Ethel.

We two against the world, she thought.

Chapter Twenty-three

With the *cocomacaque* that had saved him before, Jeff Gordon tapped the boulder he had just rolled away from the cave mouth on the knoll. "Remember," he said, "we don't have a clue as to what may be in here, so be careful."

Verna Clark touched his hand and nodded.

Jeff followed the beam of his flashlight into the tunnel. With a light of her own, Verna followed. Though it was daylight, the sun was not yet up, and behind them the knoll was gray with mist.

As he groped his way along the passage, Jeff realized he was tired. He had spent most of the night staring at the ceiling, catching only catnaps while the hours crawled by. Knowing it would be his last night at the Everols' had made him even more apprehensive than before, in that room where Jacob had been so brutally slain.

There had been no real good-byes when he left the house at daybreak. All but Everett were still asleep when he descended the stairs with his few possessions. The snow-haired patriarch of the clan, appearing from out of nowhere, had simply stood there in pajamas and a robe, disdaining to reply to a civil, "Well, good-bye, Mr. Everol. I'm sorry I couldn't be of more help to you."

Did old skull-face in fact know more about what was going on than he was admitting, as the little bird woman, Susan, had suggested?

So . . . no good-byes. Not even from Susan. And after exploring the cave, he would be following Verna back to the Four Pines Motel to find out whether the owner, Gwen Towson, had a vacant cottage he could rent. But first there was this possibly dangerous job that Verna and he had decided to tackle this morning to deal with.

He waited for Verna to catch up to him. "Is everything all all right, love?"

"Yes. How big did you say this cave was?"

"Who knows? That's one of the things we'll be trying to find out, I guess."

He went on again, and presently came to the chamber from which he had taken the *cocomacaque* that was now comfortingly clutched in his left hand—the voodoo stick that had saved him first from the saber-tooth and then from Earl Watson. When his light revealed the ruined *vèvés* and the wrecked altar, he stopped in his tracks.

"There's something here I think we should look into, Verna."

She followed him in. "This is the room you told me about? The *hounfor*?"

"Yes. And evidently someone doesn't want the Haitians using it. As I told you, on my way from the sinkhole I found another one that seemed to have been violated."

"Earl?" she suggested.

"He knows about the cave, at least. We're sure of that." Again Jeff played his light around the chamber. "Has he ever been to Haiti, do you know?"

"He never said so."

"He'd have mentioned it if he had. A visit to the land of voodoo isn't something you keep quiet about. And he isn't a reader. So maybe this is just a show of ignorance. I mean with his kind, when you don't understand something and it scares you, you fight back by trashing it."

"I don't like this," Verna said uneasily. "Can we go on, Jeff?"

On his belt Jeff carried the reel of cord he had used before, with more than half of the line still on it. Saying, "We'd better start using this now, so we don't get lost in here," he tied one end to an outcrop of rock beyond the voodoo chamber. Then, for the next ten minutes, the only sound was that of their footsteps, stirring up ghostly echoes.

Confronted by a familiar scene, Jeff stopped again. The stretch of tunnel ahead was the one in which he had picked up the bone fragment he had handed to Verna at the Drowning Pit after tangling with Earl Watson on the knoll.

Apparently nothing had been touched here. Parts of animal skeletons still littered the floor and were imbedded in the tunnel's walls. He motioned Verna forward.

She examined those on the floor first, going slowly from one group of bones to another. "This was a huge snake of some kind, Jeff. I think this must have been a bird, a big one like the vulture I told you about." Turning to the walls, she added, "It's a fantastic find. When I tell my prof about it, he'll want to bring a team here."

"There's something else," Jeff said. "Come on."

A little farther on he stopped again, this time at the wolf's head imbedded in the wall. Shining his light on it, he waited for Verna's reaction. It was, after all, a complete head, so real it seemed about to leap out of the wall and attack them. And the creature it belonged to had surely been bigger than any member of the wolf family now living on Planet Earth.

Verna's first response was a sharp intake of breath as she stepped forward. In silence she studied the thing. Then, still staring at it, she said in a voice of awe, "Jeff, this is incredible! A prehistoric wolf, almost perfectly preserved? If I weren't looking at it, I wouldn't believe it."

"And I saw one alive at my window," he reminded her. "Just as Amanda did."

"And before that you saw a huge snake."

"There were other such things, too—shadowy things some of us saw but couldn't identify. And whatever it was that made those enormous tracks near the pond, the time you picked up the marijuana cigarette. What are we dealing with, Verna? Have you any idea?"

She shook her head.

"Well, maybe the answer is somewhere in this cave. Let's go."

"I wish we'd brought a camera," she said.

"Some other time. Come on. Please."

With the cord unwinding behind them to guide them back out of the cave, they spent the next hour exploring side tunnels, retrieving the line after each dead end to make it last. Several such tunnels were difficult, with water or low ceilings finally blocking them. When the roof dipped sharply at what appeared to be the end of the last one, Jeff dropped to his hands and knees and ventured in a few yards, aiming his light ahead of him. Crawling back out, he shook his head in defeat.

"This seems to be it, love. A wasted morning."

Verna turned aside to pick up an empty bottle. "Look at this, Jeff. We're not the first to come this far."

They examined the bottle together. Holding his light behind it, Jeff said with a frown, "There's still some liquor left in it. If alcohol evaporates as fast as I think it does, that ought to mean—" He shook his head. "No, not necessarily. It might have had more than a little in it when it was left here."

"I doubt that," Verna said. "Is this a common brand?"

"I've never heard of it."

"Well, it's what Earl drinks. There was always a bottle of this on the kitchen counter."

Reduced to silence by his disappointment, Jeff led the way back out, winding up the cord as he went. The second voodoo room seemed a logical place to stop and rest. While Verna sat on the floor with her back against the wall, he stepped into the chamber for another look around.

"Verna, come here, will you?"

She pushed herself up and went to him.

"Look." He played his light over the rubbed-out *vèvés* on the floor, the wreckage of the altar. "Someone's been in here since we checked it. The altar cloth is gone. The *asson*."

"Was it Earl again, do you suppose?" There was apprehension in her voice. "If it was, he found the boulder moved away at the entrance and knew we were in here. Knew someone was, anyway."

"It wasn't Earl."

"How do you know?"

"It had to be the Haitians, or one of them." He pointed with his light. "See what's missing? Only things that could be patched up and used again—the altar cloth, the *asson,* some of the urns." Jeff turned to look back at the passage. "They must

HUGH B. CAVE

have known someone else was in here, too. Yet they came in."

"Maybe they didn't know their *hounfor* had been wrecked," Verna suggested.

"Maybe. Then, on finding it like this, they salvaged what they could to set up a new one."

"But probably not in the cave again, Jeff. That would be foolish."

"Right, probably not in the cave. Why is it so important, anyway, to have another *hounfor* right away? In Haiti ordinary ceremonies can be held at home without all the trappings." Jeff looked at her. "Should we pay Lelio and his wife a little friendly visit, do you think?"

Verna ignored the question, as though her thoughts were on something she considered more pressing. "Jeff," she said with a frown, "are you going to tell the Everols about this cave?"

"Not until I find out whether they already know about it," he replied without hesitation. "Because if they do, why didn't they tell me?"

Chapter Twenty-four

Rock and roll with news breaks. And commercials, of course. It was the station Nick and he had always listened to while tooling around in the old clunker looking for easy marks. Now Nick was gone and Dan Crawley was stretched out on the bed in his room, listening alone through headphones.

It was nine-thirty A.M., the DJ said. Nine-thirty in the fucking morning and Ma and her latest dude were already out boozing somewhere, probably at the same bar at which she'd picked him up in the first place, a week ago.

The news came on.

He shut his ears to it and reached for the burning joint on the table beside the bed. But before he could take a drag, the voice got through to him and he lay there listening, the joint suspended in space above his open mouth.

". . . and, according to the police, some of the more clearly defined footprints seem to indicate that the creature was a giant alligator or lizard. Along the route it traveled, stones in the Clandon cemetery were either shattered or trampled into the ground, as if by something as heavy and powerful as a tank. On the highway nearby were found pools of fresh blood and a woman's shoe with the severed foot still in it. The foot appeared to have been chewed off, not cut with an instrument. Also on the highway, police found a locked, abandoned car that has been traced to a Mrs. Schuyler Deering of Mobile, Alabama. The investigation continues. We will have further bulletins for you as soon as they are released."

Dan Crawley gazed wide-eyed at the joint in the air above his face, then mechanically reached out to put it back in the ashtray on his bedside table. Behaving more like a robot than a living seventeen-year-old, he dragged the headphones from his head, extended his hand again, opened his fingers, and let the headphones fall to the floor. Then, with his face dead white and his mouth still open, he sat up and forced himself to think.

It had never been easy for him to think. With fear causing his whole body to shake, it was even more difficult now. But after a while he made a decision.

Still shaking, he got off the bed and reached under it to drag out a suitcase. It was the one he had taken from the car that Nick had run off the road beyond the cemetery. The same cemetery the guy on the radio had just been talking about. The stuff he'd lifted from the driver's pockets was now in the suitcase. All but the money from his billfold, of course. They had spent that even before Nick was swallowed by the 'gator as they'd tried to loot the two cars at the pond.

Before picking up the suitcase and leaving the room, he took time to snuff out the joint. Not that his mother would say anything if she found it; she smoked more of the stuff than he did. But even if the house was a dump, it was all the house they had, and he'd catch hell if he set it on fire.

In the yard he tossed the suitcase onto the back seat of the clunker and got in behind the wheel. Ten minutes later, on Clandon's main street, he stopped in front of the town's police station.

A big, muscular man in a brown uniform, bent over something he was reading at the front desk, looked up when Dan stumbled in with the suitcase. Turning to a younger man who was hunched over a typewriter at the only other desk, he said, "Clay," and Clay stopped typing. Both silently stared at their caller.

Both knew him. He was the kid who bummed around with Nick Indrotti, who'd been reported missing. The two of them were almost always in some kind of trouble.

Dan Crawley set down the suitcase down and returned their stares. "There's somethin' I gotta tell you," he said. "About what I just heard on the radio. What happened at the cemetery."

Giving them their full attention, the two men waited for more.

"Awhile back," Dan said, "Nick Indrotti and me seen a car that had went off the road out there past the cemetery. We stopped, and it was a car from out of state and the guy in it looked dead. So we—" Forgetting the rest of what he had rehearsed on his way here, he stopped in fear and confusion.

"So you what?" the man at the front desk said.

"We—that is, Nick—well, we emptied the guy's pockets and took this suitcase out of the car's trunk. Everything's in here now." Dan looked down at the bag and began shaking again, the way he had in his bedroom. "I'm bringin' it in, that's all." Having trouble this time because his mouth had gone dry, he sucked at his lips. "No, that ain't all. I have to tell you about Nick."

The man named Clay said in a sneering voice, "He has to tell us about Nick, Marvin. Okay, what about Nick?"

Dan Crawley tried to stop shaking but couldn't. "That—" He swallowed. "That thing at the cemetery got him. Or one just like it."

"How do you know about the thing at the cemetery?" the big man at the front desk challenged.

"The radio just now. And I seen what got Nick."

"You saw what?"

"I seen the 'gator that got Nick. Or maybe it was a crocodile, if we got such things around here. Anyway, it was big and fast. Jeez, was it fast!

It caught Nick like he was standin' still, and I seen part of him hangin' out of its mouth, and then it swallowed him."

Marvin turned to look at the younger policeman, who frowned back at him. Clay said, "Where did this happen?"

"That road by the pond."

"What pond?"

"Out near the Everol place. The one with the quicksand."

Marvin said sarcastically, "And what were the two of you doin' out there? Checkin' out some other car you maybe could strip?"

Dan Crawley had stopped shaking but had to wet his lips again. "We just happened to stop and walk in there, that's all." When the men only continued to stare at him, he swallowed again and said in a hoarse whisper, "All right. There was a couple of cars in there and nobody around."

"Did you strip them?" Marvin asked.

"No! They was locked. It was when Nick was lookin' for a rock to—" Jeez, Dan thought, don't say that.

"A rock to smash the windows with?" Clay said.

"Well . . ."

"Let's see the suitcase. Hand it up here," Marvin said.

Relieved that the inquisition seemed to be over, Dan swung the suitcase onto the desk. "It ain't locked," he said. "The key's inside of it, on the ring with his car keys."

Opening the bag, Marvin half rose from his

chair to see what it contained. Pushing aside clothing and shoes, he took out a notebook and a billfold.

"The guy's name is Jeffrey Gordon," Dan volunteered. "We never used the credit cards."

"I'll bet," said Clay, leaving his typewriter to come over and have a look.

"No, we never did. Honest."

"You have any idea where this Jeffrey Gordon is now?" Marvin asked. "If he was dead like you thought he was, or like you claim to've thought, we'd know about it."

Dan shook his head.

But Clay had taken the notebook and opened it, and said now, "Most of this seems to be about Haiti, Marv, but there's something here about the Everols, too. Listen to this, Marv. 'Ethel Everol, age sixty-eight, was visited in December by psy— psychi—psychiatrist R. J. Walther at the institution where she is a patient. Claimed she actually saw the creature that killed her brother and tried to kill her. Dr. Walther says he is inclined to believe her.'" Clay's gaze traveled on down the page. "There's more about the Everols. Looks like he was headed for there, Marv. Should I phone them?"

"Take a run out there. They're not the kind to tell you much over the phone. Here, take the bag in case the Gordon guy is there." Marvin returned the notebook and wallet to the suitcase and closed it. "While you're at it, better ask him if he wants to press charges against this kid. You," he said to

Dan Crawley, "sit down on the bench over there and tell me again what happened to your buddy. And take it slow this time, so I can write it down."

At the Everol house, Clay left the suitcase in the police car when he went to the door. Everett Everol answered his ring.

"Mornin', Mr. Everol," Clay said. "We're lookin' for a feller named Jeffrey Gordon. He here by any chance?"

In the doorway Everett looked more like a scarecrow or a dressed-up skeleton than a living human being. "He was here till this morning, Clay. He's gone now." Behind him, Clay saw Blanche and her sister Susan step from the living room into the hall, apparently to find out who had rung the bell and what was wanted. They kept their distance, though.

"Would you know where he is, Mr. Everol?"

"Uh-uh." The old man shook his head. "He came here from Connecticut, promisin' to give us the benefit of his fancy knowledge about the kind of thing's been troublin' us, if you know what I mean, as I'm sure you do. Never did much and left at daybreak this mornin', I suppose to drive back there."

"Tell me some more about him, if you will," Clay said. The wife's sister, he noticed, was no longer in the hall listening. Apparently wasn't interested.

"Tell you what?"

"Well, we have a suitcase belongs to him, along

with his billfold and a notebook he done a lot of writing in. I'd like to let him know we have them if I can. Seems he had an accident on his way here and both him and his car were stripped by a couple of town kids who do that kind of thing."

"That's right," Everett said. "When he showed up here he was in pretty bad shape. You want to come in, Clay?"

"For a minute. Thanks."

Everett stepped aside. Going past him, Clay saw Blanche quickly retreat into the living room. When he himself walked into the living room he found her sitting in an easy chair with a magazine. She looked up as if surprised.

"Why, hello, Clay," she said. "What brings the police here? Or is this a social call?"

"Just tryin' to find out about your Mr. Gordon, ma'am."

"Oh. Well, you'd better—" She smiled as her husband followed Clay in from the hall. "I was just going to say you'd better talk to Everett."

For a while Clay did that, but he learned little more than he had already been told. It seemed the Gordon fellow had asked if he might come and try to find an answer to the Everol mystery, as the town folks called it. Then he'd shown up after his accident with his mind affected and his memory gone and, being stripped of his billfold and everything, hadn't known who he was until the Everols told him. That, at least, was the Gospel According To Everett, and Blanche backed the old man up by nodding every few seconds.

Anyway, Gordon had now gone back to Connecticut, where he was a professor at some university.

Clay thanked the old man and went back out to his car and was halfway out to the road when Susan stepped out of some bushes and flagged him down. He slammed his foot on the brake pedal.

There'd been Everols in Clandon since before there was a Clandon on the map, and nobody liked them much, but Susan was different. After all, she wasn't really an Everol, only the sister of a woman who'd married into the clan.

She leaned into the car window, which was open because the air-conditioning had gone bad and the department hadn't gotten around to getting it fixed yet. "Clay," she said, kind of breathless because that was the way she was, "do you really want to find Jeffrey?"

"Huh?"

"Jeffrey Gordon, Clay! You were asking Everett about him."

"Why, yes. Sure I do. You know where he is?"

"At the Four Pines," she said. "That's where he is, Clay, at the Four Pines Motel. And Clay"—she stepped back, with a sort of lost expression on her face—"you'll tell him it was me that told you, won't you? Please?"

Chapter Twenty-five

Jeff Gordon, too, heard a report of the cemetery tragedy, though not from a rock and roll radio station.

After exploring the cave with Verna, he had followed her back to the Four Pines Motel and obtained a cottage two doors down from hers. They had gone to a small nearby restaurant for dinner, then spent the evening in her cottage trying to put the pieces of the puzzle together.

Just before eleven, Jeff had returned to his own place and switched on the TV while getting ready for bed. Then, after hearing essentially what Dan Crawley later heard over the radio, and seeing some graphic video coverage of the destruction at the cemetery, he had slept badly, waking every little while to find his mind still searching for answers.

Up at daybreak, he was in the shower when one of the missing bits of the puzzle fell suddenly into place. The bottle, he thought. Why would Earl Watson have gone to the end of a dead-end passage to empty a whiskey bottle and throw it away?

The crawl there must lead to something.

Lead to what?

While poking through the wreckage in the voodoo chamber yesterday he had scratched a finger and caused it to bleed. Reluctant to take chances, he had stopped for a bottle of Mercurochrome on his way to the motel. The little bottle of red stuff was still in the motel bathroom. After drying himself, he stood before the washbasin mirror with it and carefully painted a pentagram on his chest. Then, on his way to the door, he picked up the *cocomacaque.*

Always play the percentages. More than once that philosophy had paid off for him.

Should he wake Verna and tell her where he was going? No, he decided. He would not be taking her anyway—only the presence of the fossils in the cave had persuaded him to let her share the risk before—and if she knew where he was going, she would insist on accompanying him. He had better leave a note of some sort, though.

The Four Pines was not the kind of motel that supplied stationery for its guests. He had bought some notebooks, however—planning to write a book someday about his activities, he always kept notes—and now tore a page out of one and wrote on it, "Gone to check on something. Back soon." Before going to his car he slid the paper under Verna's door.

At the quicksand pond, before climbing the knoll, he took the reel of cord he had used before from the trunk of his car, but not until he reached the place where they had found the bottle did he feel a need to use it. With one end of the cord made fast to a rock, he dropped to his hands and knees and began to crawl.

When the ceiling slanted upward after a hundred yards or so and he was able to stand again, he was not surprised. His light revealed a continuing tunnel as wide and high as the one behind him, its floor strewn with rocks and rubble.

He should have a compass, he thought then. And a tape or pedometer. Well, he had always been blessed with a good sense of direction and distance. Unless the passage had too many bends, he would come close to determining where it went. One thing he was sure of even now: It was headed in the general direction of the Everols' house.

A niche on his right was choked with the rocks and rubble that seemed to be everywhere. He stopped to peer into it. His light disclosed nothing but more boulders, however, and he went on.

Soon he began to find fossils and bone fragments.

It was like the stretch of passage in which Verna

had become so excited. One cluster appeared to be another huge bird. A second, with four legs and a skull, might have been a wolf, or perhaps a saber-tooth like the one that had threatened him. Some bones were even imbedded in the tunnel's walls.

There was quicksand at the pond. Had this whole area been something like a sea of quicksand in the old days? That might explain the presence of so many dead things here.

He would have to bring Verna here after all, to record these new discoveries. She would never forgive him if he didn't. But that must wait until later, when the Everol mystery and that of her sister's disappearance had been solved.

A piece of the Everol puzzle seemed to be falling into place right now, as he continued along the tunnel. He had come about half a mile, he estimated. There had been no significant change of direction. Unless he encountered such a change, he would very soon be under the Everols' yard. Or—who could say?—even under the house.

Think, he told himself. This tunnel is part of an underworld full of fossils from an age when Florida was a stamping ground for all kinds of nightmare creatures. Above it is a house where some of those creatures are preying on the inhabitants. What the hell is bringing those long-dead monsters to life?

He stopped. In front of him the passage ended in a solid wall of rock. And, yes, if he wasn't under the Everols' house, he was certainly close to it.

Time to go back.

Back along the tunnel.

Back on his hands and knees through the crawl, and to wind up the cord for the next visit.

Now back past the trashed voodoo room to the entrance on the knoll, and then to Verna for a discussion of what he had learned.

But as he neared the voodoo room, he heard something in the darkness ahead and froze in his tracks.

What stopped him was a deep-throated growl or snarl that seemed to make even the walls of the passage tremble. Nothing even remotely human could have made it. He knew what had.

He had been trudging along with the light in his right hand, the *cocomacaque* in his left. Now he switched them and aimed the light at the entrance to the *hounfor,* where he had been confronted by a saber-tooth before.

One was there again, in the same menacing crouch, with jaws open and long, and sharp teeth agleam. When he saw the tawny haunches quivering he knew he had only a split second to react before the monster would come hurtling at him like a battering ram. Knew, too, that if it did spring, he would be slammed to the tunnel floor like something made of cardboard and killed by a single snap of those awesome jaws.

He sank to his knees. Dropping the light, he thrust the *cocomacaque* in front of him with both hands, as he had done before when facing this beast or one like it. But this time the great cat did not retreat. For some reason the voodoo stick had lost its power. He dropped it and tore at his shirtfront, ripping the fabric apart to bare the red pentagram on his chest.

The light had fallen to the floor in such a way that the *hounfor* and the crouching cat in its entrance were left in darkness. He could see nothing now but a pair of fiery eyes as he held his breath in an agony of suspense. His heart was an air hammer, his hands and face clammy with sweat.

Then the growling subsided. There were receding sounds of huge paws slapping the stone floor. And silence.

Reaching for the light and the *cocomacaque,* Jeff struggled to his feet, the light's beam wobbling over walls and ceiling before he could steady it. The tunnel ahead was empty, thank God. Shaken, he peered into the *hounfor* as he passed it. It, too, was empty.

On he hurried to the entrance, praying the huge cat would not suddenly reappear. With the boulder rolled back into place, he ran down to his car and, still shaking, drove back to the motel.

Standing in the doorway of her cottage when he pulled in, Verna waved, then ran to him and was at the car door when he opened it. "I was just beginning to get scared," she said. "Your note didn't say what time you left, so I couldn't know how long you'd been gone. Where did you go?"

"To the cave again, and let me tell you what I

found." Taking her by the hand, he led her to his unit. There, while she sat on a chair and he on the bed, he told her of the tunnel that ended somewhere under the Everols' yard or house. "Did you watch the TV news last night after I left you?"

"Yes," she said. "The cemetery."

"I'm betting some part of the cave runs under there, too."

She nodded.

"Verna, listen to me. When I was in Haiti last summer I attended a very unusual voodoo service. It wasn't something tourists get to see. I told you before that I'd become friendly with certain voodoo people through a Haitian student of mine, didn't I? Well, I was invited by one of them to go to this affair in a place called Petit-Goave, out on the southern peninsula."

He paused. "Actually, I suppose the fellow just wanted a ride out there to save him a bruising trip on a *tap-tap* or *camion,* and he knew I had a rented car. But never mind. I got there and saw what happened.

"What happened," Jeff went on, "was that the old *houngan* in charge of the service called upon one of the old, old voodoo gods—gods most *houngans* don't even know about and wouldn't dare call up if they did—for help in obtaining revenge for his own son. The son had been a shopkeeper there in Petit-Goave. His best friend had somehow taken the shop away from him, stolen his wife as well, and left him with nothing. The son was there at the ceremony, along with some friends of his who sympathized. No one else, except my friend and I, the usual servitors, and a large black dog that belonged to the officiating *houngan*. This was forbidden stuff, you understand. All of us could have been jailed for it."

Verna stared at him in silence.

"All right," Jeff continued. "The ceremony was long and more than usually ritualistic, with drumming and chanting I'd never heard before, and *vèvés* I'd never seen. And for a long time nothing happened. I mean, there was no indication that the ancient *mystère* who was being sent for would answer the summons. Then, just before daybreak, after a whole night of it, something finally happened. The black dog, who'd been asleep on the swept-earth floor near the bench I was sitting on, suddenly sprang to life. He leaped up and raced to the central post, which in voodoo is the link between the spirit world and that of humans, and began sniffing and growling around it. It was as if the post had called to him. Then—"

He paused to glance out the window. A police car had turned into the motel drive and stopped in front of the office.

"And?" Verna said, leaning toward him.

Jeff turned back to her. "A servitor lunged at the dog to chase it away, and it turned on him. It bit him on the hand badly before the *houngan* could intervene. Then, while the *houngan* was helping the fellow, shouting at him that this was the *loa* they'd been waiting all night for, the animal took off and disappeared into the darkness."

Again Jeff paused. "On the way back to Port-au-Prince my voodoo friend, the one I'd taken to the service, explained to me that the very old gods don't have to appear as themselves when they're summoned. They can take any form they wish, and this one had chosen to become the dog. Or to possess the dog, if that's a better way to put it."

A knock on the door interrupted him. Jeff went to it and found a policeman standing there with a suitcase. It was his own suitcase, the one that had been stolen from his car after he was run off the road.

"Mr. Gordon? Jeffrey Gordon?"

"Yes, I'm Jeff Gordon."

The policeman stepped inside and put down the bag. He was Officer Clay, he said. At some length he explained how the bag happened to be in his possession. "I hope everything's here that was taken from you, Mr. Gordon. Check it, please, if you will. If anything's still missing, I'll go and see if it's at Crawley's house."

Jeff opened the suitcase and looked, taking out a notebook as he did so. "Everything seems to be here except the money that was in my billfold, Officer."

"Which there's not much chance of us getting back, I'm afraid. You want to file charges against this young man, Mr. Gordon?"

"Should I?"

Clay shrugged. "You'd have to appear as a witness, of course. And even if he's found guilty, chances are he'll be out again before you can figure what the loss of your time cost you. Up to you, though. He's guilty, all right, and a conviction might scare him some."

"Let me think about it," Jeff said.

"Right." With a nod to Verna, Clay departed.

Jeff turned to Verna, holding the notebook he had taken from the suitcase. "It's all in here, what I've been telling you," he said. "All the notes I took that night in Petit-Goave, the names of the old *loa* the *houngan* called on, everything. You know what I'm thinking?"

With her gaze still on his face, she moved her head slowly up and down. "That someone here has been calling on some of those ancient voodoo gods, and they've taken the forms of creatures that lived here when the gods did. Right?"

"Especially if the ceremony or ceremonies were held in the cave, where the remains of those ancient creatures are still present," Jeff said. "What we ought to do, I say again, is have a talk with Lelio Savain."

"Tell me something, Jeff."

He looked at her, waiting.

"What happened after the possessed black dog disappeared?"

"There was a story two days later in the Port-au-Prince newspapers. I have it at home. Soon after the ceremony, the man targeted for vengeance was found in his yard. The papers said most of the body had been eaten, and the remains were barely recognizable."

Chapter Twenty-six

It had been a long, tiring journey. Oh, people had given her rides now and then—very short rides, mostly—but she had paid for those dearly with moments of stress.

Like the time the young man who looked so presentable, so absolutely safe, had stopped his brand new Cadillac and picked her up. "Even Blackie?" she had said. "I can't leave Blackie."

"The cat, you mean? Of course. I have two of my own."

"Oh, do you?" She had climbed in with alacrity, thinking how nice it would be to ride in a big car and rest her feet. "What are their names?"

She knew now he didn't really have cats. A man like that would never be a cat person. But he had rattled off two names, Princess and Pudge, as glibly as you please. And in less than two minutes, while he was still asking questions about where she had come from and where she was going—neither of which she was about to tell him, of course—she felt his hand on her knee.

Would you believe that? A man not even thirty, trying to seduce a woman of sixty-nine? And trying to keep it up even after she cried, "Stop this car, young man, and let me out this minute!" Even forcing her to use her newfound power on him—to turn on the seat and stare at him the way she knew how to now—before he would bring the car to a stop. Oh, he'd been glad enough then to stop the car and had been shaking all over, blubbering apologies, when she opened the door and got out, but would you believe such a thing? What was the country coming to, with people like that in it?

There'd been others. The old man with such a beard you couldn't really see his face, only his beady little eyes, driving a car almost as old as he was. He'd kept looking at her in such a queer way that in the end she'd said, "This is where I'm going, thank you; I'll get off here," and then she'd had to stare at him, too. And when she did he froze at the wheel and almost put them in a roadside ditch before regaining control of the car at the very last second.

And what about the red-haired young man, on foot, who had insisted on walking with her for more than a mile, all the time eyeing Blackie as if cats were something to eat and he was half starved? And the blond girl in the expensive red

car who'd started right in talking about drugs and
how she, Ethel, ought to learn to use them so she
could forget all her troubles . . . and all the while
the blonde was talking she was taking her gaze off
the road and missing oncoming cars by only a
hair. On her the look hadn't worked. She was off
in another world somewhere, a sick one.

Of course, after learning how to use her power
on people, she hadn't been too frightened except
when it seemed she might be involved in an accident. But she was certainly glad to be trudging
up the Everol driveway now after having walked
most of the night. What time was it, anyway? She
lifted her wrist. Her watch said 11:10 A.M.

"This is where you're going to live, Blackie," she
said, turning her head to smile at the kitten now
crouching on her right shoulder. "Will you like it,
do you think?"

Almost from the beginning of their friendship,
Blackie had seemed to know what she was saying.
He answered her now by sort of nodding his head
and voicing his usual "Mrreow."

"Of course, I may have to use my power on Everett," she said. "He doesn't like cats. At least he's
always said he doesn't, but so far as I know he's
never had one, so how can he be so sure?"

"Mrreow," Blackie said, probably meaning, "Yes,
how can he?"

"Anyway, nobody's going to take you away from
me, so don't you give it a thought. Not Everett,
not Blanche, not Amanda, not Susan. Susan
wouldn't want to, of course. She loves animals."

"Mrreow," Blackie replied, and together they climbed the steps to the front door, where Ethel rang the bell.

It was Blanche, Everett's wife, who opened the door.

"Hello," Ethel said. "I'm home."

"My God." The words came out of a mouth that sagged open and stayed that way. Blanche's eyes, too, went wide. Her gaze traveled slowly from Ethel's face to the kitten on her shoulder, then down over the now shabby sweater and outdoor dress to the almost ruined black shoes. And, "My God," she said again. "Ethel!"

"Yes, I'm Ethel."

"Where have you—how did you—"

"I escaped. It took me this long because I had to lose weight. Don't you see how thin I am now?"

Blanche's gaze went to the kitten again. "What's this?"

"His name is Blackie. He's my friend."

"You mean you've brought him from the home?"

"Oh, no. We met on the road. May I come in, please? You are going to ask me in, aren't you? This was my home long before Everett married you and brought you and your sister here, you know."

Coming out of her trance, Blanche stepped aside but continued to stare as Ethel stepped past her. She closed the door as if unaware that she was doing so.

"Where are the others?" Ethel asked.

"Susan is in the kitchen. Amanda and Everett are upstairs."

"Upstairs? It's almost noon."

"Well, Amanda isn't herself. She saw one of—something like what you saw—and hasn't been right since. Everett—well, I don't know what's the matter with Everett. He came down for breakfast looking just awful, as if he was all worn out, then said he couldn't eat anything and went back upstairs. To tell the truth, he hasn't been himself at all lately. Something's troubling him." Blanche eyed the kitten again. "Are you going to keep that creature?"

"Yes."

"Here? In the house?"

"Yes."

"You know Everett doesn't like cats."

"I don't care what Everett likes. After putting me in that awful home he owes me a few favors." In the living room Ethel went to a chair and eased herself into it with a heavy sigh of relief. Turning her head to smile at the kitten on her shoulder, she said, "There. We're home. Are you hungry?"

Blackie meowed.

"Well, in a minute I'll get you something to eat, but first just let me sit awhile. Don't you want to go exploring?"

Blackie jumped from her shoulder to her lap and stayed there, looking around the room. From the kitchen came Susan, as wide-eyed as Blanche had been.

"My goodness, it is you, Ethel! I thought I recognized your voice in here!" With her hands fluttering in front of her face, she stopped in her tracks. "Are you—what happened? How did you get here?"

"Wait, wait," Ethel said. "I'll tell you all about it, the whole long story, after I've fixed Blackie and myself something to eat. We're hungry, both of us. The last time we ate anything was yesterday afternoon."

Susan stopped staring. "You just sit there. I'll fix you something." Turning, she trotted back into the kitchen while Blanche walked silently to a chair and sat down.

"So, tell me what's been going on here," Ethel said to Blanche. "My story can keep until you're all together, so I won't have to tell it over and over."

"Well—"

"Go on, tell me. You said Amanda saw something."

"A wolf. At least that's what—oh, I don't know." Everett's wife flung her hands apart in a gesture of despair or impatience. "Mr. Gordon saw it first at his window and then—"

"Who?"

"Mr. Gordon. He's a college professor from Connecticut who came down here to see if he could help us find out what killed Jacob and drove you—well, anyway, he wrote and asked if he could come and Everett finally let him, and right away things began to happen again. I mean, the very first night he was here he saw a huge

247

snake at his window, and then this wolf that attacked Amanda, and he put those things on all the windows to protect us." She pointed to one of the living room windows, and Ethel saw what looked like a star inside a circle painted on each of its two panes. "But that's all he did, and when he got friendly with a girl who'd been prowling around the property, Everett lost patience and ordered him out."

"Which, if you ask me, was a terrible mistake," said her sister Susan, coming in from the kitchen in time to hear that part of the story. "And frankly, I don't see why Everett gets so touchy whenever anyone dares to set foot on the property. Privacy is one thing—we've always cherished that—but my goodness gracious, next thing you know he'll be putting a fence around the whole place and buying pit bulls for watchdogs."

"I know what to do with pit bulls," Ethel said.

"You what?"

"Three of them tried to kill Blackie and I showed them."

"Showed them how?"

"Never mind. What's wrong with Everett?"

"Well, if you ask me, he just can't cope anymore," Blanche said. "First this Gorden fellow and the snoopy girl, then Amanda being scared out of her wits, and the awful thing that happened at at the cemetery where Jacob is buried—"

"What happened at the cemetery?" Ethel demanded.

Blanche told her about it. "It was on the TV;

that's how we know about it. And, as I said, it's my opinion that poor Everett just couldn't keep fighting back any longer."

Ethel looked at the two of them in silence for a moment; then Susan suddenly said, "Oh, dear, your soft-boiled eggs will be hard!" and leaped up and ran back to the kitchen.

Ethel said with a frown, "What happened to this Mr. Gordon you've been talking about?"

"I suppose he went back to Connecticut."

"Oh." It might have been exciting to have some man other than Everett in this house. Since Jacob's death Everett had ruled the place as if the rest of them did not even belong here. Stroking the kitten in her lap, Ethel said, "Did the vulture come back while I was away?"

"Not the vulture. At least, we're not sure. Other things just as terrible, though."

"What other things?"

"A huge snake, a wolf, some shadowy things we couldn't put a name to."

Ethel realized she was very tired. "I'd better see what Susan is doing," she said. Lifting Blackie to her shoulder, she started for the kitchen.

"I'll go upstairs and tell Everett and Amanda you're here," Blanche called after her. "Come up when you're finished, won't you?"

"Yes. Of course."

Susan had set a place at the kitchen table and put out orange juice, eggs, toast, and coffee. While Ethel ate, she sat at the table too, every now and then shaking her head as if unable to believe

Ethel could be home again. Suddenly she said, "I don't care what the others say, I think Mr. Gordon is a nice man."

"Oh? How old is he?"

"Too young for me, if that's what you're thinking. But that's not what I mean. I think he really tried to help us."

"Why did Everett send him away, then?" Ethel had put half of an egg in her saucer and now smiled at the kitten on her shoulder. "That's for you, Blackie. Go on, eat it."

Blackie jumped to the table and went straight to it.

"Yes, why?" Susan said. "First Jeffrey wrote to ask if he could come here and try to help us, and Everett was—well—reluctant. Then Jeffrey telephoned a few times and Everett finally said all right, come on down, and we were all excited about having someone who really might know what to do come to Clandon. And then for no reason at all Everett suddenly changed his mind. I mean, he did a complete turnabout. Jeffrey had an accident on his way here and didn't know who he was when he arrived. And would you believe it, Everett didn't even want us to tell him who he was." Silent for a moment, she watched while Ethel ate. "You're really better, aren't you? I mean, no one would ever know you—"

"Had been crazy? I wasn't crazy. I just went away for a while."

"You what?"

"Never mind. We'll talk about it later. But I'm

250

glad you noticed." Susan had always been the sensitive one in this house, hadn't she? Always the first to see a raccoon or rabbit in the yard, or to worry about the birds getting enough to eat when the weather turned cold.

Her breakfast finished, Ethel rose to her feet and spoke to Blackie. The cat jumped to her shoulder again. "I'll go upstairs now and say hello to Amanda and Everett," Ethel said.

Susan nodded. "And I'll go for Lelio and Lucille. Your room ought to be—"

"Go for who?"

"Lelio and Lucille. You remember our Haitians, don't you?"

"You mean they're still here?"

"Well, why not? It was March, wasn't it, when we found them living in the old cottage and Everett said they could stay if they'd do some work around the place." Susan counted on her fingers. "That's only three months ago. Anyway, I'll go and get them while you run along upstairs. That is, if you've had enough breakfast, the two of you."

"We've had enough. Haven't we, Blackie?"

The kitten leaned forward on Ethel's shoulder to rub his face against her cheek.

"Just don't be shocked when you see Amanda," Susan warned on her way out of the kitchen. "That wolf or whatever it was actually broke through the wall of her room and was about to attack her when Jeffrey saved her. She's improved a little, but she's still a long way from being right again."

Admitting to herself that she was now almost too tired to stay awake, Ethel climbed the stairs. Blackie must be tired, too, the poor little thing. Just as soon as she'd said hello to Everett and Amanda, both of them ought to lie down somewhere for a good, long nap. Her own bed would be nice, but if the Haitians were coming to look after her room, she and Blackie would just have to use some other bed. Or even the sofa in the living room.

She walked into Everett's room first and found Blanche seated there beside the bed.

"He's asleep," Blanche warned.

"No, I'm not," Everett said in a husky voice, as if he had a bad case of laryngitis. "Welcome home, Sister. Let me look at you." He tried to sit up but couldn't maintain the effort and, with a heavy sigh of surrender, fell back again.

"What's the matter with you?" Ethel said.

"Weary, that's all. Been trying to fight it off, but it got the best of me."

"He tried to drive to town yesterday," Blanche said. "Got so weak and shaky, he had to turn the car around and come on back. I begged him not to go in the first place. Told him I could run any errand that had to be run. He wouldn't listen."

"Everett, you always were mule stubborn," Ethel said.

"How'd you get out of the home?" he managed after another struggle with his inflamed larynx.

"Never mind that now. It's a long story."

"Are they after you?"

252

"I suppose so. We'll cross that bridge if they come here. You can see for yourself there's nothing wrong with me anymore. I was just away for a time."

"Away where?" Everett demanded, gazing up at her owlishly.

"Well, I don't know exactly. But it was a learning place, I know that. I learned things there, anyhow. And now I'm back. I can help you after you're rested, most likely. First you have to rest. Anyone can see you're just worn out from all the frightening things that've been going on here." Ethel reached out to pat Everett's hand. "You rest now, you hear? I'll come back later."

Despite the near loss of his voice, Everett managed a few last growly words. "Is that a cat on your shoulder?" he demanded.

"It is."

"You know how I feel about cats. Get it out of here. Out of the house, I mean."

"Why?"

"Because I say so."

"You know," Ethel said, "you're really something. Just because you took Daddy's place when he died and have been looking after us all these years doesn't give you the right to play Hitler about every little thing, you know. Now be quiet," she added quickly and wagged a finger at him as Everett opened his mouth to argue. "Be quiet and look at me."

Scowling, he did that.

For a moment the two of them gazed at each

other in silence, while the wife of the man on the bed watched them both with an expression of bewilderment on her face. Then Everett's mouth began to tremble and his bony, long-figured hands clenched on the old patchwork quilt that covered him. Finally he said in a voice that barely escaped his lips, "Well, all right, if that's how you feel. Just let me rest."

Ethel left the room smiling but waited in the hall for Blanche to catch up with her. Blanche said, "How in the world did you do that, I'd like to know?"

"Never mind. What room is Amanda in?"

"Her own now. We had the wall fixed after the thing smashed through it."

"Let me talk to her alone, please." Ethel went down the hall and opened Amanda's door. The woman on the bed had her eyes open but seemed unaware that the door had been opened. Ethel went to the bed and stood there looking down at her.

"Hello, Amanda. Remember me?"

The open eyes focused on her hovering face, and Amanda reached out to clasp her hand. "Ethel." It was only a whisper. "You've come back!"

"And now that I have, you're going to be all right again."

"I wish I thought so." The voice was full of sadness. "I keep thinking of it, Ethel. The way it burst through the wall over there."

Ethel turned to look and saw that a patch had

been applied over what must have been a really big hole. A wolf, had Susan said? No wolf could ever be that . . . but the vultures had been bigger than life, too, hadn't they? Seating herself on the edge of the bed, she took one of Amanda's hands in both of her own. "We're going to help you, Sis." Turning her head to the kitten on her shoulder, she added, "Aren't we, Blackie?"

"Mrreow," Blackie said.

"Is that a kitty?" Amanda said.

"It is, indeed. A very special one."

"Everett will be furious. Can I hold it?"

Ethel took the kitten from her shoulder and laid it gently on her sister's breast, where Blackie looked into Amanda's face and began to purr.

"He likes you," Ethel said with a smile.

"He really does!"

"Amanda, look at me."

While stroking the kitten, Amanda did so. Blackie went on purring. After a while Amanda said. "I'm glad you came back, Ethel. Oh, I'm so very glad! I'm going to be all right now. I just know it."

Chapter Twenty-seven

Susan had to wait a long time for the door to open after she knocked at the caretaker's cottage. The Haitians were at home, no doubt of that. She could hear them moving about inside. Had she caught them doing something they didn't want her to know about? Something they had to clear away before letting her in?

The door opened at last and Lelio, standing there with a look of unease on his face, said, "Please excuse us for making you wait, Miss Susan. The room was such a mess, we would have been ashamed for you to see it."

The table was bare, Susan noticed as she entered. Well, maybe it had been littered with the remnants of a meal. And maybe not.

"I'd like you to come to the house," she said. "Ethel is home and we need to fix up her room."

Standing by the bare table, Lucille opened her eyes wide and said, "Ethel? You mean from the—"

"From the place where she's been for the past few weeks. Yes."

Lelio and Lucille looked at each other but neither spoke.

"So, can you come?"

"Of course!" Lelio said. "Right away!"

Susan returned to the house and, true to their word, the Haitians arrived a few minutes later. She led them upstairs to Ethel's room and told them what she wanted done. Leaving them there, she went back down. Ethel, she noticed, was asleep on the divan in the living room, with the little black kitten curled up close to her face. Going into the kitchen, Susan sat at the table to think about what everyone might have for lunch.

She was still sitting there when the front doorbell rang not once but three times, as if whoever was ringing it was both ill-mannered and impatient.

Getting there as fast as she could, she jerked open the door and found herself face-to-face with a lean, husky-looking man with dirty, uncombed hair and a face that appeared to be made of old leather. "Who are you?" she demanded.

"Name's Watson. Earl Watson." The words were thick and slurred, and she could smell the liquor that made them that way. "Want to see Mr. Everol."

"I'm sorry, but Mr. Everol can't see you. He's not well."

"He has to see me." The voice was a threat now. "I tell you—"

"Lady, you listen to me." Earl pushed her aside as he lurched in. "Mr. Everol and me got business to do and I aim to see we do it. You tell him I'm here or by God I'll tell him myself!"

Frightened, Susan said in a low voice, "Wait here, please. I'll go up and talk to him." She looked again at the matted hair and leathery face. "What did you say your name was?"

"Watson. You tell him Earl Watson is here. And make it quick, lady. I ain't got all day."

She hurried upstairs and found Everett asleep. Waking him, she said, "Everett, I'm sorry, but there's a man downstairs who says he has to see you. He's drunk and I'm afraid of him. He says his name is Earl Watson."

Everett's face took on a look of sheer fright as he struggled to sit up. Twice he fell back, gasping, but on the third try, with Susan's help, he managed to brace his back against the headboard. "Oh, my God," he said.

"What shall I tell him, Everett?"

"Tell him to go away! I'll see him as soon as I'm better!"

"Everett, he's not going away. I've just told you, he's drunk and nasty. I knew it even before I opened the door to him—the way he rang the bell so hard."

"Then—then bring him up here," Everett said.

His voice was a moan now. "Bring him here and leave the two of us alone. Oh, my God, I knew I shouldn't have turned back yesterday."

"You were going to see him, you mean? What about?"

"Never mind, never mind. Just go bring him here before he starts tearing the house apart. I've seen him drunk before."

Susan hurried back downstairs and found Earl Watson leaning against the wall in the hall. The front door was still open. Fearfully, she stepped past him and closed it, then said, "All right, Mr. Watson. Come with me, please."

With him thumping up the stairs behind her, all she could think of was a movie she had seen once of that scary novel by Mary Shelley. That story in which Dr. Frankenstein created a monstrous human being out of parts of bodies, and the creature was so big and clumsy he made the floor shake with every step he took. This Earl Watson wasn't that big, but he certainly made the stairs shake. She thought they'd collapse.

He followed her along the upstairs hall the same way, and when she stepped aside at Everett's door he stomped past her without even a thank you. Everett was still sitting up in bed, braced against the headboard.

"All right, Susan," Everett managed in spite of his laryngitis. "Shut the door and leave us alone now."

Susan shut the door and walked briskly back down the hall, making sure to do some stomping herself so they would hear her. Then she turned and tiptoed back, hoping Everett would trust her enough not to suspect anything. Earl Watson, being so drunk, would not even think of it.

"All right," Mr. Watson was snarling, "where the hell's the money? I told you last time if you kept me waitin' again I'd quit foolin' with you and go to the cops."

"I was sick," Everett said. "My God, can't you see I'm sick?"

"I don't take no excuses!"

"But I'm only one day late. One day!"

"One day is one day too damn many. How am I supposed to know you ain't plannin' on goin' to the cops yourself?"

"Planning on—what?"

"Goin' to the cops about me keepin' quiet about that girl's body when I found it, 'stead of reportin' it like I should've. You know what I'm talkin' about, Goddamn it. Don't play stupid with me."

"Earl, for God's sake, you know I wouldn't do that. Listen, I'll give you a check."

"I don't want no check. Where the hell would I cash a check that big without bein' asked questions? I want cash, like always."

"But I can't get to the bank, Earl." Everett's voice was full of pleading now.

"Send one of your women, then. You don't have to tell 'em what it's for. Just get the cash here so I can come for it."

"I—I'll go myself, Earl. I'll manage somehow."

"You don't know which one of 'em to trust, is that it? You still ain't figured out which one of 'em shut that girl up in the cave. By God, I'd have found out long ago if I was you. I'd have stood the lot of 'em up against a wall till the guilty one broke down and admitted what she done. But even if you knew, you'd still be payin' me to keep my mouth shut. Don't you forget that. 'Less you want the guilty one charged with murder."

"Earl," Everett moaned, "I'll go to the bank right now. You can come for the cash this evening. Now go, please go, so I can get my thoughts together and plan how to handle this."

"For Christ's sake, they're only women, ain't they?" Earl said. "Just say you're feelin' better and go."

"You don't under—"

"All right, all right. I'll be back this evenin'. You better believe it."

At the door, Susan was off and running. Down the hall she sped, and on down the stairs. Before Earl Watson reached the top of the stairs and began to blunder his way down them, she was in the kitchen with one hand hovering over the telephone.

When the front door slammed shut behind him, she snatched up the phone and dialed the Four Pines Motel.

A moment later she was talking in whispers to Jeff Gordon.

Chapter Twenty-eight

Earl Watson had left the Everol house about noon. Ninety minutes later Jeff Gordon and Verna Clark arrived. Susan opened the door to them.

"I was beginning to think you wouldn't come," the bird woman said accusingly. "What on earth took you so long?"

Jeff said quietly, "We had some talking to do first, Susan. Miss Clark is really Linda Mason."

"Linda—what?"

"Mason. She is the younger sister of the woman who is missing." Jeff put his arm around Verna's shoulders. "Now you know why she has been 'prowling around here,' as you people have been calling it, since Kimberly disappeared."

"Oh." Susan shifted her gaze to the face of

Verna Clark. It was expressionless now, or at least under tight control, but there were unmistakable signs of recent tears. "I'm so sorry, Miss Clark." She reached out to touch Verna's hand. "I really am."

"May we see Everett?" Jeff asked.

"He went out right after Mr. Watson was here, but he should be back soon. I'm sure he only went to the bank for the money that terrible man demanded." She shuddered. "Please come into the living room. Amanda and Ethel are there, and the Savains. We've been talking about what I overheard and trying to decide what really happened."

Jeff and Verna followed her. In the living room, the two Haitians sat together on the divan, the woman looking frightened. Amanda and Blanche sat in two of the old easy chairs. Ethel occupied a third, with the black kitten on her lap.

"Please sit down," Susan said. "I'm sure Everett won't be—"

"He's coming now," Ethel said.

Jeff looked at her. He had heard nothing before she spoke, but the cat was peering alertly toward the hall. Now—yes—he heard a car in the drive. It stopped, and he heard its door thud shut. The front door of the house opened. Looking exhausted, Everett walked slowly into the living room and stopped.

His gaze took in the Haitians and the Everol women before it finally settled on Jeff and Verna.

"What's going on here?" he asked in his sandpaper voice.

Susan said, "Sit down, please, Everett. We want to talk to you."

"Talk about what? I'm sick. Can't you see I'm sick?"

She stood before him with her hands on her hips. "You've been putting some of it on, Everett, and we know why. You didn't want to pay that man again and were hoping—"

"What are you talking about?" Everett's voice made the windows rattle.

"I listened outside the door while he was talking to you. And you're wrong, Everett. You've been wrong from the start. None of us shut that woman up in the cave."

Amanda said, "She's right, Everett. We didn't."

Ethel said, "We've been talking about it since you left."

Everett sank onto the unoccupied end of the divan and again slowly turned his head to scowl at them all. "No one else knew about the cave," he challenged. "We agreed never to mention it outside of this house, so we wouldn't have people coming from all over to investigate the fossils. Are you trying to tell me you broke that agreement and other people do know about it?"

His wife said, "You know better than that, Everett. Now suppose you tell us what's been going on between you and that Watson man. We all want to know."

"No." Everett clamped his lips shut after the word was uttered.

"Everett, we have to decide what to do about him. Because he's coming back tonight for more money, and you're not going to pay him. That's final."

Everett sat in silence for a moment, looking them over. "Which one of you did it?" he demanded. "Who shut that woman up in there?"

"None of us," Susan said.

"I don't believe you. One of you must have!"

They shook their heads. Ethel said, "I would know if one of us did it, Everett. I have a way of knowing such things now. It's something I learned when I was in the learning place."

"Huh?"

"Never mind," Susan said briskly. "It's not important. Everett, can't you see that if one of us had done it, we would certainly own up to it now to save this family from ruin? We could always say it was an accident—that whoever did it just happened to find that boulder rolled away from the entrance one day and rolled it back in place without knowing anyone was in there. You can't charge a person with a crime when it was only an accident."

"Anyway," Amanda said, leaning forward on her chair, "none of us did that. Found the boulder rolled away and put it back, I mean. We've talked about it and we're positive."

"So who did lock her up in there?" Everett said. Speaking for the first time, Jeff Gordon frowned at the two Haitians on the divan. "Lelio, do you and Lucille know anything about this? Two of the rooms in that cave have been used for voo-doo ceremonies, and you're a *houngan*."

Every pair of eyes in the room focused on the Haitians.

"Well, Lelio?" Everett demanded.

"It—might have been us," the old Haitian admitted. "But if we did it, we did not know what we were doing."

"Suppose you tell us about it," Jeff said quietly.

"Well, I discovered the cave by accident, m'sieu. I was up on the knoll one day, seeking a stone I could use as a *pié loa*. You know about the *pié loa*?"

Jeff nodded. To the others he said, "It's a special stone, with special powers, that is used in certain ceremonies."

"And while I was searching for one on the knoll," Lelio said, "I felt a powerful force flowing from behind one of those big rocks. When I went to investigate, I discovered the cave entrance." Silently he begged for understanding with his eyes and outspread hands. "Lucille and I, we had been afraid to serve the *loa* in our cottage, thinking Mr. Everol would probably send us away and we would be homeless. But thinking no one knew about the cave, we made one of its chambers into a *hounfor*."

"When was this?" Jeff asked. "I mean, when did you discover the cave?"

"In March, soon after we came here." The old Haitian looked at his woman, and she nodded.

"And when did you hold your first voodoo service there?"

"In May, m'sieu. There was much to do first, because we had none of the things we needed. Not even an altar."

"Then did you—well, never mind now. Tell the story your way."

"Well, m'sieu, we used the cave from that time on. Always we left the stone rolled away from the entrance when we went in because for an old man like me it is very hard to move from the inside." He looked at the others. No one interrupted. "So I suppose this woman you are all talking about—I suppose she could have found the stone rolled away from the entrance one day and gone in. And when we came out, we could have rolled it back without knowing she was inside. I am sorry if that happened, m'sieu. Believe me." He paused, then almost defiantly added, "But an active young woman should have been able to move the stone away and escape from there! Even I would have been able to get out if I had been trapped like that!"

Jeff looked at Verna. Her face was wet with tears again.

"My sister broke her wrist in March, in the college gym," she said almost inaudibly. "She could still hardly use it when she was here."

With a look of bewilderment on his face, Lelio said, "But m'selle, if she had been shut up in there that way, would we not have found her at the entrance when we went again? Would she not have been trying to get out?"

"How often have you been using the cave?" Jeff asked.

"We have tried to hold a weekly service, but sometimes two weeks pass before we can go there."

Jeff turned to Everett. "Evidently, after Miss Mason was trapped Watson was the next to go in, and he found her. What happened then, Mr. Everol?"

But the patriarch of the Everol clan had something else on his mind. In a voice full of despair he said, "So it was you, Lelio. You. And all the time I thought—"

"All the time you thought it was one of us," Susan snapped indignantly. "And instead of calling a family meeting and asking us, you stupidly paid that horrid man to keep quiet. It was he who found the body, wasn't it?"

Alone at his end of the divan, Everett let his head droop and talked to the patch of carpet between his feet. "He told me that when he dived for the Shelby girl's body, he discovered an entrance to the cave near the bottom of the sinkhole. Being the kind of man he is, he kept the knowledge to himself but went back. That's when he found the entrance on the knoll. Then he discovered Miss Mason's body at the boulder one day, as Lelio has suggested, and assumed one of us must have shut her up in there to put a stop to her snooping. So be began to blackmail me.

And I, too, thought one of us must be guilty. How could I have known that Lelio and Lucille were using the cave? So I—well, I've been paying him to be quiet."

Still gazing at the floor, the old man wagged his head and exhaled another long sigh. "He showed me where he'd hidden her. I mean, he couldn't expect me to pay for him to be silent without proving to me there actually was a body, could he? She—" Lifting his head, he glanced at Verna Clark, then quickly looked down again. "He had her wrapped in canvas, and it's always cold in there. I suppose the constant temperature . . . I'm sorry. I don't know about such things. Anyway, I agreed to pay him and he promised to keep quiet."

Jeff said, "And that is why you changed your mind about me, isn't it? After giving me permission to come, you suddenly found yourself with this secret to protect. So you did everything you could to persuade me to leave."

"Yes," Everett mumbled.

"You knew who I was but thought if I didn't know, I'd hurry out of here to look for medical attention."

"I was afraid you would find out what was going on."

Verna Clark said in a controlled voice, "Is my sister still in the cave, Mr. Everol?"

"Unless he has moved her."

"Will you take me there—Jeff and me—and show us where she is, please? Now?"

"Oh, Lord," the old man groaned. "I'm so tired, so sick. I almost didn't make it to the bank."

Jeff reached for Verna's hand. "She's been dead for weeks, love. A day or two more . . ."

With her eyes shut and tears on her face, Verna nodded.

Little Susan said sharply, "Everett, that man is coming here this evening for more money, isn't he?"

"Yes."

"And blackmail is a crime, isn't it?"

"Of course."

"Then I think I should telephone the police, don't you? So they can have someone here to arrest him?"

"I suppose."

"Is this family conference over? Can I use the phone now?"

"Wait," Jeff said, fixing his gaze on the Haitians.

Startled, Susan said with a frown, "What, Jeffrey?"

"I want to ask these two about something. Give me a few minutes more before we break this up, will you?"

The room was silent. A look of fear widened Lelio Savain's eyes and changed the shape of his face. Reaching out to the woman beside him, he clasped her hand.

Jeff continued to stare at him. "Lelio, there are some *loa* in your voodoo who are not very nice, and some of them, when summoned, are able to take strange forms. That's so, isn't it?"

Lelio's look of fear intensified. "Y-yes, m'sieu," he whispered.

"I found the stumps of black candles in the room you first used for a *hounfor*. Did you use those in a ceremony?"

"Y-yes."

"Which *loa* did you send for?" Blessed with a near photographic memory, Jeff had only to close his eyes to see a certain page in his notebook. "Was it by any chance Ogoun Dan Petro, who eats people?"

"He—he was one of them."

"I think I'm beginning to understand. Because, Lelio, I once attended a service to Ogoun Dan Petro in Petit-Goave, and he took the form of a large black dog that killed a man. Black candles were used at that ceremony, too. Now tell us, please, why you sent for such a *loa*."

Lelio wet his heavy lips. "It was not just Dan Petro I sent for. I made *vèvés* for other Petro *mystères* who are known to help in righting wrongs."

"What wrong did you want justice for?"

The old man shut his eyes. "They drowned our people, m'sieu. The two men on the boat that brought us from the Bahamas—when the boat's engine failed, they were afraid of being caught and forced us into the sea. Seven of us. One was but a baby. Only Lucille and I reached the shore alive."

After a little gasp from Susan, the silence returned. But now the sound of breathing was heavier. All in the room gazed at Lelio, including the yellow-eyed black kitten on Ethel's lap.

"So . . . when our *hounfor* in the cave was ready, I called on the *loa* for vengeance," Lelio said. "Vengeance against those two evil men. And for the humiliations and sufferings Lucille and I were made to endure on our way here to the Panhandle, where I hoped we could survive because I worked here once before."

"Sufferings on your way here?" Jeff said.

"It was no easy journey for an old man like me and a woman who does not speak the language. It was January when those two evil men tried to drown us. The weather was cold. We had little money. Most of the time we were hungry. And while we had papers that those men had sold us, we were afraid to ask for help because people might question us."

He paused. The others waited in silence for him to stop trembling, but Jeff said gently, "Go on, please, *compère*."

"We were questioned anyway by suspicious policemen wanting to know why we were walking along your roads that way," Lelio continued. "Only the papers we had paid such a high price for saved us from being taken to prison, I am certain. For weeks we just walked and rested, walked and rested, always cold and sick and frightened, always hungry. We even ate food from restaurant garbage cans. And then when we reached here, I could not find work after all. No one would even talk to me about work. But *Le Bon Dieu* led us to the empty cottage here and persuaded M'sieu Everol to let us stay. If that had not happened, we might have died."

"And then," Jeff said, "you fixed up a *hounfor* in the cave and asked the *loa* for revenge."

"Yes."

"Petro *loa*, you say."

Lelio nodded. "The Ogoun Dan Petro you mentioned, who eats people. Marinette Pieds Cheches. The Ge-rouge *loa* with the red eyes. Some others. But, m'sieu"—a shudder seized the old man and he closed his eyes—"it was not those who answered."

"Who did answer?"

"I don't know. We should not have held the service in the cave, I think . . . all those bones in there, of animals and birds from some ancient time. The *loa* who came in response to our summons must have been from that time, too— nameless ones that I have heard about but never dealt with before. I think the cave must be some kind of doorway to that world. And because we were calling upon wicked *loa* to avenge our people, the ones who came were evil also, able to take the shape of the most terrible creatures who lived here then. Yes, that is surely what happened. Seeking simple justice for the wrongs done to us, we let loose an even greater evil."

"And then, after Jacob was killed and Ethel so badly frightened, you tried to send them back, didn't you?" Jeff said. "In that second voodoo room I found white candles, not black ones."

"Yes. We called upon Papa Legba and Maitresse

Erzulie to close the gate we had opened. And they did so, I think. But whoever destroyed our first *hounfor* found the second one as well and destroyed that, defiling the *vèvès* and everything else the *loa* hold sacred. And the gate opened again. That happened the day you arrived here, m'sieu."

Susan broke the silence that followed. "And, of course, we know who did it, don't we? It was that awful Mr. Watson, afraid his ugly secret might be discovered and he would no longer be able to blackmail Everett."

"So what are we to do about all this?" Everett said. "Now, I mean." His gaze shifted from the two Haitians to Verna and Jeff.

"I would like to find my sister," Verna said.

Jeff touched her hand and shook his head. "With Lelio's ancient ones on the prowl, the cave is too dangerous, love. Twice I've met some kind of saber-toothed cat in there. We should try to make it safer first." He frowned at the *houngan*. "Would it help, Lelio, to call on Legba and Erzulie again?"

"I wonder, m'sieu."

"What do you mean?"

"So many of those things have crossed over now. Only a few were on this side when Legba and Erzulie closed the gate for me before."

"I say it's worth a try. Can you set up a *hounfor* here in the house?"

"Yes . . . but it will take time."

"How much time?"

"The rest of the day, at least."

"Even if we help you?"

"There is not much you can do, m'sieu. I alone must do most of it."

"Then I suggest we break up this meeting and let you get started," Jeff looked around. "Is everyone agreed?"

There were murmurs of assent.

But Lelio shook his head. "M'sieu, at the cottage I have most of what we will need, but there remains a big problem. When I called for help before, I had my *cocomacaque* to use for a *poteau-mitan*. It has special powers. You know what a *poteau-mitan* is, no?"

Jeff nodded. "The link through which you communicate with the *loa*. And I have your *cocomacaque, compère*."

"You, m'sieu?"

"It saved my life against that cat I mentioned. Then against Watson. It's out in my car. I'll get it for you."

Chapter Twenty-nine

"I am ready, m'sieu. Shall we begin?"

For hours Lelio had worked to make the Everol living room as much like a voodoo *hounfor* as he could. He and Jeff had carried the big table from the dining room and placed it against a wall to serve as an altar. It was covered now with a clean white sheet. On the sheet stood two earthenware jars—*govis*—freshly painted with the colors and designs of Legba and Erzulie. And an *asson*, newly made to replace the one defiled by Earl Watson. And a dish of cornmeal, a *pié loa*, certain other items of less importance. Lelio had changed into a long-sleeved green shirt—green in honor of Legba—and was barefooted.

The living room itself was to be the peristyle. "Such as it is," Lelio said with a look on his face that said he was not hopeful. "If we had a true *poteau-mitan* . . . but again, we have only the *cocomacaque*."

"The *cocomacaque* worked before, you said," Jeff reminded him.

"Yes. But it has been handled by you since then, m'sieu. It is no longer wholly mine."

The stick that had twice saved Jeff's life now stood upright, as before, in a *govi* newly painted with the *vèvé* of Papa Legba, the *loa* who at every service opened the gate through which the *mystères* would make contact. By careful measurement it was in the exact center of the room, where it belonged.

All else in the room—divan, overstuffed chairs, chairside tables, everything—had been removed. Smaller chairs had been brought in from the dining room and placed against two of the walls for those who would witness the ceremony.

The preparations had taken hours. Now by Jeff's watch the time was 9:15. Three white candles flickering on the altar provided the room's only light. A hard, steady rain beat against windowpanes still marked with the pentagrams. Outside, the night was unbroken blackness.

"We begin," Lelio said. "We lack many things, but we begin. May *Le Bon Dieu* be with us, for what we do here tonight is almost too dangerous to think about."

Beckoning Lucille to join him, he began a slow *yanvalou*, less a dance than a procession, around the *govi* in which the *cocomacaque* was set upright.

With his knees bent and his hands on them, he circled the improvised *poteau-mitan* counterclockwise, all the while voicing a low, almost inaudible chant. Lucille followed him in silence but imitated his every movement. All the others—Jeff, Verna, the members of the Everol clan—sat on the chairs against the walls and watched.

The kitten on Ethel's lap, Jeff noticed, was equally attentive. Its gaze followed Lelio's every move.

Now Jeff caught some of the words Lelio was whispering. *"Papa Legba, ouvri bayé! Papa Legba, Attibon Legba, ouvri bayé pou nou passé!"* Over and over the same words, rising in volume as they were repeated. Then the dance and the chanting came to an end, and silence took over.

Motioning Lucille to be seated, Lelio went to the altar. From it he took up his *asson* and a glass of water. As though walking in his sleep, he paced about the room, dipping a finger into the glass and flicking drops of water onto the floor, then shaking the gourd rattle over them. In the center of the room he circled the makeshift *poteau-mitan* three times, performing the same ritual. A salute to the *loa,* Jeff thought. Especially to the two he would call upon: Legba to close the gate on the evil ones and Erzulie to protect this home as she protected all homes.

Lelio had fallen to his knees. He leaned forward to touch his lips to the *cocomacque.* His chanting was now in *langage,* the old African tongue that no one could translate anymore, not even the *houngans* and *mambos* who used it. But the gods knew its meaning. They would respond.

The old man rose, visibly tired and trembling. He motioned to Lucille again and she got up from her chair and went to the altar. Taking up a dish of cornmeal, she carried it to him.

Rain pounded the windows. A gust of wind rattled one of the pentagram-marked panes of glass.

With the dish of cornmeal in his left hand, the *asson* in his right, Lelio turned to face each of the room's walls in turn, shaking the rattle each time. Then he laid down the *asson* beside the urn with the stick in it and stepped back to begin the drawing of the same two *vèvès* he had drawn in the cave.

The *vèvé* to Legba slowly took shape—the cross with mystic sybols. Then the one to Erzulie— oddly like an elaborate Valentine heart with wings. It was a long, slow process. For a man of his age, bending from the waist and reaching out in that manner, with his knees held straight, must have been pure torture. But he persisted. The *vèvés* were completed. He sprinkled drops of water on them and shook the *asson* over them.

Then he and Lucille, standing side by side, intoned the usual prayers in Creole. The Hail Marys from Haiti's Catholic Church, the Aposties' Creed, the Lord's Prayer. And the voodoo prayers, over and over, with Lelio shaking the *asson* and looking as though he might collapse from exhaustion.

Silence, at last. He turned to look at Jeff.

"I know nothing else to do, m'sieu. And they have not come."

The doorbell rang. Those in the room looked at one another. "Mr. Watson," Blanche said. "You should have let us call the police, Everett."

Lelio shook his head at her. "No, m'selle. Your Clandon police would never have understood what we are trying to do here. In their ignorance they probably would have arrested me."

Susan stood up and marched out of the room, saying over her shoulder, "Well, anyway, I suppose he'll be drunk again."

With the others waiting in silence, she went to the front door and opened it. And, yes, the caller was Earl Watson and the whites of his eyes were red.

"Where is he? I told him I'd be back this evenin'."

"Come in, please," Susan said briskly. "Everyone is in the living room."

Weaving a little, he followed her into the living room and, like Everett before him, stopped in his tracks at the sight of so many people seated there. "What the hell's goin' on?" he demanded. "What is this?"

Jeff Gordon got to his feet and faced him. "Why don't you sit down, Watson?" he said quietly. "Mr. Everol has something to say to you about the blackmail."

"Huh?"

"We know about the money he's been paying you. Now it's time for some talk before we call the police and press charges against you. Sit down."

His mouth twitching, Watson went to the nearest empty chair and slumped into it. With an obvious effort he pulled himself together. His gaze traveled slowly from face to face, like that of a man on trial seeking to read the minds of his jury.

Jeff looked at the aged head of the Everol clan. "Everett?"

"I'm—so tired, Jeffrey. Can you handle this for me? Please?"

"Gladly." Hands in his pockets, Jeff confronted Watson again. "What happened, Watson, is that Susan overheard what you said to Everett in his bedroom." He paused, waiting.

"So what?" Watson growled. "One of these women murdered the college dame. You ain't callin' no cops, mister."

"I think we are. Because we're not talking about a murder here. It was an accident."

Watson's face changed again, turning the color of putty. "A what?"

"An accident. No one meant to shut Miss Mason up in the cave. The person who rolled the stone over the entrance on the knoll didn't know she was in there. And it wasn't one of Everett's people."

Watson's gaze went the rounds, to settle at last on the face of Lelio Savain. He licked his lips. "You tryin' to tell me—"

"I am telling you. It was not an Everol who shut Miss Mason up in there; it was Lelio and Lucille. And they didn't know they were doing it. So you see, Watson, there's no secret for you to keep any more. No reason at all why Mr. Everol shouldn't let the truth be known and charge you with blackmail."

Watson took in a breath that swelled his chest. Half rising from his chair, he let himself fall back again. "There's no way you can prove I blackmailed anyone!" he snarled. "It'd be his word against mine."

"And mine," said Susan. "Remember, I overheard the two of you talking upstairs."

"You're his sister. Nobody's gonna believe you."

"His wife's sister, Mr. Watson. There's a slight difference. Besides, I think when the bank produces proof that Everett drew certain sums of money at regular intervals—"

"Wait." The interruption came from Ethel.

Everyone looked at her.

Lifting the black kitten to her shoulder, she rose from her chair and walked to stand at Jeff's side, facing the house painter. "May I?" she quietly asked Jeff.

Jeff stepped back.

Standing there with no display of hostility, her hands limp at her sides and a faint smile on her lips, the woman from the institution said, "Mr. Watson, look at me, please."

Watson did so, then looked away again.

"No. Keep looking. I believe you have something to tell us, and I want you to look at my eyes while you do. Let me tell you something, Mr. Watson. Just a little while ago I was attacked by pit bulls who were far more ferocious than you, yet there isn't a mark on me. Think about that while you look at me."

Watson's gaze returned to her face. Evidently it had to. His hands gripped his knees and his mouth trembled.

"It wasn't Lelio and Lucille who shut that poor girl up in the cave was it, Mr. Watson?" Ethel said.

Except for his trembling he was like a statue, sitting there looking up at her.

"Was it?" she repeated.

"I—I don't have to—"

"Oh, but you do. Doesn't he, Blackie?" She turned her head to smile at the kitten on her shoulder.

Blackie voiced a shrill, "Mrreow!"

"It was you who shut Miss Mason up in the cave, wasn't it Mr. Watson?" Ethel continued.

"No! You're crazy!"

"Don't stop looking at me. And I'm not crazy, Mr. Watson. I was never crazy. I only went away to learn." Again Ethel glanced at the small black animal on her shoulder. "I've even taught Blackie some of what I learned. Haven't I, Blackie?"

"Mrreow!" This time the kitten bared its teeth.

They looked a little like the teeth of the saber-tooth in the cave, Jeff Gordon thought. Smaller, of course, but just as threatening. Perhaps just as dangerous.

"Tell us, Mr. Watson," Ethel said. "Tell us how you saw Miss Mason go into the cave one day and decided you didn't want her to discover the fossils there and tell the world about them. Because, at the right time, you planned to 'discover' them yourself and become rich in some way. And so you rolled the boulder over the entrance while she was inside, and everything you have said about finding her body in there has been a lie. Come, Mr. Watson. Tell us."

Mouth open, he stared up at her with eyes that appeared to be made of glass.

"All we need from you is a simple 'That's right,' " Ethel murmured. "Come now."

The rain pounded the windows. Watson licked his lips.

"Mr. Watson, we haven't all evening." Ethel's voice was a shade less casual, a little more biting. "For your information, we have other things to do here this evening."

He remained silent.

"Very well." Lowering herself to one knee, she looked again at the kitten on her shoulder. It meowed once more and jumped to the carpet only a yard or so from Earl Watson's feet. With its teeth bared, it crouched there with its gaze fixed on his face.

Watson suddenly lurched erect, flailing the air in front of himself with both hands. "No!" he cried hoarsely. "Keep it away from me!"

"You must be aware, Mr. Watson, that one snap of those terrible jaws could take your head off." Ethel's voice mocked him. "All I need to do is give a command."

"My God, all right, I did it! I locked the Mason woman up in there!"

"Say it again, Mr. Watson."

"I did it! I admit it!"

Ethel turned, letting her gaze touch the faces of the others in the room. "You heard that, all of you? Everett? Blanche? Amanda? Susan? You, Jeffrey? You, Miss Mason?"

Some nodded; others only stared. Jeff Gordon's gaze was fixed on the kitten, and he wondered what Earl Watson was seeing there. Was it only a kitten or had it become to Earl something more like the tawny saber-toothed cat of the cave?

"So, then, we have witnesses," Ethel said. "You have confessed to a murder, Mr. Watson. A murder for which you have blackmailed my brother Everett. We know all we need to know, except where you have hidden the poor woman's body. Tell us that, please."

"It—you go into the crawl, if you know where that is."

"I know where it is," Jeff Gordon said.

"You go through the crawl on your hands and knees. Just beyond it, on the right, is a niche choked with boulders."

Jeff nodded. "I know about that, too."

"She's in there, wrapped in canvas."

Jeff looked at Verna Clark, beside him, and reached for her hand. But there were no tears now. As she gazed at the man who had killed her sister, her face revealed only loathing.

Ethel said, "All right, Mr. Watson. Now, because

we have other things to do at the moment, you
will continue to sit here quietly, please, until we
are finished and have the time to deal with you."
She leaned forward to stroke the crouching kitten. "Guard him, Blackie. If he tries to get out of
his chair, you will know what to do."

The kitten's "Mrreow!" was too savage a sound,
too threatening, to have come out of that small
mouth, Jeff Gordon decided. There was something going on here that only Ethel and Watson—
and the cat?—seemed to understand.

Apparently Ethel was finished. Turning to the
Haitians, she said quietly, "Lelio, I believe the time
has come for you to try again. We need the presence of your *loa* to close the book on all this. If
you think I can be of any help, please call on me."

Chapter Thirty

"Papa Legba, ouvri bayé! Papa Legba, Attibon Legba, ouvri bayé pou nou passé!"

Over and over Lelio intoned the words.

The three white candles burned on the altar. In the center of the room the *cocomacaque* stood upright in the *govi*. The *vèvés* to the keeper of the gate and the protector of homes still lay undisturbed on the carpet. The sound of rain at the windows was much like the sound of whisper drumming that normally would accompany this stage of the ceremony. So much so, in fact, that when Jeff Gordon closed his eyes he could easily convince himself he was in Haiti, not Florida.

But, of course, this was not Haiti and what Lelio was attempting to do had already failed once.

Something was not correct. Was the old *houngan* himself at fault?

Not likely, Jeff decided, watching the man as he walked slowly about the room with his glass of water, sprinkling the floor as a salute to the *loa*. He had been in voodoo all his life and had probably been taught by a father who had learned from his father, all the way back to Africa. That was how it went.

It must be something else, then. The altar, perhaps—Lelio had suggested a service to consecrate the old table, but there had not been time. The *govis?* Lucille and he had had a supply on hand, made, of course, by themselves, but were they made of the proper kind of clay? And should they, too, have been blessed after Lelio added the symbols of the *loa* he was so desperately trying to contact?

The *cocomacaque.* Such a stick had certain powers, granted. And this one had worked at first when Lelio called upon the old gods for vengeance and unleashed horrors he had never dreamed of. Then it had worked a second time when he realized his mistake and called on Legba to close the *bayé* on the horrors so innocently let loose. But, as the old fellow himself had suggested, the *cocomacaque* had been handled by a certain Jeff Gordon since then. And the *poteau-mitan,* for which it was being used here as a substitute, was perhaps the most important part of any voodoo ceremony. It *was* the *bayé.*

On his knees now, Lelio was kissing the *cocom-*

acaque. Except for the drumming of raindrops at the windows marked with circles and stars, the room was still as a tomb. Every eye was on the *houngan.* Even Earl Watson stared at him in silence now, instead of at the black cat crouching before him with its gaze fixed on his face.

Lelio staggered up from his knees. His voice was only a hoarse whisper as he spoke the ancient *langage,* the meaning of which even he could not know. Again Lucille brought him a dish of cornmeal from the altar. Again, stiff-kneed, he bent from the waist and drew the *vèvés*—easier for him this time because he had only to dribble the cornmeal over the same designs he had so carefully created before.

Again he sprinkled the completed symbols with water and shook his *asson* over them.

Again, with Lucille, he chanted in Creole the Catholic prayers and the voodoo invocations.

Again, after an anxious wait that seemed to last forever, he intoned words of despair.

"They—are not coming."

Silence.

Earl Watson, with a sneer on his face, leaned back in his chair and said with a snort, "Who ain't comin'? What the hell's this crap all about, anyhow? What you think you're doin'?"

Lelio seemed to feel he must answer. With his head lowered and his gaze on the floor, he said wearily, "I have asked Legba and Erzulie to come and help us. They have not heard me."

But little Susan, the bird woman, suddenly

leaned forward in her chair to stab a finger at one of the windows. "Look!" she cried shrilly. "Oh, my God, all of you! Look at what *is* coming! Look!"

Shapes. Shapes out there in the darkness pressed forward to peer in through the glass, with only the pentagrams between them and those in the room. What revealed them was not the flickering light of the candles on the altar; that was too faint. It was the glow of their own eyes, red as burning coals and bright enough to identify some of them.

One window framed the face of a huge vulture. Another that of the monstrous snake, or one like it, that had appeared to Jeff Gordon the first night of his stay here, when he had not even known who he was. At a third appeared a wolf's head with gaping jaws and a mouth like a passage in the cave, with stalactites and stalagmites for fangs.

Jeff recovered first from the paralysis that seized them all. In a voice so steady it surprised him, he said, "All right now. Let's not panic. The pentagrams have worked before." He stood up. "I'll check around, see what's going on in the rest of the house."

Before he reached the hall, Verna Clark was at his side. No need for her to say, "Where you go, I go." It was in her eyes. In the touch of her hand.

They hurried together through the rest of the downstairs and found shapes, shadows, at almost every window. Not all had eyes. Some were only swirling lumps of black mist apparently seeking a way in. But no longer was the pounding of the rain the only sound. At every window the besiegers had voices now. Some snarled, some growled, some hissed. Some that looked like giant lizards even screamed like birds.

As Verna and Jeff stood before a window that framed one of those—behind, of course, the pentagram that made it safe at the moment for them to be there—Verna spoke as if unaware of what she was saying. "Jeff . . . a professor of mine once said that all the birds we know today are descended from dinosaurs. Dinosaur means terrible lizard, Jeff. Maybe the vulture that killed Jacob in this house wasn't a bird at all. . . ."

Jeff took her hand. "Come on, love. We have to get ourselves and the others out of this trap. Let's see what's upstairs."

They hurried there together, first to the room Jeff had occupied—the one in which Jacob's face had been mangled by the beak of a huge vulture—then to the one in which Ethel had been driven to her "learning place." Then they went to Amanda's, and Susan's, and the room shared by Everett and his wife.

In all of them it was the same. Shapes, shadows, globs of swirling mist at the windows. Some with glowing red eyes, some with eyes of other colors or no color at all, merely bright round holes like tunnels. Again the rain drumming was overpowered by snarlings, spittings, and ear-splitting bird cries from the throats of things that looked like lizards.

"No way out here," Jeff said. "No way out anywhere, it looks like. Let's go back to Lelio."

As they hurried back down the stairs, he asked himself a question: If the house were under siege, as it seemed to be, how long would the siege last? More important, would the traditional power of the pentagrams, many of them now blazing as brightly as the fiery eyes they held at bay, continue to be effective that long?

He and Verna had more to protect them than the magic symbols on the windows. They wore the stars on their bodies, as well. Back at the motel, after his last adventure in the cave, Verna had stood naked before the mirror in the bathroom and painted one on herself with the Mercurochrome, as he had. How could he forget it when, feeling she might not be doing it correctly, she had asked him to come and help her?

Would he ever again take her in his arms the way he had then? Would they ever get out of this hell house alive, to even think about such things?

In the living room the others had not moved. Not even Watson, whose gaze was fixed again on the cat. Still seated, staring at the windows like a group of people turned to stone by some kind of curse, they did manage to turn their heads and look at him as he and Verna entered. But no one spoke. The only sounds were those made by the specters in the night outside.

Quietly Jeff said, "There's no way out. Lelio, try to think what you may have done wrong and begin again. But first"—he turned to Susan—"have you some iodine or Mercurochrome here? Something you can paint pentagrams on your bodies with, for extra protection?"

Susan said calmly, "We have already done that, Jeffrey."

"You what?"

"Blanche and Everett said I was being foolish, but I pointed out that those on the windows had already proved their worth, and we would have nothing to lose in going a step farther." She nodded briskly. "I helped you with the windows, if you remember. This time I used some blue paint that was left over from painting a bedroom. There is some of the paint left if—" She looked at the two Haitians. "In the kitchen closet we have some white, too. Shall I get it, Lelio?"

"Thank you, m'selle. Lucille and I will use it, yes."

Jeff turned to the man who had murdered Verna's sister. "Watson?"

"What the hell you talkin' about?" Watson snarled.

"We're talking about the symbols you see on the windows here. They seem to be keeping those creatures out there from breaking in and destroying us. For now, at least."

"And you want to paint one of those dumb things on me?"

"I don't want to paint one on you, Watson. I wouldn't touch you with plastic gloves and a brush with a ten-foot handle. But if you want to apply one to yourself, Susan will bring you what you need."

"You got to be crazy. All of you, you got to be crazy!"

"Have it your way." Jeff shrugged and turned away.

Susan hurried to the kitchen. Returning with a pint can of white paint already opened, she handed it and a small brush to Lelio, who stepped into the dining room. Lucille followed. They had not asked how to draw a pentagram, Jeff noticed. Had not even glanced at a window. Apparently they knew about such things. Among the many truths his summer in Haiti had taught him was that there was much, much more to voodoo than chanting and drumming. And very little of it took place in most voodoo movies.

In a few moments Lelio and his wife returned. Because the sounds outside the house had become louder, Lelio had to speak loudly to be heard. "I am ready to try again, m'sieu. But without knowing what is wrong, I have little hope." Shaking his head in anticipation of failure, he stepped to the altar. Lucille followed to assist him. Jeff, who had been standing, turned to go to an empty chair.

A low, throaty growl stopped him. He spun about to face the dining room doorway. There, filling the whole doorway, was the monstrous wolf he had faced before, or one just like it. Even as he threw up his arms and took a backward step, the slavering jaws opened wide to reveal a forest of fangs.

Blanche and Amanda screamed. Little Susan wailed "Oh, my God!" Everett tried to yell but could produce nothing more than a strangled moan of fear.

The two Haitians merely stared.

Ethel, calmly rising from her chair, voiced only one word. "Blackie!"

Before the wolf could launch itself in a leap that must have brought it hurtling into the room with the door frame draped around its neck, the black cat obeyed Ethel's command. Leaving its place in front of Earl Watson, Blackie sprang to confront the intruder. The kitten's "Mrreow!" was a challenging scream that made the windows rattle. Jeff Gordon thought his eardrums had ruptured. The thing in the doorway froze.

Something strange happened then. At least, Jeff thought it did. One moment what he saw was a small black kitten in a crouch, facing a prehistoric monster whose head alone filled the whole doorway. Then, its tail horizontal and swishing from side to side, the kitten began to grow larger.

No, not the kitten itself. Ethel's tiny companion was as small as before. But something like a shadow of the same shape began to flow out from it: an opaque shadow that even while retaining the kitten's form expanded until it was as big as the wolf. From where Jeff stood, the prehistoric thing in the doorway was hidden by it.

The voice of the spectral cat made the windows

shake again. That of the wolf this time was only a whimper.

Then Jeff found himself rubbing his eyes and asking himself if he had imagined it. The wolf was gone. What he saw was an empty doorway— nothing there at all—and little Blackie turning to look up at his mistress as if for a word of approval.

The whole thing had taken no more than a minute or so, Jeff was certain. Long enough, though, for something else to happen. Long enough, while all eyes were on the drama in the doorway, for Earl Watson to have seized his chance to get away.

His chair was empty. A gust of wind from the hall had to be coming from the front door he had left open behind him in his flight.

But was that important? More so, surely, was the revelation that some part of the cave did, indeed, run underneath this house, as Jeff had suspected. And if that was so, the pentagrams on the windows might offer no protection against some of the creatures from the cave.

But why had the wolf appeared inside the house when the other horrors were still trying to get in from outside? Was it because Lelio had moved his *hounfor* into the house this time, and because the wrong *loa* were answering his summons again?

Chapter Thirty-one

Stumbling down the veranda steps in rain and darkness, Earl Watson made for his pickup truck in the driveway. Then he saw he could not escape that way.

Beyond the truck, the usual route to the main highway was alive with the same kinds of things that had been snarling and hissing at the windows of the house. They themselves were almost invisible in the dark, but their eyes were not.

It was some trick, of course. Some trick that the Everols or Gordon—or maybe those voodoo creeps from Haiti—had cooked up to scare him. But, by God, he'd show them he didn't scare so easy. There were other ways of getting out to the main road. Not with the truck, no. He'd have to come back for that later. But he still had two feet, and sitting there with that damned black cat staring at him had sobered him up enough to use them.

With the driveway blocked, the shortest way to the highway was over the knoll where the cave entrance was. The entrance where he'd seen the Mason woman go in and locked her up to keep her from telling the world what he had in there. Though how Ethel Everol could have known about that, he'd be damned if he could figure out. She must be one of those weirdos who could read a person's mind.

Blast the cave, anyway. He wished he'd never been called on to recover the Shelby girl's body. Wished he'd never discovered the entrance down there in the sinkhole. The stinking cave had been nothing but trouble. The Everols had been smart to keep it a family secret, even if they'd only done it so strangers wouldn't come around to explore it.

The hell with them. To hell with them all. Especially that Gordon guy, whoever he was. Gordon was just shit lucky to have had the stick with him that time at the cave mouth, and even luckier to have escaped when the net was dropped on him. Some people were born lucky.

Too bad he didn't have the time right now to set the Goddamn house on fire, with all of them inside it. They deserved it, siccing that damned black cat on him the way they had.

With one last glance at the shadow shapes blocking the driveway—their eyes like hot coals floating in the rainy dark—Earl took off through brush and trees, en route to the knoll.

A tree came to life in his path and lunged at him. No, not a tree. It was a huge snake of some kind, with beady eyes and a flicking tongue, so high off the ground it seemed to be walking on its tail. With a strangled cry he leaped to one side and fell on his hands and knees in a thicket of prickly wild fern but managed to scramble to his feet again just in time. The snake lunged again but missed him.

Sobbing for breath he ran on, and as he ran, he thought of the time he'd fixed the brakes on Verna Clark's red car so it would roll down the slope into the quicksand pond with her inside it. He hadn't been certain she was a real danger to him then, only figured she might be, and he'd be stupid to take any chances.

Sending for that college catalog to check on her had been a real smart idea, too, one that paid off. Whatever she was—a friend of the Mason dame he'd murdered, a snoop for the broad's insurance company, even a lady cop—he'd found out she wasn't a professor at the college like she'd claimed to be.

The knoll. And no more shadows with fiery eyes. Whatever they were, those shadows, maybe they'd take care of things for him back there at the house. That wolf—Jeez. But the people back there had crazy Ethel and the black cat, didn't they? Crazy Ethel who'd been just another old woman when she went away, and now was some kind of . . . kind of . . . some kind of what?

Climbing the knoll in the dark, he lost his footing a few times where the going was steep and had to wobble along sideways before he could regain his balance. As he passed the boulder at the cave entrance he turned his head and cursed it. Then he thought about how he'd found that Mason after shutting her up in there.

After staying away for days to be sure she'd be dead when he went back, he'd found her just inside the entrance, cold and stiff, with her fingernails gone and her hands rubbed to the bone from trying to claw the rock aside. She never could have clawed it aside. Nobody could. Not after he'd wedged a couple of others against it on the outside.

But had she been there all the time, right there at the boulder? He'd wondered. After finding herself trapped, wouldn't she have looked for some other way out? Her flashlight had been dead when he found her, but it must have been okay for a while. Anyway, there wasn't any way for her to escape except through the sinkhole with scuba gear. Finding that out was all she would have got for her trouble.

Cursing the rain and the darkness, he stumbled past the cave entrance, then went sliding and lurching down the other side of the knoll toward the pond road that would lead him out to the highway. But twenty feet from the road he stopped in his tracks, suddenly wanting a drink so badly he would have given an arm or a leg for one.

Blocking his way were a human shape and a crouching cat, both of them glowing in the dark like they were made of glass or clear plastic with lights inside. The cat was no little one like the one at the house either. It was bigger than his pickup truck and glowed like it was a kind of dirty yellow with dark stripes. Its wide-open mouth looked like a room in the cave, filled with white teeth. Two teeth in its upper jaw were so long and sharp, they could probably bite right through a man.

Standing there, trying to summon enough strength to turn and run, Earl saw the cat's rump and hind legs twitching. Saw its long tail whipping from side to side with such force that he could hear brush being scythed down by it on both sides of the road. The creature's huge front paws dug holes in the ground as it got ready to spring. From its cavern of a mouth came a warning growl that turned his whole body ice cold and made his hair stand up.

"Run!" he silently screamed at himself. "For Christ's sake, run!"

He couldn't.

The human shape at the cat's side was not so clear but in a different way was even more scary. A woman, glowing the same way but made of mist or fog. The same woman he had shut up in the cave. The one whose cold, stiff body he had first wrapped in canvas and carried to a niche just short of the crawl, then later dragged through the crawl to a safer hiding place where it was supposed to be now.

It wasn't there now. Holy Mother, no! And it wasn't a dead body anymore, either. Alive again, even though made of mist or whatever, the woman was here between him and the road to the highway, standing alongside the cat, with a hand on the cat's head. Like they were pals. Buddies. And she was staring at him like she hated him. Her eyes were twin lasers burning holes in his brain.

Earl's mouth opened and he screamed, but no sound came out. His mind told him again to turn and run before it was too late. The cat was ready to leap. The woman's eyes would turn him to ash. From somewhere he at last found the strength, the will, to lurch around and run for the pond.

The pond, yes. Even in the dark he knew where the pond was, and it was his only chance. No way could he get past those two and go down the road, and with the knoll behind him he couldn't retreat. With his legs shaking the way they were, he couldn't even climb the damned knoll. But if he could reach the pond and dive into that black water, maybe they wouldn't follow. And he was a good swimmer. Once under water, out of sight, he could maybe change direction and come up where they wouldn't expect him to. . . .

Racing down the slope into the water, he flung his arms over his head for the dive, then realized his mistake and tried to stumble back out but was too late. He had run into the pond at a place where the bottom was soft—the very place he had hoped the red car would end up, with its owner inside it. When he tried to scramble back out for a try at a different spot, his feet were trapped in soft ooze that was already over his ankles. Wildly he waved his arms about, trying to pull himself free.

No good. Nor was there anything he could grab on to. No tree limb was close enough even if he could see, though he all but turned himself into a corkscrew trying to reach for shadows.

Full circle. His luck had come full circle. The Clark girl had escaped being drowned here and he, Earl Watson, was about to take her place.

He began to cry.

The ooze was up to his knees now, and the more he struggled, the deeper he sank into it. He stopped struggling and still went on sinking. At the edge of the pond the huge, glowing cat crouched just back from the water's edge, watching him, and the woman stood beside it, still with one hand on its head. The woman who was really back there in the cave, stiff and cold, wrapped in canvas, in the niche beyond the crawl.

Was she the cat's mistress? If she let go and gave the word, would it spring at him? It could reach him in one bound, he was sure, a tiger cat that huge. Even if the quicksand trapped it, those god-awful jaws would close on him first.

In his terror he was moaning now. The ooze, sand, mud, whatever it was, had reached his ribs. Below the ribs everything was so numb it seemed not to be there anymore. He flung his arms about. He began screaming for help. His past, or parts of his past, took over his mind, as if to add to his punishment.

That day back in February when the cops had come to ask if he would try to recover the body of the Shelby girl, and he had taken his scuba gear to the sinkhole and found her on the bottom. And noticed what looked like a cave opening there.

A cave. He would keep it a secret, at least until he had a chance to find out how big it was and what could be done with it. You never knew. A man would be stupid to blab about a thing like that, and maybe pass up a chance to make some big money. That was the way he'd always worked, grabbing at opportunities that came along from out of nowhere. A chance to peddle crack one time, though he was too smart to use the stuff himself. A chance to make a couple of grand by helping a guy get out of the state when the cops wanted him for rape. A little here, a little there; you took what came along and made the most of it. To live any other way was just plain dumb.

So he'd kept quiet about the cave but gone back to explore it every now and then. Easy enough after he'd found the entrance on the knoll. Then the Mason dame; he'd have been stupid to risk losing everything because of her. And even more stupid to pass up the chance to get some dough out of Everett after getting rid of her.

And Everett, believing one of the Everol women

had done it. Yeah. But what the hell, why wouldn't he? Before Mason disappeared she'd been around town for quite a while, staying at the inn and snooping around the Everol place. Everybody knew that. And everybody knew the Everols were death to people who trespassed on their property. One time they'd even tried to have the sinkhole fenced in so people wouldn't go there, and they didn't even own it. And here was this woman shut up in their cave to die, and who else would have done such a thing except one of them, to put an end to her prowling around?

One of the Everols. So you got on the phone and you called the old man and you said, "Hey, I got somethin' to show you, Mr. Everol. Somethin' mighty important." And after a lot of talk you took the old buzzard into the cave and showed him the body and, yeah, convinced him he'd better co-operate. It wasn't hard to convince him one of his women had done it.

"So, Mr. Everol, you pay me and I'll keep quiet about this. We leave the body right here in the cave—I'll hide it where no one will ever find it—and you pay me to keep my mouth shut. What, Mr. Everol? If you take any big sum of money out of your account, the folks at the bank might wonder what's up? Well, all right, here's what we'll do. You take out a smaller amount every week, see, and drop a hint you're fixin' up that old house of yours. Nobody's gonna question that."

It all came back. Not slowly but in a rush, like a sudden gust of wind when you were out on the

Gulf in a boat sometimes. Whoosh, and all that part of his past raced through his mind and was gone, and he was still right there in the pond, up to his armpits now in the ooze, and the woman of mist was still standing there at the pond's edge watching him, with one hand on the head of that huge, crouching cat.

And he, Earl Watson, was now pleading for help in a voice that had become little more than a whine. "Oh, God, get me out of here! Help me, somebody! Jesus, I'll drown in this stuff. I'll drown!"

The ooze reached his shoulders. He felt it slide in and slither around his neck. Only his head and arms were still out of it, the arms waving feebly now and his voice reduced to a whimper.

"Lady . . . you on the shore . . . I know I shouldn'a done it to you. I was wrong. Jeez, lady, please . . . don't let me die like this. . . ."

She answered him by lifting her hand from the head of the cat.

In one swift, fluid glide, with its awesome jaws agape, the monstrous feline leaped out over the black water toward the parts of Earl Watson that were still visible. A loud crunching sound cut off Earl's blubbering as the jaws snapped shut. Then with an enormous splash, the prehistoric monster disappeared into open water beyond what was left of its victim.

The parts of Watson it left behind were the bloody stumps of his upthrust arms and a third stump, spouting blood like a fountain, where his head had been. In another moment these, too, disappeared into the now crimson water. Then the misty figure on the shore slowly dissolved, leaving nothing there but rain-filled darkness.

And silence. An eerie silence that flowed in to swallow the echoes of Earl Watson's last whimpering pleas for mercy.

Chapter Thirty-two

Rising from its crouch, the black kitten turned from the now empty doorway in which the wolf had appeared. Ethel Everol went to it and picked it up. Holding it in front of her face, she said to it softly, "Thank you, Blackie. You were wonderful." Then she put the cat on her shoulder and, with a frown, went to the center of the room and lifted the *cocomacaque* out of the earthenware jar that held it upright. "Now help me with this, Blackie," she said while frowning at it.

The cat rubbed its face against hers.

After studying the voodoo stick for a moment, Ethel turned to Jeff Gordon. "You say you handled this, Jeffrey?"

He nodded.

"How, exactly? If I may ask."

"To hold off a creature in the cave, a saber-toothed cat of some sort, when it was about to attack me. And to defend myself against Earl Watson."

"Did you injure Mr. Watson with it? Enough to draw blood?"

"I'm sure I did. When Verna and I saw him a little later, he was wearing a bandage with blood on it."

"Ah! Then this stain on the stick could be his blood!" Ethel turned her head toward the cat on her shoulder. "Do you see it, Blackie?" She held the *cocomacaque* close to the cat's eyes and touched a dark spot on it. "Right here. See? And don't you agree with me that the blood of such an evil man might be the cause of Lelio's problem?"

Blackie put his nose against the stain. His ears flattened. His tail bushed out. His "Mrreow!" was louder than the animal sounds outside the windows.

Lelio stepped forward. "I should have washed it, m'selle. Let me wash it now."

"No." Ethel shook her head. "Such pollution can't just be washed off, I'm sure. Throw the stick away, Lelio."

"But we must have a *poteau-mitan*, m'selle! Without one, we cannot have a service!"

"I will be your *poteau-mitan*," Ethel said.

"You?"

"Yes. Get rid of the stick."

Lelio tossed the stick into the dining room. Jeff

Gordon saw it land on a rectangle of carpet, slightly less faded than the rest, where the big dining table had stood. Ethel kicked off her shoes, leaving herself barefoot, and took a step forward. The movement placed her with one foot on each side of the *govi*, which by careful measurement was already in the exact center of the room.

With the kitten still on her shoulder, Ethel folded her arms. "Proceed with the service, Lelio. Let your *loa* come through me."

"From—the beginning, m'selle?"

"I think so, yes. From the beginning."

For the third time that evening the two from Haiti went through the ritual of a service summoning Erzulie and Legba while the others sat on the chairs against the walls and silently watched. But the room itself was not silent. Accompanying the small sounds made by Lelio and his wife were the louder ones voiced by the creatures outside. Not a moment passed when at least one of the room's windows did not frame some shadow shape darker than the night itself, with eyes like blazing coals. Would-be intruders, determined to get in but held at bay by the pentagrams.

But for how long, Jeff Gordon asked himself, would those circled stars on the windows be effective? They blazed now with a life of their own. Could they continue to blaze that way without burning themselves out?

Lelio sprinkled drops of water about the room again. When the moment came for him to kiss the *poteau-mitan*, he dropped to his knees and pressed his lips to the bare feet of the woman who had taken its place.

He retraced the *vèvés* and sprinkled water again. He shook his *asson* over them, filling the room with its rhythmic maraca music. Now for good measure he repeated the invocation to the guardian of the gate.

"Papa Legba, ouvri bayé. Papa Legba, Attibon Legba, ouvri bayé pou nou passé. . . ."

But the prayer was intoned in a different voice this time. One heavy with despair. One that said he had lost faith in his ability and was merely going through the motions.

Leaning toward Jeff, Verna Clark whispered, "What will happen if he is successful?"

"Someone will be possessed. Perhaps more than one."

"Possessed?"

"Mounted, they call it. By the spirits of the *loa* he is calling up."

"How will we know?"

"By what they say. How they act. But when it's over they won't remember."

Suddenly the person on the other side of Verna, the little bird woman, Susan, began to tremble. Her eyes closed and she stood up. Her arms, dangling at her sides, shook so violently it seemed they would break off at the shoulders.

Lelio, still chanting the prayer to Legba, became aware of what was happening and was silent. He turned slowly to face her. His eyes doubled in size and he sucked in a breath. In a voice totally different from the one he had been using, he began a new chant.

Jeff Gordon had learned enough Creole in Haiti, and enough about voodoo, to know the words were an improvisation.

"Erzulie, you have answered! You are here at last. Thank you; oh, thank you! But now you must protect this house of sorrow from the evil old ones I called up by mistake! You must send them back! You must intercede for us with Papa Legba and ask him to close the gate on them!"

Trying to watch the bird woman and the *houngan* at the same time, Jeff felt himself becoming dizzy. More than dizzy—confused. He rose from his chair and fell back again, aware that Verna Clark was staring at him in alarm. He lifted a hand and slapped the side of his head, hard, hoping to clear his mind and his vision.

Suddenly his attention was diverted by a sound from the adjoining room.

He staggered to his feet again. Beside him, Verna also rose but clutched his arm and voiced a gasp of horror. He and she were the ones directly opposite the dining room door, best able to see what was happening in that room where Lelio had tossed the discarded *cocomacaque*.

In that room where Lelio had thrown the once sacred stick, now defiled by the blood of a murderer, a section of the floor had suddenly heaved upward. There was a hump in the old carpet where the big dining table had stood. The floor heaved again as Jeff took a step forward. This time the ends of splintered boards ripped the carpet and shot up into the room.

At Jeff's side, Verna still clutched his arm, silent now but trembling from head to foot with her mouth open in a silent scream. Blanche and Amanda had seen and were screaming aloud. Ethel, with the kitten on her shoulder, had not moved, in fact seemed incapable of moving now that she had elected to become the link between two worlds. Old Everett was saying over and over in a scratchy whisper, "Oh, God; oh, my God!" Lelio and Lucille, hand in hand, were statues facing the upheaval.

Up through the broken floor and torn carpet in the other room rose a monster from another world, another time. A huge, scaly head burst into view, its mouth a tunnel bristling with teeth. As the rest of the creature rose up from beneath the house, the whole dining room floor exploded into fragments, the walls of the room wobbled and burst apart, the ceiling broke into a score of cracks and began to rain chunks of plaster.

An earthquake, Verna Clark thought. It was like an earthquake. But the thing causing it was alive, monstrous, deadly. Her schooling told her what it was. Of all the creatures from that bygone time, all the giant cats, wolves, birds, and reptiles, nothing had been more feared than the tyrant lizard, the huge carnivorous dinosaur that walked erect on its hind legs. Already this one had wrecked the dining room and was causing the rest of the house to shake like a child's toy made of cardboard. Its head alone had done that. If the rest of it rose from that ancient world beneath the house, the whole place would quickly become a heap of rubble and splinters from which the thing would pluck the living morsels of its next meal one by one and gulp them down.

This thing ate other dinosaurs, for God's sake. A human being wouldn't even be a mouthful.

The awful head filled half the dining room now. Those eyes from eighty to a hundred million years ago had seen them and focused on them. The living room floor on which she stood at Jeff's side, still clutching his arm in her terror, had become a heaving sea.

The monster was not even going to wait until it stood erect, she saw then. With a body that would weigh five or six tons, why should it? The great head, jaws agape, simply bulldozed its way toward them like that of a giant white shark seeking a meal in a school of small fish.

Why, if Susan had become Erzulie, didn't she do something to stop it? Dear God, why? Erzulie was supposed to be a protector of homes, wasn't she? She had answered Lelio's call and was here. Why didn't she do something?

Because the whole voodoo thing was nonsense, of course. What other answer could there be? Yet if Lelio hadn't called upon evil voodoo gods for vengeance in the beginning, none of this would be happening at all, would it?

Jeff. The man at her side. The man she knew she loved. He had suddenly shaken off the paralysis that gripped him. Was suddenly in motion. What was he doing?

He had freed his arm from her grip and was no longer paying any attention to her. He seemed not to know she even existed. Slowly, as if unaware that anyone in the room existed, he was striding toward the monster and speaking in a voice that was not his own.

She knew his voice. Loved it. But this was not the voice she knew and loved. It was much more— what was the word?—more commanding than his. Or was he just speaking loudly to be heard above the thunderous sounds now roaring out of the cavernous mouth that was about to swallow them all?

Creole. He was speaking in Creole. Or was he? How could she know, when she knew nothing more of that Haitian peasant tongue than she had heard here in this house? She caught some familiar words, though, even through the bellowing that seemed designed to drown them out. The word *bayé*—that meant gate or door, didn't it? And *femé*. Creole was a kind of French, wasn't it? She knew a little French. Would *femé* mean shut?

"M'ap femé bayé la!" he was shouting in the voice that was not his. Standing there closer to the advancing horror than any of them, yet seemingly unafraid, he had both hands extended, palms outward, as if commanding the huge, meat-eating monster to halt.

Yes, that was what he was saying: *"M'ap femé bayé la!"* With the words *gate* or *door* and *close* or *shut* in it, it must mean he was doing what only Legba could do. He was Legba! And he was responding to Lelio's plea to close the gate.

No one else had moved, not even Lelio. Ethel still stood over the *govi* in the center of the room, though with the floor heaving she was having trouble holding her balance. The cat still clung to her shoulder. Little Susan had returned to her chair and was simply sitting there, staring wide-eyed into space as though in a trance. Blanche and Amanda had stopped screaming. Everett was silent. The two Haitians watched Jeff intently.

The monster seemed to be watching him, too. No longer moving forward, it was suddenly more like a man-made replica of itself than a real, live tyrant lizard. The kind of replica you saw in museums, marked TYRANNOSAURUS REX, THE GREAT, with a crowd of wide-eyed schoolchildren looking up at it in disbelief.

It had even begun to fade.

Jeff was still speaking Creole, if it was Creole. The words *bayé* and *femé* still crept into what he was saying. As he stood there with his back to her, facing the now cowed creature from that other world, he seemed taller than he really was. Older, too. How tall was Legba? How old? She wished she knew more about such things, so she could be sure of what was going on here. What had he said to her a while ago? "Someone will be possessed. Perhaps more than one. But they won't remember it."

She found herself turning to look at the windows. There were no eyes outside them now. And the monster who had wrecked the dining room and might in another few moments have destroyed the whole house . . . that ghastly creature had become only a blurred ghost of itself, a misty, smoky shape that was fast losing even an outline.

Even as she stared at it, it faded away completely and was no longer there at all. And all the sounds outside the house had ceased. Silence flowed in like a blessing.

No one moved.

No one spoke.

She saw Jeff shake himself, like a dog coming out of water. He turned and looked around the room at the Haitians, at Ethel, at the other Everols, finally at her. As though tired, very tired, he walked slowly back to her.

He took her by the arm. He led her to the empty chairs from which they had risen an eternity ago. When she sank onto hers, he lowered himself onto the one beside it, saying nothing.

Lelio came over to peer into his face and nodded.

"He is all right," the *houngan* said.

"Was he—possessed?"

"Yes. By Papa Legba. But he will remember nothing."

"Is it over, then? All over?"

"He closed the gate. Yes, it is finished."

Verna looked toward little Susan. "And she was possessed, too?"

"By Erzulie. With Miss Ethel acting as a *poteau-*

mitan for us, which is a thing I have never seen done before. But I have never known a woman like Miss Ethel before, either. With her as the *poteau-mitan,* both Erzulie and Legba answered our prayers. Thank *Le Bon Dieu.*" His voice faltered. He seemed very tired. "But Miss Susan will not remember being mounted, either."

He was right.

When the fear had passed—when those in the room felt they could safely move about again—neither Susan nor Jeff could answer the questions put to them. "They will never remember," Lelio said with a shrug. "Never. After all, they were not themselves for those few moments. They were gods."

Chapter Thirty-three

When they realized at last that it was all over, they talked. The Everols, the Haitians, Jeff, Verna, all of them talked about what had happened. It was nearly midnight when, with his woman at his side, Lelio said quietly, "Most of this was my fault and I am sorry. I am not sorry that I sought revenge for the cruel thing done to my countrymen by those two men on the boat, you understand. Those two were more evil than anything we have seen here. But I regret the troubles I have caused."

After a silence Everett said with a shake of his head, "I made mistakes too, Lelio."

"We may go now, then? Back to our cottage?"

"But be ready in the morning to talk to the police. I have to call them, of course, and tell them—show them—what happened here. They will want to know who did all this. And about other things, like that woman and child who disappeared near the cemetery. You'll have to help me tell them."

"Yes, of course, m'sieu." The old Haitian solemnly nodded. "We will say good night, then."

He and Lucille departed.

Jeff Gordon said, "And we—Verna and I—will be going into the cave tomorrow to find her sister. So we'd better say good night, too, and go back to the motel."

Little Susan, who for a few moments had been the voodoo goddess of love—chosen for the role with good reason, perhaps—gazed at him in sadness but said nothing.

Jeff looked at Ethel, at the small black kitten now on her lap. "Before I return to Connecticut, Ethel, I'd like very much to talk to you about what you call your 'learning place.' May I do that?"

She glanced down at the cat and smiled. "We'll be happy to talk to you. Won't we, Blackie?"

Hand in hand, Jeff and Verna departed.

In the morning they found the body of her sister Kimberly where Earl Watson had hidden it in the cave, and brought it out. And in response to a telephone call from Everett Everol, most of Clandon's small police force came to the house to gape in awe at the damage done and hear what had happened. But Lelio Savain and his wife played no part in telling them. When Everett went to their cottage to get them, it was empty. A note signed by Lelio said simply, "We thank you all but must say good-bye. It was a mistake for us to come to your country. We have decided to go home."

After hours of talk in the Everols' living room—that room where Lelio had conducted the last of his services the night before—the police at last decided they had learned all they were likely to, at least for the present. The man called Clay said with a shake of his head, "Well, this clears up some of the questions, I suppose—like what happened to that Deering woman and her daughter near the cemetery. And I guess it proves Dan Crawley was tellin' the truth about what happened to the other kid who robbed you, Mr. Gordon. God only knows what's become of Earl Watson, though. His pickup's here in the driveway and he didn't come home last night, his wife says. We don't have a clue where he could have got to." He shrugged. "Anyway, we'll put out the the word on the Haitians. Most likely they'll be walkin' or tryin' to hitchhike to the coast. They won't dare take a bus, knowin' we want to question them."

Jeff Gordon talked to Ethel Everol. So did people from the institution. The latter were not summoned by anyone; they came in the knowledge that patients escaping from such a place usually headed for home. Amazed at her recovery, even more at what one of them called her "totally new personality," they offered no argument when the Everols insisted she was herself again and need not go back with them.

Jeff Gordon and Verna Clark followed a

funeral-home vehicle transporting the body of Verna's sister to Fort Lauderdale, where Jeff met Verna's mother and liked her. There, for a week, Verna and he discussed a future that would include all three of them.

And a few days later, in another part of the state . . .

"Joe, listen. Will you please listen to me, Joe? There is no such lake on this road, I'm tellin' you."

Looking up from the map spread open on his knees, the pimply faced man gazed entreatingly at his companion hunched over the wheel of the almost-new Cadillac. "There just ain't any Lake Revanche on here, Joe," he persisted. "We are not only on the wrong road; we ain't even close."

"Must be an old map," the tall man said with a shrug.

"Joe, this is the latest gover'ment map of this here district. Look at it. Over here"—Pimples jabbed a finger at the left side of the paper—"are lakes we know about: Placid, Huntley, Grassy, Clay, June-in-Winter, all o' those. Even the littlest ones like Lost Lake and LaChard. But there ain't no lake along this road. Look for yourself, for God's sake."

Joe turned his head for a second to glance down. "It's here," he insisted. "I never make mistakes about fishin' spots."

"Well, if it's such a hot place to fish, why didn't you never mention it before, huh? Tell me that.

How come the first time you ever thought about it was the day before yesterday?"

"It just slipped my mind."

Pimples heaved a sigh of surrender and slumped down on the seat, ignoring the map now and staring straight ahead through the windshield. At five in the afternoon the road was deserted. It was only a narrow ribbon of blacktop anyway, scarcely wide enough for two cars to pass without one of them running off onto a shoulder of soft sand. Most of the time it was probably deserted. The scenery on both sides was a monotonous blend of scrub and palmetto, with only an occasional oasislike cluster of oaks or pines standing stark against the cloudless sky.

"We shouldn't be out and around so soon anyhow," Pimples suddenly whined. "We ought to've laid low a lot longer after what happened this last time. Suppose one o' them people made it to shore and told what we done to them?"

"Nobody did."

"How do you know nobody did?"

"It would've been in the papers the day after," the driver said calmly. "As quick as any survivor talked, it would've been in headlines a foot high, and that would've been three weeks ago, so forget it."

Pimples was silent again for a few minutes. Then he said "I still say we shouldn't be on any fishin' trip."

"Why not? Give me one good reason."

"It just don't seem right. All them people losin'

their lives and us drivin' all this way to some crazy lake you just remembered. One that don't even exist, I bet. And Jesus, Joe, this is the second time we done that. Made 'em swim for it, I mean." He wagged his head. "You remember that first bunch? The old guy that grabbed the watch off your wrist?"

"It wasn't our fault, either one," Joe said with a touch of annoyance. "We didn't ask the damned engine to quit that first time. We didn't ask the Coast Guard 'copter to show up the second. You realize where we'd be this minute if those Haitians had been on deck when that the 'copter guys took a notion to make a pass over us? Huh? Do you?"

Through an extended silence the Cadillac approached a gentle curve in the road.

"You hear me?" Joe said. "It was not our fault, Goddamn it!"

"Sure, sure."

"It could've happened to anyone!"

"Sure."

"So forget it, will you? We're on a fishin' trip."

"If we can find the stupid lake," Pimples growled. Then, as the car came out of the curve, he jerked his frail body to a more upright position and said, "Hey! There's a sign!"

Joe eased his foot off the gas pedal.

The sign was a yard-long board, crudely cut in the shape of an arrow and nailed to a cypress post. It said DARBY'S FISHING CAMP, and in smaller letters under that, LAKE REVANCHE.

Joe stopped the car to make sure his companion would have time to read it. "Now do you know what you can do with that map?"

Pimples wagged his head from side to side in disbelief. "Jeez, I never thought a gover'ment map could be wrong. That's a real old sign, too. You'd think somebody would've told 'em by now, huh?"

"Put the damned map away," Joe said, letting the car move on again, but more slowly now. This road was unpaved and only one car wide.

"Joe, what's *revanche* mean?"

"Hell, I don't know. Some French Canadian's name, most likely, like Lake LaChard. There's lots o' Canadians in this part of Florida."

"It's a big lake, Joe?"

"Not so big. Maybe a mile and a half long and half a mile wide, the way I remember it. But a beauty, and full of bass. The biggest lunkers you ever fished for."

Pimples looked out at more sandy flatland bristling with palmetto and stunted scrub. "It's real queer you never brought me here before," he said then. "Or even mentioned any such lake. We sure been to a lot of places where the fishin' wasn't so great."

"I told you—I just remembered."

"That's what I'm sayin'. It's queer you only just remembered, when we been workin' together for more'n five years now." Pimples slowly inhaled, let his breath out in a kind of snort, and added, "Oh well, hell. We're here, so let's have us a time. We going to this Darby's camp?"

"It's the one I recall."

"How far in is it?"

"About a mile."

Joe's memory was unflawed. A mile farther on they came upon a second sign, larger but just as weathered as the first and with the same words on it. It led them along a pair of grassy ruts into a clearing. In the clearing, spaced about thirty feet apart, stood three old cottages of silver-gray cypress.

From the nearest of these, as Joe stopped the car in front of it, came a man in his seventies, if his almost white hair and bent shoulders were any indication of his age. His wrinkled white face had been so long burned by the Florida sun that Pimples, on watching him approach, said, "Jeez, Joe. If he was only a little darker, he'd look like one of our customers."

"Shut up, will you?" Joe said under his breath. Sliding out of the car, he thrust out his hand. "Mr. Darby?"

"I am Orville Darby." The fellow looked Joe over, from costly desert shoes to handsome yellow sport shirt. "I don't think I know you, though," he said, not quite frowning.

"Joe Janarek. Been here before. This is a buddy of mine. We'd like to rent a cabin for a couple days and do some fishin'."

"Janarek?" Again the scrutiny, which ended this time in a relaxing of the not quite frown. "I remember now. It was a long time ago."

Joe glanced impatiently toward the lake. "Well,

anyhow—I been here before, like I say, and if it's all right with you—"

"Joe only just remembered your place," Pimples said. "I been tellin' him for the past hour there wasn't no such lake as this one on the map, but he kept sayin' I was crazy, and—"

"All right!" the tall man said impatiently. "Well, Mr. Darby?"

"Of course. Take number two and stay as long as you like. No one is here right now."

"Are the bass bitin'?"

"The same as always, Mr. Janarek." The white-haired man started to walk away, then stopped and looked back. "I'm sorry I don't have more than one boat this evening. The others are being painted and won't be returned until tomorrow. One will be enough for you, though, won't it?"

"Yeah, yeah, sure."

"If I were you, I would try to get out there right now. This is the best time of the day."

Joe drove the car through the clearing to the second cottage and flipped the lever that opened its trunk. They carried in their luggage, fishing gear, and food. It was a pretty nice cabin, Pimples remarked. "Old, but you can see he looks after it real good. The old guy, I mean. I take back what I said about you bein' crazy, Joe."

"Thanks."

"I still don't understand why you never brought me here before, though. We been to a lot o' worse places."

"Let's go look at the lake," Joe said.

They walked the fifty yards down to the lake-shore, and Pimples was again impressed. "Hey, a real beauty," he said. "A mile and a half long, did you say? It looks longer'n that to me. Deep, too. And look at all them cypresses and live oaks, would you? I'd have swore there was nothin' like this in here."

"Well, now you know."

"Awright, I'm dumb. So let's wet a line, huh?"

Returning to the cottage, they changed into the fishing clothes they had brought and readied their spinning rods for the evening's action. "No need for live bait here," Joe said with authority. "Darby probably charges all outdoors for it, so to hell with him. Just tie on a plastic worm."

"Any special color, you think?"

"I bet it don't make the slightest bit of difference. You could use a hunk o' shoelace."

First to finish his preparations, Pimples glee-fully pranced around the room, even leaping onto a bed and jumping from that to the other one. "Jeez, Joe, this is great! A lake like this all to our-selves, a swell cabin; oh boy, oh boy." Still stand-ing on the second bed, he suddenly became thoughtful. "There's just one thing."

"What?"

"That feller Darby. I never been here before, Joe, but I swear I know him from someplace."

"There's a million old guys like him, for Pete's sake. Come on, let's catch us some bass."

According to Joe's watch—the one he had bought to replace the fancy French one snatched from his wrist that time by the old Haitian—there was an hour of daylight left when they pushed the rowboat into the water. Pimples took up the oars. Joe sat in the stern and gazed with pleasure at the massed oaks and sweet bays on one shore, the swamp maples and colorful ground cover on the other. He prided himself on having an eye for beauty.

Selecting what appeared to be a likely spot some eighty yards from shore, alongside an expanse of lily pads, they began to fish. After only a few minutes Pimples, with a yelp of triumph, set his hook and hauled in a bass. A big one.

Joe caught one. Pimples caught another. As the sport continued, they filled the evening with whoops and loud talk, and the white-haired man came down from his cottage to stand at the lake's edge and watch them for a while. This time he was not alone. There was a woman with him.

Joe waved to them and the old fellow waved back before he and the woman returned to the cottage.

There were more than a dozen big bass in the boat when the sport began to pall. Time had passed unnoticed; the lake was turning black and the tall trees framing it began to lose their identifying shapes against a darkening sky.

Pimples put down his rod and lit a cigarette. "Have you noticed a funny thing about this place, Joe?" he said. "There's no birds."

Joe thrust a cigarette between his lips and

leaned forward to take a light from his companion. "So what?"

"There ought to be, with all these trees and water. Lots of birds."

"We're scarin' 'em off."

"You don't even hear any birds. If we was scarin' 'em off, they'd still be around, singin'. Birds almost always sing this time o' the evenin'."

"You can think of more damned things to complain about," Joe said, shaking his head from side to side in mock amazement.

"I'm serious, Joe. This is a spooky place." Pimples reached for his rod but stopped in midmotion. "Hey, look. The old guy's watchin' us again."

Joe turned to look and saw the man and woman on shore again. He shrugged. "What of it?"

"I still say I know him from someplace." Pimples took up his rod. "Hey, this boat's leakin'."

"It's been leakin' since we got into it," Joe said.

"I mean bad. Look here, for God's sake! He must've had it patched with somethin' and the stuff is washin' out." Pimples moved a leg so the tall man in the stern could see the waterspout under his thwart. At the rate the water was spurting in, the small craft would be unmanageable in only a few minutes. "Jeez," he said. "We better get out o' here!"

"It's time we quit, anyway," Joe said.

Reaching for the oars, Pimples dipped the blades into the dark water and pulled with a strength born of uneasiness. The right-hand oar broke just above the blade and he tumbled backward off the seat, letting go of both handles. The oar that had not broken jumped from its lock and was out of reach in the lake before either man could grab for it.

"You clumsy fool!" Joe yelled. "Now look what you done!"

Pimples pulled himself back onto the seat and looked helplessly at the lost oar. Then he saw something beyond the oar and said in a whisper, "Jeez, Joe—look! And see the size of it!"

Joe looked and was silent with dread. Ten feet from the boat, a foot from the floating oar, a snake all of four feet long swam toward the boat with its broad, flat head creating a wake. It was a dark olive brown with darker bars and blotches along its heavy, slithering body. In a place like this, so far from help, a bite from a cottonmouth moccasin that big would leave a man no chance.

"Make for shore!" Joe cried hoarsely. "Use your hands!" Twisting sideways, he leaned over and plunged his own cupped hands into the water.

But Pimples was incapable of movement. "Joe," he whispered, staring now beyond the snake. "There's more of them. There's dozens more. And look what's happenin' to the lake."

Joe snatched his hands from the water as though it had suddenly become boiling hot. His eyes bulged. All about the crippled craft now, as it filled from a swiftly increasing number of leaks, the dark surface of the lake was in motion. Everywhere he looked, those broad, flat heads moved toward him trailing long, slithering shadows.

The silence complained of by Pimples no longer existed. An eerie hissing had taken its place.

Wrenching himself out of his trance, Joe stumbled to his knees and tore loose the rotten board on which he had been sitting. Clutching it with both hands, he thrust one end into the water and used it as a paddle.

The boat lurched ahead for a few yards, then slowed to a crawl. Slowed because the water he sought to drive it through was no longer open but choked with reeds, lily pads, and cattails. Lake Revanche had shrunk in size. The surrounding forest of tall trees had vanished. The boat struggled like a trapped and frightened animal in a shallow, snake-infested slough less than a hundred yards in diameter.

Exhausted, Joe at last stopped trying to paddle.

Shaking with fear, Pimples put his hands to his face and moaned through his fingers. "Joe, Joe, we're sinkin'. This ain't no real lake at all, and it's full o' snakes! And look, Joe—they're back again, the old guy and the woman, watchin' us!" Despite his near delirium, he managed to remove one hand from his face and point to the shore.

Joe looked up and saw the two people standing there. Just standing, watching, not making any move to help them. If, indeed, there was any way the pair could have helped.

"Joe, look at him," Pimples whimpered. The boat had filled with water and was settling among

332

the swamp growth, still sixty feet or more from the standing figures. "You know who he is, Joe? It's the old Haitian who grabbed your watch that night!"

Joe could no longer use the ripped-up board; the boat was resting on the bottom with only an inch or two of its sides above water. "You're crazy!" he bellowed in a rage of frustration. "He's white. Those Haitians were black!"

"I don't care what color he is, Joe. He could be makin' us think he's white, couldn't he? You talked to him about bass fishin', so he knew you was big on it. And he could've made you think you remembered this lake that ain't no lake, and made both of us believe anything he wanted us to believe when he got us here, couldn't he? Maybe these aren't even real fish we got in the boat, Joe. Jesus, Joe. He said he was a voodoo priest, didn't he? They got powers!"

"You're crazy."

"No I ain't, Joe. They get ahold of somethin' that belongs to you; they can do all kinds of things to you!"

"What's he got that belongs to us, for Christ's sake?"

"Joe, he took your watch."

Joe stood up. "To hell with him," he snarled. "We can walk ashore from here."

"No, Joe! Jeez! The snakes!"

"How do you know he isn't makin' us see the snakes, too?" Joe yelled. "You want to stay here, that's your business. I'm gettin' out."

HUGH B. CAVE

Stepping from the boat into the slough's dark water, he stumbled but regained his balance and began his struggle to reach the shore.

From the boat Pimples watched him, softly whimpering.

On shore the old man and the woman had disappeared into darkness.

At the junction of the dirt road and the narrow blacktop, a boy of eleven stood by the old arrow-shaped sign. His bicycle had been leaning against the signpost for nearly an hour.

Hearing a car coming along the blacktop, he stepped forward. When he waved the driver down, the car stopped. It was a police car with a young uniformed officer at the wheel.

"Hi, Duane," the policeman said. "What you want?"

"There's somethin' you ought to look into down at Mr. Darby's old place," the boy said.

The officer glanced involuntarily at the sign above the lad's bike. An old, weathered thing that had been there for years, it said simply ORVILLE DARBY, FROG LEGS. "What you mean, something I ought to look into, Duane?"

"Well, there's an almost new Cadillac there and nobody around but two dead men. I been waitin' here to tell you."

"Two dead men? Get in!"

"What about my bike? I don't want it stole."

The officer got out, opened the car's trunk, and put the bike into it. He held the car door open for the boy to squirm onto the seat. On the way down the road he said, "When did you discover this, Duane?"

"On my way to town for Ma. The car was there and I called out to the two black people that's been livin' there, like I been doin' since they got here. When they didn't answer, I took to wonderin' if they was all right and went on in."

They arrived at what Joe and Pimples had believed to be a fishing camp on a lake. There was no lake—only a round glimmer of dark, shallow water filled with swamp growth, about a hundred yards across. On the edge of it stood three all but falling down shacks of cypress, in a yard overgrown with weeds and tall grass. The Cadillac stood in front of the second shack.

The boy led his policeman friend past the buildings and the car to the edge of the slough, where a tall man lay half on the bank with one leg in the water. He had ripped his pants to expose the other leg, and both of his hands still gripped it, with fingers and thumbs imbedded in purple flesh, as if struggling to hold back the pain. The leg was swollen to more than twice its normal size and the man's face was a gargoyle of agony and terror, with the mouth and eyes wide open.

"He's been snake-bit," the officer said. "Cottonmouth, looks like. They hang out here, I've heard."

"They sure do," the boy said. "It was a cottonmouth killed Mr. Darby when he was after frogs one night. And the old black guy told me they come out every evenin', a whole slew of them. He even had one come into his cabin. But you know what he said, Terry?"

"What did he say?"

"He said he wasn't scairt of no snakes. That's right. Honest. He said, 'The snakes will not harm me, little boy. I serve them. I serve Dam—Damballa—and all the snakes do his bidding.' " Perhaps unconsciously the lad had imitated the old man's deep, slow voice. In his own he added, "Who's Damballa, Terry?"

The officer's last name was LeClerc and he was from Louisiana, where voodoo is not unknown. He said quietly, "Damballa is a voodoo god, Duane. One of the big ones. His symbol is a snake. If your old guy said he served Damballa, I'd guess he was a *houngan,* a priest."

"Anyway," the boy said, "I expect more'n likely it's on account of all the snakes that nobody never tried to take over here when Mr. Darby died." He tugged at the man's arm. "Look out there at the boat, Terry."

The morning sun was bright, and Terry had to shade his eyes to see the rowboat in the slough and the second body in it. "I just don't believe this," he said. "Why, that old tub's been laying here since Orville Darby died. It couldn't have even floated unless somebody patched it up. Even the oars were too rotten to steal. Duane, what do you suppose happened here?"

"You'll notice there's two fishin' rods in the

boat," the boy said with a show of pride at his ability to observe such things. "See 'em stickin' up there behind him? What I think, these two men was out there fishin'—though Lord knows what for—and the boat sank and this one tried to walk ashore but got snake-bit, whilst the other was too scared to try it and got bit where he sat. You see how swole his arm is, hangin' down in the water?"

"I see," Terry said. "And I think you're probably right. Anyhow, I'm not wading out there after him and I'm not touching this one either. I'll call in for help. Let's have a look inside those shacks first."

They went together into the shack that had been assigned to Joe and Pimples and found the suitcases and food on a wreck of a table in there. The two beds in the shack were only rusty springs laid on rustier iron frames—no mattresses, no bedding of any kind. The rundown condition of the place led the officer to say wonderingly, "Now how did those two men figure to stay in a place like this? Can you answer me that, Duane?"

"No, sir, I can't."

They looked at the third cabin and found it in even worse condition but empty. Then with the officer in the lead they walked into the first cabin.

"This must be where the old black fellow and his woman were living," Terry said.

The boy nodded. "They were here about a week, all told."

"Doing what? Trying to make a living hunting frogs, like Orville Darby did?"

"Uh-uh. The old guy said they were on their way home and just staying here awhile to rest up. First time I talked to him, he asked me real polite was it okay for them to use the place, seein' as how nobody was here, and I said why not but stay out o' the slough because there was so many snakes in there." The boy interrupted himself. "Hey, looka this. I never seen any o' this stuff before."

He had walked around the shack's one bed, on which its occupants had constructed a mattress of grass that still bore the imprints of their bodies, and halted before a table. Except for the bed and a single wobbly straight-backed chair, the table was all the shack contained.

On it stood an assortment of curious objects—curious to the boy and his policeman friend, at least. One was a miniature hand-carved signpost. Shaped like the one where the boy had been waiting with his bike, it said DARBY'S FISHING CAMP. LAKE REVANCHE.

"I never heard Mr. Darby call this place a fishin' camp," the boy said. "Never heard of any Lake Revanche around here, neither. Did you, Terry?"

"Never."

"What's it mean, that word?"

"It's French. Means revenge."

A second object was even more curious. It was a postcard picture of a mid-Florida lake surrounded by tall trees. A place of unusual beauty.

And in front of that, laid out on an oblong of green palm fronds like a jewel on a bed of velvet, was a wristwatch. Its expansion band was broken and it had the words LOUVAN, PARIS on its dial.

The room's single chair was placed at the table in a position from which anyone seated on it could have concentrated, without distraction, on the carefully laid-out objects.

Perhaps for hours on end.

THE DAWNING

HUGH B. CAVE

In the all-too-immediate future, the day has finally come when crime, drugs, and pollution have made the cities of the world virtually uninhabitable. Gangs roam the streets at will, the police have nearly surrendered, and the air and water are slowly killing the residents who remain. But one small group of survivors has decided to escape the madness. Packing what they can carry, they head off to what they hope will be the unspoiled wilderness of northern Canada, intent on making a new start, a new life. But nature isn't that forgiving. For far too long mankind has destroyed the planet, ravaging the landscape and slaughtering the animals. At long last, nature has had enough. Now the Earth is ready to fight back, to rid itself of its abusers. A new day has come. But will anyone survive . . . the Dawning.

___4739-X $5.50 US/$6.50 CAN

Dorchester Publishing Co., Inc.
P.O. Box 6640
Wayne, PA 19087-8640

Please add $1.75 for shipping and handling for the first book and $.50 for each book thereafter. NY, NYC, and PA residents, please add appropriate sales tax. No cash, stamps, or C.O.D.s. All orders shipped within 6 weeks via postal service book rate. Canadian orders require $2.00 extra postage and must be paid in U.S. dollars through a U.S. banking facility.

Name_____
Address_____
City_____State_____Zip_____
I have enclosed $_____ in payment for the checked book(s).
Payment <u>must</u> accompany all orders. ❏ Please send a free catalog.
     CHECK OUT OUR WEBSITE! www.dorchesterpub.com

HEXES

TOM PICCIRILLI

Matthew Galen has come back to his childhood home because his best friend is in the hospital for the criminally insane—for crimes too unspeakable to believe. But Matthew knows the ultimate evil doesn't reside in his friend's twisted soul. Matthew knows it comes from a far darker place.

___4483-8 $4.99 US/$5.99 CAN

SERVANTS OF CHAOS
DON D'AMMASSA

The isolated little fishing village of Crayport, Massachusetts, might seem almost normal at first glance, but appearances can be deceiving. You would never be welcome there. Outsiders never are. The inhabitants of the village are unusually hostile toward strangers, and you might notice some of them share an odd physical trait. . . .

If you look very closely, though, you might discover the hideous secrets of the mysterious island off the coast. And if you aren't careful, you'll meet the powerful group that dominates the town, the ones known only as the Servants. Just pray you never catch a glimpse of the Servants' unimaginable masters.

Dorchester Publishing Co., Inc.
P.O. Box 6640   ___5069-2
Wayne, PA 19087-8640   **$5.99 US/$7.99 CAN**
Please add $2.50 for shipping and handling for the first book and $.75 for each book thereafter. NY and PA residents, please add appropriate sales tax. No cash, stamps, or C.O.D.s. Prices and availibility subject to change.
Canadian orders require $2.00 extra postage and must be paid in U.S. dollars through a U.S. banking facility.

Name _____
Address_____
City_____ State_____ Zip_____
E-mail_____
I have enclosed $_____ in payment for the checked book(s).
Payment <u>must</u> accompany all orders. ❏ Please send a free catalog.

CHECK OUT OUR WEBSITE! www.dorchesterpub.com

T. M. WRIGHT
LAUGHING MAN

In their own way, the dead tell Jack Erthmun so much. Jack is a New York City police detective with his own very peculiar ways of solving homicides, and those ways are beginning to frighten his colleagues. He gets results, but at what cost? This may be Jack's last case. He's assigned to a series of unspeakable killings, gruesome murders with details that make even seasoned detectives queasy. But as he goes deeper into the facts of the case, facts that make it seem no human killer can be involved, Jack begins to get more and more erratic. Is it the case that's affecting Jack? Or is it something else, something no one even dares to consider?
